BONFIRE

krysten ritter
BONFIRE

A NOVEL

CROWN
ARCHETYPE
NEW YORK

Library of Congress Cataloging-in-Publication Data is available upon request.

ISBN 978-1-5247-5984-1
Ebook ISBN 978-1-5247-5986-5
Export edition ISBN 978-1-5247-6245-2

Printed in the United States of America

Jacket design by Will Staehle
Jacket photograph by Volodymyr Baleha/Shutterstock

10 9 8 7 6 5 4 3 2 1

First Edition

BONFIRE

Prologue

My last year of high school, when Kaycee Mitchell and her friends got sick, my father had a bunch of theories.

"Those girls are bad news," he said. "Nothing but trouble." He took it as a matter of faith that they were being punished. To him, they deserved what they got.

Kaycee was the first. This made sense. She was the first to do everything: lose her virginity, try a cigarette, throw a party.

Kaycee walked in front of her friends, like an alpha wolf leading the pack. In the cafeteria, she decided where to sit and the others followed; if she ate her lunch, the rest did, too; if she pushed her food around on her tray or just ate a bag of Swedish Fish, her friends did the same.

Misha was the meanest and the loudest one.

But Kaycee was the leader.

So when she got sick, we, the senior girls of Barrens High, weren't horrified or disturbed or worried.

We were jealous.

We all secretly hoped we'd be next.

The first time it happened was in fourth-period debate. Everyone had to participate in mock elections. Kaycee made her way through three rounds of primary elections. She was easy to believe in the role of politician, convincing and quick-witted, a talented liar; I'm not even sure Kaycee knew when she was telling the truth and when she wasn't.

She was standing at the front of the room delivering a practiced stump speech when suddenly it was as though the tether connecting her voice to her throat was cut. Her mouth kept moving, but the volume had been turned off. No words came out.

For a few seconds, I thought there was something wrong with *me*.

Then her hands seized the podium and her jaw froze, locked open, as if she were stuck, silently screaming. I was sitting in the first row—no one else ever wanted those seats, so they were mine to take—and she was only a few feet away from me. I'll never forget how her eyes looked: like they'd transformed suddenly into tunnels.

Derrick Ellis shouted something, but Kaycee ignored him. I could see her tongue behind her teeth, a wad of white gum sitting there. Some people laughed—they must have thought it was a joke—but I didn't.

I'd been friends with Kaycee, best friends, back when we were young. It was only the second time in my life I'd ever seen her look afraid.

Her hands began to shake, and that's when all the laughter stopped. Everyone went quiet. For a long time, there was no sound in the room but a silver ring she always wore clacking loudly against the podium.

Then the shaking traveled up her arms. Her eyes rolled back and she fell, taking the podium down with her.

I remember being on my feet. I remember people shouting. I remember Mrs. Cunningham on her knees, lifting Kaycee's head, and someone screaming about keeping her from swallowing her tongue. Someone ran for the nurse. Someone else was crying; I don't remember who, just the sound of it, a desperate whimpering. Weirdly, the only thing I could think to do was pick up her notes, which had fallen, and reshuffle them in order, making sure the corners aligned.

Then, all of a sudden, it passed. The spasm apparently left her body, like an ebbing tide. Her eyes opened. She blinked and sat up, looking vaguely confused, but not displeased, to find us all gathered around her. By the time the nurse came, she seemed normal again. She insisted it was just a weak spell, because she hadn't eaten. The nurse led Kaycee out of the classroom, and the whole time she was glancing back at us over her shoulder as if to be sure we were all watching her go. And we were—of course we were. She was the kind of person you couldn't help but watch.

We all forgot about it. Or pretended to.

Then, three days later, it happened again.

Chapter One

State Highway 59 becomes Plantation Road two miles after the exit for Barrens. The old wooden sign is easy to miss, even among the colorless surroundings. For years now, on road trips from Chicago to New York, I've been able to pass on by without any anxiety. Hold my breath, count to five. Exhale. Leave Barrens safely behind, no old shadows running out of the dark woods to strangle me.

That's a game I used to play as a kid. Whenever I would get scared or have to go down to the old backyard shed in the dark, as long as I held my breath, no monsters or ax murderers or deformed figures from horror movies would be able to get me. I would hold my breath and run full speed until my lungs were bursting and I was safe in the house with the door closed behind me. I even taught Kaycee this game back when we were kids, before we started hating each other.

It's embarrassing, but I still do it. And the thing is, it works. Most of the time.

Alone, locked in a gas station bathroom, I scrub my hands until the skin cracks and a tiny trickle of blood runs down the drain. It's the third time I've washed my hands since I crossed the border into Indiana. In the dinged mirror over the sink, my face looks pale and warped, and the memories of Barrens bloom again like toxic flowers.

This was a bad idea.

I shove open the bathroom door and squint into the early sunlight as I get back into my car.

At the turnoff I pass a deer carcass buzzing with flies, its head still improbably intact and almost pretty-looking, mouth open in a final sigh. Impossible to say whether it was hit by a car or struck by a passing bullet. Typically fresh roadkill gets scooped up by a good ol' boy, loaded into a smoker, and made into venison jerky. I hit a deer in my old Ford Echo when I was seventeen; it was picked up even before I was. But this deer is, for some reason, undisturbed.

Hunting game is a main activity in Barrens—*the* main activity, actually. It's built into the culture. If you can call it that. Hunting season isn't officially until winter but every year kids sneak out with a six-pack, a spotlight, and their fathers' guns to scout for a big buck or watch a few fawns and a doe grazing. And after a few beers, they take shots at whatever they can aim for.

My dad used to take me with him to hunt; our father-daughter bonding activities usually involved an outing to the taxidermist. Deer, coyote, and bear heads adorn the walls of our house like trophies. He taught me to step on the bodies of the pheasants he took down while he snapped their necks in one hand. I remember how annoyed he was when I cried over the first deer I watched him kill, how he made me place my hands on its still-warm body and the blood pulsing out of the hole that had ripped its life away. "Death is beautiful," he said.

My mother was beautiful once, too, until bone cancer did its work. Chewed off her hair, carved her body into a shell of muscle and bone, took her cell by cell. After she died, my father told me it was the ultimate blessing and that we should be thankful, because the Lord had chosen her to be part of his flock in heaven.

I turn from Plantation Road onto Route 205, which eventually becomes Main Street, struck hard by the smell of cow manure in the heat. It's mid-June, end of the school year, but it feels like high summer. Fields brown beneath the sun. Another mile on, I pass a brand-new sign: *Welcome to Barrens, population 5,027.* The last time I was here, ten years ago, the population was barely half that. Main Street is in fact the main street, but even on a nine-mile stretch, passing three cars is high traffic.

I count telephone poles. I count crows swaying on the wires. I count silos in the distance, arranged like fists. I turn my life into numbers, into accounting. For ten years I've lived in Chicago. I've been a lawyer for three. After six months in private practice, I landed a job at CEAW, the Center for Environmental Advocacy Work.

I have a future, a life, a clean and bright condo in Lincoln Park with dozens of bookshelves and not a single Bible. I meet friends in downtown Chicago bars and clubs and speakeasies where the cocktails have ingredients like lilac and egg white. I *have* friends now, period—and boyfriends, if you can call them that. As many as I want, nameless and indistinguishable, rotating in and out of my bed and life and on my own terms.

Most nights, I don't even have nightmares anymore.

I swore, many times, that I would never go home. But now I know better. Any self-help book in the world will tell you that you can't just run your past away.

Barrens has its roots in me. If I want it gone forever, I'll have to cut them out myself.

MAIN STREET. WHAT used to be the chapel—a one-story concrete building with no windows where we used to go on Sundays, until my dad decided that the pastor was interpreting scripture as he pleased, infuriated particularly that he seemed too lax on "the gays"—is now a White Castle. The library where my mother used to take me to story hour as a kid now touts a sign for Johnny Chow's Oriental Buffet. When I was growing up, we had practically no sit-down restaurants at all.

But so much is the same: the neon light from the VFW bar still flickers, and Mel's Pizza, where I would ride my bike sometimes to get a slice after school, is still churning out pies. So much might have tumbled out of memory intact—the Jiffy Lube Pit Stop, Jimmy's Auto Parts Supply, the run-down porn shop Kaycee Mitchell's father used to own. Might still own, for all I know. Temptations has a new roof, though, and a new electric sign. So business has been booming.

I spot a crow on a telephone wire and another one nesting farther along. *One crow for sorrow, two crows for mirth . . .*

Past Main Street nothing looks the same: brand-new condos, a Jennifer Convertibles, a sit-down Italian place advertising a salad bar in the window. Everything is unfamiliar except for the salvage yard and, just beyond it, the drive-in movie theater. Site of many birthday parties with kids from Sunday school and even a depressing Thanksgiving right after my mom was buried. Our claim to fame, prior to the arrival of Optimal Plastics.

More crows perched on a pylon. *Three, four, five, six. Seven for a secret, never to be told.* A murder of crows.

Being back is giving me that tight-chest, lumpy-throat feeling. I grip the steering wheel tighter. At the first red light—the *only* red light in Barrens—I hold my breath and close my eyes. *I am in control now.*

The guy behind me lays on his horn: the light has turned green. I press the gas pedal just a little too hard and shoot forward into the intersection. When a familiar orange sign flashes in my peripheral vision, I signal to turn without thinking and swerve into the parking lot of the Donut Hole—this, like the drive-in movie theater, is totally unchanged.

I turn off the ignition. Sit in silence. After just a few seconds of no air-conditioning, it's painfully hot. It must be eighty degrees—much warmer than it was in Chicago. The air is chokingly heavy with moisture. I wrestle off my leather jacket and grab my purse from the floor of the passenger seat. I could use a water.

As I'm opening the car door, a blue Subaru pulls up next to me, jamming its brakes at the last second and making me jump. The driver honks twice.

I slide out of the car, annoyed by how close the other driver has parked, and then notice the woman in the car is smiling at me and giving a frenzied, two-handed wave. She motions toward the Donut Hole and I have a split second to decide if I should turn back toward Chicago and forget this whole thing. But suddenly I am paralyzed. Somewhere along the line, my fight-or-flight instinct turned into *freeze, turn invisible, wait for it to pass.*

Misha Dale. Blonder, heavier, still beautiful, in her small-town way. *Smiling.* I used to dream of her smile—the way, I imagine, bottom-feeding fish must dream of the long dark funnel of a shark's throat.

Misha at twelve: getting all her friends to pelt me with stale lunch rolls when I walked through the cafeteria. Misha at fourteen: planting an animal femur in my locker, claiming it was one of my mother's bones, whispering that I kept body parts in my freezer, a rumor that achieved such aggressive popularity that Sheriff Kahn came over to check. At fifteen, she organized a campaign to raise money for the treatment of my acne. At sixteen, she circulated an online petition to have me suspended from school.

A sadist with a beautiful smile. She, Cora Allen, Annie Baum, and Kaycee Mitchell fed on me for years, grew fat and strong on my misery, ecstatic when junior year I tried to swallow half a bottle of Advil and had to spend a week at Mercy mental hospital—something my father refused to ever acknowledge and of which we have never spoken.

Next time, I'll help, Misha whispered to me in the hall when I finally got back to school.

Terrible girls. Demonic.

And yet, I'd envied them.

"I DON'T BELIEVE it. I heard you might be coming back." Her eyes have softened but her smile is the same—sharp, and slightly crooked. "And your car! Lord knows *you've* done well." She folds me briefly into a one-armed hug. She smells like cigarettes—menthol—and the heavy perfume used to mask them. "Don't you remember me?

It's Misha Jennings. Dale," she corrects herself, shaking her head. "You'd know me as Dale. My Lord, it's been a long time."

"I remember you," I say. Panic flashes in me, quick as the baring of teeth. She heard I was coming back—but how? And from whom?

"You coming in?" She gestures toward the Donut Hole. "They've added about a million varieties in the past year. All thanks to Optimal, I guess. We've had something of a population boom around here, at least by Indiana standards."

The mention of Optimal is bait—it must be. But this time she's not the one who gets to stand on dry land and cast.

"Yeah," I say. "Yeah, I'm coming in."

"The jelly is still my favorite." Her voice has softened, too. She genuinely appears happy to see me. "Do you keep in touch with any of the old group?"

I hesitate, suspecting a trap. But she doesn't seem to notice my confusion. There is no "old group." At least not that I was a part of. I just shake my head and follow her inside. I notice that when she yanks open the door, she makes sure to step ahead of me.

The Donut Hole is home to its namesake, the donut, as well as a truly random assortment of drugstore supplies and our historical society "museum," a corner display with pamphlets for the taking. There's even a small, unofficial free library in the Donut Hole— you leave one, you take one. The particular odor of artificial air freshener, musty old travel guides, and baked goods is like the barrel of a gun, shooting me into the past.

"Must be fun coming back after so long." Misha bypasses the donut counter and heads instead for a wall of pharmaceutical products, where a handwritten sign blandly announces *No Pharmacist/No Suboxone/No Sudafed Sold.*

Misha picks out antacid, baby shampoo, lilac-scented body lotion, a box of Kleenex: all so normal, so domestic, and so at odds with the vicious girl who preyed on me for years.

"*Fun* isn't the word I would choose." *Mistake* is closer to it, especially now as I'm standing in front of Misha at the Donut Hole. "I'm here for work."

When she doesn't ask me what kind, I know for sure she's heard.

"Well, *I* think it's fun to have you back," she says. Her tone is warm, but I can't help but feel a current of anxiety. Misha's fun was always the kind that drew blood. "Your dad must be glad to have you home after all this time. He worked on our fence for us just last summer, after that big tornado came through. Did a great job, too."

I don't want to talk about my dad. I definitely don't want to talk about my dad with Misha. I clear my throat. "So you married Jonah Jennings?" I ask, with a kind of politeness I hope she'll interpret, correctly, as fake.

Misha only laughs. "His brother, Peter."

The new Misha is unpredictable. It's as if the rules to the past have been rewritten, and I'm still learning the game. All I know of Peter Jennings is something I saw in the *Tribune*, a year or two into college—that he'd been arrested for dealing heroin.

Misha fiddles with the magazine rack. "Held out for as long as I could, but he was persistent." She hesitates for just a fraction of a second. "We have a baby, too. Kayla's out in the car. We'll say hi on the way out."

Even inside, with the air-conditioning going, it feels like standing inside a closed mouth. "It's so hot," I say. Misha's not my business. Misha's baby's not my business. But still, I can't help it. "You sure she'll be okay?"

"Oh, she's just napping. She'll scream like anything if I try to wake her. God. Listen to me. Can you believe it? I swear, you blink and ten years go by and it looks nothing like you thought it would." She eyes me as if we're sharing a secret. "You know I work over at Barrens High School now? I've been vice principal for a few years now."

This shocks me. Misha hated school almost as much as I did, though for different reasons. She found class to be an inconvenience, and the mandatory homework a distraction from getting felt up by random guys on the football team.

"I had no idea," I say, although what I really want to ask is:

How? Then again, Barrens High, a tiny school with a graduating class of about sixty, probably isn't attracting the best and the brightest in the education system. "Congratulations."

She waves a hand, but she looks pleased—pleased, and proud. "We make plans and God laughs. Isn't that what they say?"

I can't tell if she's kidding. "I didn't think you believed in all that religious stuff. In high school, you hated the Jesus freaks."

But of course she didn't: she only hated me.

Misha's smile drops. "I was young then. We all were." She lowers her chin and looks up at me through lashes thick with mascara. "It's all water under the bridge now. Besides, you're our big star around here. The girl who got out."

Of course it's bullshit. It has to be. She tortured me, tortured my family, got pleasure out of making me cry. I didn't make that up. I can't have made it up. She left a razorblade taped to my homeroom desk with a note saying, "*Just do it*." That's not water under any bridge I know. She spread rumors, humiliated me, and why? I had no friends anyway. I wasn't a threat. Back then I was barely even a *person*.

Still, when she takes my arm, I don't pull away. "I could use an iced coffee. How about you?"

"Nah," I say. I swing open the cooler door and stare at the rows of bottled water, gripping the handle to steady myself. Six bottles, side by side. Three in each row, except the last, which has only one. That's the one I grab. "Just this."

Even though I really want to say, *Stop touching me. I've always hated you*. But maybe this is Misha's ultimate power, like the witch in *The Little Mermaid*: she steals your voice.

I watch her fill up an iced coffee. I'm trying to figure out how to excuse myself, how to say, *Good-bye, have a very mediocre life, hope I never see you again as long as I live*, when she suddenly blurts, "You know, Brent still asks about you sometimes."

I freeze. "Brent O'Connell?"

"Who else? He's a big shot at Optimal now. Regional sales manager. Followed in his father's footsteps and worked his way up."

Brent was from one of the richest families in town, which for

Barrens means a basketball hoop, aboveground pool, and separate bedrooms for Brent, his older sister, and their parents. Brent's father wore a tie to work, and his mother was like Carol Brady: big smile, blond hair, very clean-looking. Brent was hired at Optimal straight out of high school. Whereas the other guys had after-school jobs pumping gas or stocking shelves at the grocery store or even sweeping stables at one of the local farms, Brent had an internship at Optimal.

"He's still single. A shame, isn't it?" She stirs her coffee slowly, like it's a chemistry experiment and the wrong blend of sugar and cream will make the whole place blow up. One sugar. Stir. Two sugars. Stir. Three. Then, suddenly: "He always had a crush on you, you know."

"Brent's with Kaycee," I say quickly. I have no idea where the present tense came from: five minutes back in town and the past is invading me. "I mean, he was."

"He was with Kaycee, but he liked *you*. Everybody knew that."

Brent O'Connell was one of the most popular guys in Barrens. What she's saying makes no sense.

Except . . .

Except for the kiss, the one kiss, the night of graduation. A first kiss almost exactly like I'd always dreamed it: an unseasonably warm June day, swimming weather, almost; the smell of smoke turning the air sharp; Brent coming through the trees, lifting a hand to his eyes against the dazzle of my flashlight. How many nights had I walked the woods behind my house to the edge of the reservoir, hoping to run into him just that way, hoping he would notice me?

It was so perfect I could never be sure I hadn't made it up, like I did Sonya, a dark-skinned colt-legged girl who lived in the attic of our old house when I was a kid and used to play games with me in exchange for leaves, twigs, and branches I brought her from out-side; she had once been a fairy, I explained, when my mother found the attic nesting with rotten leaves and beetles. Like the games I made up after my mom died, to bring her back. Skipping over the sidewalk cracks, of course, but other ones, too. If I could hold my breath until five cars had passed . . . if I could swim down to the bottom of the reservoir and plunge a finger in the silt . . . if there were an even number of crows on the telephone pole, any number but ten.

Misha carefully seals a top on her iced coffee, pressing with a thumb around the edges. "Why?" she asks—so casually, so sweetly, I nearly miss it.

"Excuse me?" For a second, I really don't understand.

Finally, she looks up. Her eyes are the clear blue of the summer sky. "Why do you think Brent liked you so much?"

I clutch my water bottle so hard the plastic takes on the imprint of my fingers. "I—I don't know," I stutter. Then: "He didn't."

She just keeps smiling. "All that long hair, maybe."

And then, unexpectedly, she reaches out to tug my ponytail lightly. When I jerk away, Misha laughs as if embarrassed.

"Maybe that's where all that BS came from, Kaycee wanting us to hurt your feelings," Misha goes on. "She was cuckoo, that one."

"She was your best friend," I point out, struggling to keep up with the conversation, to haul myself out of the muck of memory.

"She was yours, too, for a little while," she says. "You remember how it was. She scared me to death."

Could it be true? Whenever I remember that time, it's usually Misha's face I picture, her crowded teeth and those big blue eyes, the look of pleasure whenever she saw me cry. Misha was the vicious one, the pit bull, the one who made the decisions. Cora and Annie, the followers: they trailed after Misha and Kaycee like worshipful little sisters.

Kaycee was the prettiest one, the one everyone adored. No one could ever say no to Kaycee. Kaycee was the sun: there was no choice but to swing into orbit around her.

Now, ten years older and ten years free of her best friend, Misha seems to be at ease. "Brent will be so happy you're back, even if you're on opposite sides now. Well," she adds, seeing my face, "it's true, isn't it? You're here to shut Optimal down?"

"We're here to make sure the water is safe," I say. "No more, no less. We're not against Optimal." But to the people of Barrens, the distinction will make little difference.

"But you *are* with that agency group, right?"

"The Center for Environmental Advocacy Work, yeah," I say. "News travels fast."

Misha leans a little closer. "Gallagher said they're going to shut off the water to our taps."

I shake my head. "Gallagher has his signals crossed. Anything like that would be way down the line. We're just here to check out the waste disposal systems." Law school teaches you one thing above all: how to speak while saying absolutely nothing.

She laughs. "And here I was, thinking you were a fancy lawyer. Turns out you're a plumber instead!" She shakes her head. "I'm glad to hear it, though. Optimal's been such a blessing, you have no idea. For a while we thought this town was turning to dust."

"I remember," I say. "Believe me."

A look of sudden pain tightens her forehead and pinches her mouth together. And for a long second she appears to be working something out of the back of her throat.

Then she grabs my hand again. I'm surprised when she steps closer to me, so close I can see the constellations of her pores.

"You know we were only kidding, right? All those things we did. All those things we said."

I guess she takes my silence for assent. She gives my hand a short, quick pulse. "I used to worry sometimes about you coming home. I used to fear it. I thought you might come back looking for—" She breaks off suddenly, and I feel a cold touch on the back of my neck, as if someone has leaned forward to whisper to me.

Kaycee. I'm sure she was about to say Kaycee.

"For what?" I ask her, deliberately trying to sound casual, spinning a rack full of cheap sunglasses and watching the sun get sucked into their polarized lenses.

Now her smile is narrow and tight. "For revenge," she says simply. This time, she holds the door open and allows me to pass through it first.

. . .

MISHA'S BABY IS fussing in the car seat. As soon as she spots Misha, she begins to wail. I let out a breath I didn't know I was holding when Misha reaches in to unbuckle her.

"This is Kayla," she says, as Kayla begins to cry.

"She's cute," I say, which is true. She has Misha's eyes, but her hair, surprisingly thick, is so blond it's nearly white.

"She is, isn't she? Thank God she didn't get Peter's coloring. The Ginger Ninja, they call him at work." Misha jogs Kayla in her arms to quiet her. I somehow can't square an image of Peter Jennings— blunt-jawed and stupid-looking—with this child. But that's always true of babies, I guess: it's not until later that they inherit their parents' ugliness. "You're helping put us on the map, you know, living all the way out in Chicago with your big job." It's half-compliment, half-command. Subtext: *Don't fuck with us.*

"You'll have to come by the house for supper. *Please.* You at your dad's? I still have the number." She turns and fastens Kayla into the back seat again. "And let me know if you need anything while you get settled in. Anything at all."

She slips into the car before I can say don't bother, and there's no way in hell I'd be staying at the old house anyway. As soon as she's gone, it's like a hand has released my vocal cords.

I will never need a thing from you.

I will never ask you for anything.

I've always hated you.

But it's too late. She's gone, leaving only a veil of exhaust that hangs in the thick summer air, distorting everything before it, too, vanishes.

Chapter Two

Senior year, Misha and Kaycee started getting sick. Their hands shook—that was one of the first symptoms. Cora Allen and Annie Baum came next. They would lose their balance even when they were standing still. They forgot where their classrooms were, or how to get to the gym. And it was like the whole town got sick, too, like Barrens spiraled down into the darkness with them.

And all of it? A joke. A prank. All just because they felt like it. Because they wanted attention. Because they *could*.

For a few months, they were famous, at least in Southern Indiana. *Poor, neglected small-town girls.* Misha's and Cora's moms went on local TV, and just before Kaycee ran away, there was even talk of interviews with big-time media. Someone from the *Chicago Tribune* was trying to link the sickness to other examples of corporate pollution. When the girls came out as liars, though, the story fizzled quickly, and no one seemed to blame them, at least not for long. *They just wanted a little attention.* That's how the newspapers spun it.

But I believed them. And there's a part of me that never *stopped* believing the sickness was real—that found myself again and again tugged to questions of environment and conservation, that brought the initial complaint to the agency's attention, cleaving to it with the small but painful, nagging intensity of a hangnail.

When I moved to Chicago, I tossed all my old clothes as soon as I could afford to replace them. I traded in my style, such as it was, for whatever was draped on the mannequins on Magnificent Mile. I ran my accent over a blade, sharpening out the long Midwest vowels, and told people I came from a suburb of New York. I slept off my hangover on Sundays, and never prayed unless it was to clear the traffic. And I stopped calling home.

I did my best to shake Barrens off.

But the more I tried, the more I felt the subtle tug of some half-dead memory, the insistence of something I'd failed to do or see. A message I'd failed to decipher.

Sometimes, coming home after one glass too many—or maybe too few—I'd return to old memories of Kaycee, back to afternoons spent target-shooting rocks at the huge mushrooms in the woods, back to my dog, Chestnut, and back to the convulsions of a town felled by sickness.

Maybe I wanted to believe there was some answer, some reason, for why she did what she did.

Maybe I just wanted to believe her, because after all this time I couldn't understand how she had suckered me so badly.

No matter how many times I swore I would stop, I found myself coming back to the same questions. *Why?* I could shake free of almost everything, but I couldn't shake free of that question. *Why?* Kaycee, Misha, the hoax. *Why?* Sometimes a month or two would go by. Other times, it was every few weeks. I'd lose hours searching Optimal, combing through the pitiful threads of what in Barrens counted for news. Mostly Optimal PR—new housing, a new community center, a new scholarship fund. All that searching over the years, and it never turned up anything of use.

Until, six months ago, it did.

WYATT GALLAGHER'S THREE hundred acres are enclosed entirely by a sagging post-and-beam fence. The drought's been bad here; the green has gone brown, and dust obscures my windshield. As I turn up the gravel drive, several chained-up hound dogs bark in the distance. I knew the CEAW was renting out temporary space for the legal team, but I had no idea we'd be moving onto Gallagher's farm—not that it's surprising, given that Gallagher is the one who first complained about the reservoir.

Considering Gallagher doesn't have a cell phone, not to mention the spotty Wi-Fi, it's a miracle the complaint ever made it past town lines.

When I first saw the post, I immediately recalled the minutes from the most recent town hall meeting to read Gallagher's complaint in detail. It wasn't just Gallagher: a few other families stood up with him and expressed concern about the water. Poring over the minutes, I felt like Alice down her rabbit hole: I tumbled suddenly into old complaints, buried reports from dozens of Barrens residents, all these old issues and complaints neatly spiraled up and bound to Gallagher's rage. I made four pages of handwritten notes just by reviewing the minutes.

And for the first time in a decade, for the first time in my whole life, maybe, I felt as if the whole world had settled down. I felt as if everything had quieted to whisper the small promise of an answer.

I put Gallagher in contact with the Indiana chapter of CEAW. There are procedures, protocols, paths meant to take us out of the entanglement of our fears and suspicions. But the Indiana team, still dealing with a tie-up in state legislation about a clean energy bill that should have been passed two years ago, leaned on us for support.

So here I am.

I pull into the grass alongside a newly painted barn, identifiable as our headquarters only by Joseph Carter's beat-up Camaro with the ubiquitous *COEXIST* bumper sticker. There are a few other cars I recognize and some I don't—Estelle Barry, one of the senior partners, told us we'd be getting some interns from Loyola.

I stuff the empty water bottle into two old gas station coffee cups and toss them on the floor of the passenger seat.

"Williams. You're late," Joe greets me as I enter the giant, airy barn, where the team has set up folding tables, filing cabinets, and a mess of computers cabled to a single power strip. The floor is a tangle of wires and dirt, warped floorboards, and cheap by-the-foot carpet.

"It's 9:02, dude."

Joe and I were hired at the same time in the Illinois office. He's pretty much my best friend, though I'd chew off my hand before I ever admitted that to his face. We were greenies together. We've spent countless nights eating Chinese takeout under the glow of shitty fluorescents, hollow-eyed with exhaustion. We celebrated our first three Christmases as lawyers together. I always had a feeling that, like me, Joe wasn't close to his family; I remember being stunned and a little jealous when he announced last year that he was taking time off for a family vacation in Florida.

"I like that morning, tousled look. It works on you." Joe leads me to a long folding table set up in the back of the barn. "Brings me right back to law school."

"Brings you right back to last weekend," I say, and Joe makes a *who, me?* expression. Joe picks up boyfriends the way corners gather dust. It just happens. "You're in a good mood."

"Maybe the country air agrees with me," he says, stretching his arms out as if he's never seen so much open space before. I wonder why the hell he's so peppy this early, after a long drive from Indianapolis. Joe refuses to sleep in one of Barrens's few motels or rentals, claiming that a gay black man belongs in Barrens, Indiana, like a dildo belongs on a dinner table. Instead, he's chosen to commute.

"Maybe the water does," I say, which makes him laugh. He's not the only one buzzing on something more than caffeine. It's that new-job, new-team energy. These pimply law students still believe we're going to change the world, one oil spill, one contaminated reservoir, one gas pipeline leak at a time.

"Hey guys," Joe speaks up. "This is Abby Williams in the flesh. She's the one who's been cluttering your inbox for the past two weeks."

The research team is a modest one: a first-year associate and a few wide-eyed volunteer law students. I swear one of the girls looks as if she's still in high school. That's CEAW—law on a shoestring budget. Fighting the good fight is always underpaid.

"I believe the correct term is *prepping*," I tell Joe.

He ignores that. "Abby," he says to the rest of the group, "as you all know, is the other lead on the team besides me. But really she's the reason we're here, so when you hate your life in a few days, blame her." He bats his eyelashes at me when I pull a face.

I can match the team to the little thumbnail images I got from Estelle Barry when she was staffing us. There's Raj, the first-year associate, fresh out of Harvard. And, already, I've given out nicknames to the interns: Flora, a perky California girl in a floral top; Portland, a bearded hipster with a flannel too tailored to be truly authentic. Interns are like one-night stands. You can pretend to listen to a name or two, but the outcome never justifies the effort.

Flora leaps to her feet. Wants to prove she did her homework. "So far we've gathered all the town hall meeting notes from the past five years, before they went digital," she says. "Several families started complaining as early as, um . . ." She glances down at her notes, and her face darkens. "As early as three years ago." She tucks her hair behind her ears. "We'll be revisiting those complaints, one by one," she adds, before sitting back down.

"What about now? Who else do we have besides Gallagher?" Gallagher is one of the largest landowners in or around Barrens—his farm's been here since long before my time—and he uses the reservoir for irrigation. According to the notes Joe sent, he's had to rely on it more than ever during the past two years' drought. When he lost whole fields of corn and soybeans, he began to suspect something was wrong with the water—a suspicion borne out by several neighbors' complaints of funny odors from the pipes, of skin inflammations and headaches.

"A half dozen people have signed the complaint he brought to the town. A family called Dawes and a Stephen Iocco seem like our best bets."

"A half dozen complaints? We'll be laughed out of the judge's chambers." Joe is underexaggerating. We'll be kicked out.

Flora looks uncomfortable. "Optimal's the biggest employer in Barrens," she says. "It's hard to sway people."

"It's a company town," I say, and think uneasily about what Misha said—*you're on opposite sides now.* I fear most people in Barrens will be on the other side. "That's going to be our biggest obstacle."

Everyone nods, but the whole team has the slick look of a city—or at least suburbia—about them, and can't possibly understand.

When I was growing up, the morning air was coated in a film of plastic ash; we breathed in Optimal chemicals every time we inhaled, and the chemical smog turned the sun into different shades of pink and orange. Our ears rang with the constant din of Optimal construction: new scaffolds, new warehouses, new storage hangars, new smokestacks. I ate my lunch in a newly added school library built by an Optimal donation and rode home on a bus purchased by Optimal, with parts made by Optimal, and went to Optimal-sponsored dances, bake sales, and cookouts. My dad was right: there *was* someone bigger than us, someone watching us, someone who even made the colors in the sky and textured the air we were breathing. I remember as a kid when the skeleton of the production plant went up. I used to sneak around the reservoir to play on the construction site and write my name in the rusty ooze along the drainpipes, when the house was full of the smell of sick and seemed as if it might fold in on me.

"A company town," Joe repeats. "How quaint."

"When is ETL sending techs?" Raj asks. He even sounds depressed. Environmental Testing Laboratories specializes in clean water supplies, with a focus on heavy metal contamination. Unfortunately, they're one of the few trustworthy labs in the Midwest, and their backlog runs months deep.

"Next week," Joe says. "But we shouldn't expect results on the water to come in before July."

"If that," I say. "What else can we look at? What about accelerated rates of cancer?"

"In the past few years? Nope." Only in our line of business is there reason to be disappointed that cancer doesn't work faster.

"Optimal moved in twenty years ago," I point out.

"You expect us to go back that far? We don't have the manpower. Besides, you know how these hospitals work. It's easier to get blood out of a quarter, and half of what you do get is restricted."

"It's data. Even if it isn't admissible later, it isn't a waste. We should do a survey of local doctors at least." This is how we work: quick back and forth, push and pull. The first time I met Joe, he pointed out that the water bottle I was drinking from was a source of chemical leach, and I pointed out that he was a dick. We've been friends ever since.

I decide to push my advantage. "What about the old cases I sent around? Do we think there's anything there?"

"You mean the Mitchell case?" Flora speaks up. Brightly, of course.

"The Mitchells, Dales, Baums, and Allens were the primary plaintiffs," Portland jumps in. He doesn't miss the chance to get some Brownie points. I like him. "Apparently their daughters— teenagers, four of them—got really sick. Tremors. Vision disturbances. Episodes of fainting. They filed a civil suit when it began to spread—"

"Right. Then dropped it." Joe tosses the stack of notes back on his desk. "It was a hoax. Just young girls trying to get rich in a corporate payout." Then, without warning, he rounds on me. "Wasn't it, Abby?"

Fucking Joe. He's always litigating.

"That's what they said." I think of Kaycee trying and failing to pick up her pencil in art class. I think of her friends, twitching through the halls like insects. "There was a lot of attention on them. One of the girls skipped town afterward. The others withdrew their complaints. I'm originally from Barrens," I explain into a room of blank stares, taking on the *originally* as if afterward I hopped around to, who knows, Paris and Rio and Santa Monica. "I was in school with the girls who got sick."

"But there was an audit." This is from Raj, our first-year associate. I suspect, from the distant courtesy with which he and Joe treat each other, that maybe they are screwing after hours. "Someone from the EPA came down and spent a month doing tests. Optimal passed. They've passed every review since then, too."

"Still, it's a pretty big coincidence, don't you think?" I say, casually, as if the idea never occurred to me before.

"But it wasn't a coincidence," chimes perky Flora again. "Before Optimal moved to Barrens they were headquartered in Tennessee for a decade. At the time, they were called Associated Polymer. I guess that's still the parent company. In the early 2000s a group of plaintiffs brought a case accusing Associated Polymer of illegal dumping. They paid out rather than fight the case, though they always denied wrongdoing." This girl is really working for her A. You gotta love overachievers.

"If they didn't do anything wrong, why would they settle?" Portland asks.

"Optimal's come close to skirting the line a few different times over the past decade," Joe says, riffling through a stack of papers as if checking his notes. It's all for show. He has a photographic memory, or close to it. "Labor violations, tax audits, even a discrimination case. But nothing sticks. No one wants to press them too hard, not when they're bringing in so much cash."

"That's small-town politics for you," I say.

Flora picks up where she left off. "Well, that's how the girls got the idea to shake them down in the first place. One of the girls—Misha Dole—said so."

"Misha Dale," I correct her.

"That wouldn't help us now unless we can prove continuity," Joe puts in. "If we want to do a deep dive on Optimal, we'll need to convince someone there's a reason we're even looking. That means sworn testimonies and affidavits from people who are experiencing symptoms *now*. It also means ruling out other causes. I do not want to put my ass on the line only to find out we got some bedbugs and a crazy old man with a vendetta."

"You have to understand." My voice echoes to the old rafters, and something startles. A bird. I can't see what kind, though. "We're not the heroes here. We're the enemy."

"Oh, good." Joe smirks. "The villains always get better outfits.

Let's get to work." When he claps, the bird alights and swoops down over our heads, beating its way out the open door. Flora screeches.

"It's just a crow," I say. And then, because I can't help it, "Crows have amazing memories. They can distinguish between human faces, too. They're like elephants. They never forget."

"No wonder they always look so angry," Joe adds, and when I look up at him he's lifting an eyebrow at Raj. Yeah, they're fucking.

I CLAIM THE empty desk and busy myself sorting through the notes that Gallagher left us: detailed notations, almost hieroglyphic, of changes to the soil pH, unfamiliar bacterial blight, unexplained crop failure.

One thing leaps out at me right away: Gallagher provided a statement from a woman named Dawes who claims that her kid has been getting rashes. But if they've been using a private well, as most families do in Barrens, it's bad news for us. If the contamination is in the groundwater it will be much harder to tie to a single source. And there's always the possibility the whole case is fluff to begin with, that some locals might be sniffing around for a payout like Kaycee and her friends tried to ten years ago.

For the rest of the team, this is just another case. For me, it's a chance to finally take on the demons. To root out the ugly secrets. I wish I could say I was here to get justice for the voiceless, for those who have no power, just like I once had no power. I wish I could even say I want the bad guys to suffer.

But I just want to know—for sure, for good, forever. For a decade the same questions have been knocking around, over and over, in my head. Only the truth can shut them up.

Chapter Three

At six o'clock I call it: type on the page has begun to collapse before my eyes. Joe packs up when I do, and watching him shove papers into a leather carryall, I wonder what he thinks of this place. I've tried to explain to him where I'm from before, in minor detail and broad generalities. Rural, sticks, wide-open spaces, twenty minutes to get a loaf of bread . . . I wonder if he sees me differently now amid the faint smell of manure and hay and the acres and acres of unpopulated land.

Gallagher's dogs are working overtime, and start up again as soon as Joe and I step outside to lock the place up. Several hundred yards away, the furnace behind the farmhouse feeds the smell of charcoal into the evening air. Gallagher must be home.

"I could use a drink. Any bad sing-along karaoke around here?" Joe gives me a nudge, and I know he's trying to make up for forcing my little confession that I'm from here earlier. That's one of the things you have to love about Joe—off the clock, he always feels guilty for being great at his job. "You can give me the tour of the ol' stomping grounds."

"I'm too wiped," I say, which is half true, and I've gotta see my dad, which I don't even want to get into with Joe. "Besides, don't you have to drive back to Indianapolis?"

"You're. No. Fun." Even his voice changes once he leaves the office, and he told me, when I once pointed that out, that mine does, too.

"Trust me, Carrigan's isn't really your scene."

Joe gives me a wave and gets into his car. I turn away from the dust kicked up by his rental.

I have a headache from puzzling over records old and new. Patterns are like truth. They'll set you free, but first they'll give you a bitch of a migraine.

THE SKY IS in that in-between phase, day and night throwing up a confused riot of blues and pinks and oranges to a soundtrack of crickets. At this hour, Barrens looks beautiful: the fields are wrapped in haze. That's how beauty works in Barrens, by sidling up to you when you least expect it.

Muscle memory takes me straight out to the Barrens Dam. I spent a lot of time here when I was growing up, especially in summer, when the water was low and the current would wrap around my ankles. It was always freezing, but that never seemed to matter. If the weather was nice, it could be pretty lively. Kids catching crayfish, swinging on ropes, floating on tire tubes, fishermen in thighwaders trying their luck with the newly stocked trout.

Today there's not a soul in sight. The water is high and rough and would surely knock me over. I close my eyes and imagine wading in anyway. I imagine the shock of the cold, the sudden weight of all that water. The pressure of the current like a long line of clutching hands trying to pull me under. I stumble backward, hardly managing to keep my balance.

Then: a distant sound of laugher makes me turn. Two girls, one dark-haired, one corn-silk blond, dart hand in hand into the trees, scattering dust and pebbles with every footstep.

Time wrenches away from the present, and instead it's me and Kaycee I see, scabby kneed and wild.

The dark-haired girl drops a sandal and twists around to retrieve it, breaking from her friend. When she spots me, suspicion tightens her face. She looks as if she might say something, but her friend grabs her again by the hand and off they go. I exhale before realizing I'd been holding my breath.

I used to see her everywhere. I grabbed a girl on the L only last year, shouldered my way through a holiday-packed train car and barely managed to hook a hand around her purse strap before she plunged onto the platform.

"Kaycee," I panted out, until she turned and I realized she was far too young—she was the age Kaycee was when she ran, not how old she would have been now.

One time, late senior year, I found her on her knees in the bathroom, the toilet flecked with blood. She kept saying the same thing, over and over, as I stood there wanting to feel vindicated but feeling nothing but panic and a hard dread: if this thing had come for Kaycee, none of us were safe.

She reached out a hand, but not as if she wanted me to take it. As if she was fumbling blind in the dark for something to hang on to. *What's happening to me?* A convulsion worked through her and she turned to the toilet to retch.

I remember thinking the blood was far too red.

I remember, later, thinking, *How would you fake that?*

Chapter Four

I know where I'm supposed to be going, but I stall a little longer and end up in the drive-in parking lot of Sunny Jay's: the seedy general store slash liquor shop where all the high school kids used to buy without ID. Myself included. Across the street, what used to be a patch of scrubby land used informally as a secondary dump has been cleared out, irrigated, and converted into a public playground: a few screaming kids coast down a bright red plastic slide and pump their legs on a spanking-new swing set while their parents wilt in the shade. A big sign on the chain-link fence reads *Optimal Cares!* Not exactly subtle.

I shift my car into park and practically jog to the door. Inside, I head straight for the meager wine section, scanning the crappy pink zinfandel box wines and the Yellow Tail and the jugs of Carlo Rossi. I'm about to pull a decent-looking albeit dusty Malbec from the shelf—hard to go wrong there—when someone speaks up behind me.

"Need help?"

"No, thanks—" I turn and the bottle slips. I barely manage to catch it.

There are a lot of things I've never forgotten about Barrens—a lot of things I can't forget. The smell of chicken farms in summertime. The feeling of being stuck in the wrong place, or in the wrong body, or both. The pitch-black night, the silence.

But I have forgotten this: you can't go anywhere in this town without running into someone. It's one of the first things you shed in a city, the feeling of being watched, observed, and noticed; the feeling of racketing like a pinball between familiar people and places, and no way to get out. First Misha, and now . . .

"You need anything, you let me know." Dave Condor—who always went by his last name—goes back to counting money into a register. His hair half obscures his face. Something about him always set me on edge, even in high school. Maybe because he was always quiet, fluid, like he'd just yawned into being.

I slide the bottle back onto the shelf and take a couple of steps toward the door, already regretting the detour. My dad would probably say this was punishment for wanting a drink in the first place.

Before I can make it outside, he looks up. "Wine's pretty old. Not in a good way. More of beer and liquor people around here," he tells me. "Not from here?"

He doesn't recognize me. It feels like an achievement. I smile. "Why do you say that?" I ask, genuinely curious. Maybe the small-town stain can be scrubbed away after all.

But he just shrugs and grins. "I know all the girls in Barrens. The pretty ones especially."

"I'm sure you do," I say, and he squints at me, as if he's seeing me through a filter of smoke.

I remember all the stories about Condor in high school. He got in trouble for dealing weed—I remember that—and he dropped out a few months shy of graduation, when I was still a junior. I remember Annie Baum getting in Condor's face the same year he got his girlfriend, Stephanie, pregnant. *So Condor*, she said, *I hear you like* putana? Because Stephanie's dad came from Ecuador. And Condor had stood up without saying a word, grabbed his bag, and walked out.

Putana was probably the only Spanish word Annie Baum ever learned.

But there was something else—something involving the Game. I never heard exactly. Condor was a slippery kind of person, always sliding through cracks just before you could pin him into place. He wasn't popular, but he wasn't *un*popular, either. He lived outside the system. Even the stories about him got refracted and rounded off, bounced back to us before they'd had a chance to solidify. Brent O'Connell and his friends supposedly went to Condor's house and beat the shit out of him. Was it something he did to Kaycee? Or tried to do? It was after Becky Sarinelli died, I know that. And I remember, too, that Condor and Becky Sarinelli were friends.

That's the thing I remember most of all: that Condor was always in trouble. Or he was always finding trouble.

He stands up. "Want something drinkable?"

He moves out from behind the counter and crosses the room in a few steps. He still has that weird graceful quality, even though he's built like a farmer, all shoulders and forearms and blunt hands.

"This one's decent." When he reaches for a bottle on the top shelf, his T-shirt rides up, and I see a tattoo wrapped around his torso: a pair of wings. "You like Bordeaux?"

"I like wine," I say. "I'll take it." I follow him up to the register. I have no cash on me, so I hand him my card. When I see him puzzling over the name, I blurt out, "We actually know each other. I'm Abby Williams. I was a year behind you and we were in the same Spanish class."

Unexpectedly, Condor laughs. "I do remember you now," he says. "So you *are* from around here."

"Originally."

"Well, I'm surprised you remember *me*. I was never in class those days. Skipped out to smoke up in the woods behind the football field, most of the time. Hence, my kingdom." He opens his arms to indicate the store, the narrow racks filled with cheap liquor, a whole aisle dedicated to the smallest bottles for the alcoholics who can afford only a little at a time. He doesn't sound bitter, though. "So what are you doing back in this charming little town?"

"I'm working on a case, I'm a lawyer now. Environmental law."

"Big time, huh? Good for you." I can't tell if he means it or not.

"Pretty junior, actually," I say, not to downplay it, just to clarify.

"Still, you got out. That's something. That's a *lot*." This time, I know he means it. "Here." He hands me the bottle without ringing me up. "On me. A welcome-home present."

"You don't have to." I reach for the bag, and as my hand makes contact with his, something passes between us, a quick transfer of chemistry and heat.

That's the whole problem with instincts: they're all fucking wrong.

"I want to."

"Thank you. That's very . . . nice of you," I say, taking the bag and walking away, fast.

"And hey, Abby," he calls, when I'm already almost out the door. "Don't be a stranger. I never forget a pretty face twice." Condor's smile is wide, and maybe, just maybe, genuine.

And I know right then that I'm in trouble.

Chapter Five

Less than a mile from my father's house, the road narrows and becomes a gravel path, so familiar it shrinks a decade into no time at all. Tiny rocks ping against the car while birds—turkey vultures, this time—pick over a carcass in the road. I lean on the horn and they look up with those dull hooded eyes before lifting into the air.

It's just dinner, I remind myself. Simple. Quick. My father has no power over me. He is just a person, even if he's a terrible one. There are bad people in the world; sometimes, they are your own parents. But he can't see into my thoughts. He can't read my sins, like I once thought he could.

I can't avoid him, anyway.

Like so many around here, my childhood home is a modest split-level dumped on a plot of land in the middle of nowhere. There's nothing strange about it, no darkness to its gabled roof or clapboard siding, nothing peculiar in the concrete porch or the patch of yard browning in the sun.

Still, the house seems to rush toward me and not the other way around. Like it's eager to get me inside. Like it's been waiting.

For the first time in nearly a decade, I'm home.

I kill the engine and fuss with my hair, which is knotted on the top of my head, killing time, buying an extra few seconds. I almost never wear my hair down, and by now it reaches midway down my back. Every few months I take scissors to it myself, trimming away the dead ends. I've always wanted to cut it short, always sworn I was going to. Several times I've even been in a hairdresser's chair before panicking at the sight of the scissors. My dad always told me that my hair is my one good quality, and somehow that idea grew into the very hair itself—that, and the memory of my mom running her fingers through it from scalp to end as she braided it so that it would later fall in waves. Somehow I fear that without long hair I'll be ugly. But even worse, that by cutting my hair I'll be cutting away this memory, one of my few very good ones. I'll have to lose her again. But this time, it really will be my fault.

I climb out of the car and stand for a second, staring out at the line of trees in the forest: acres running down to the reservoir, public land, and my private oasis when I was little. I try and remember the last time I saw my father but I get a composite of images: his hand around my throat, the time he rooted out a thong in my underwear drawer and made me wear it around my neck at dinner for a week. The moments of kindness, strange and startling and almost more painful than the abuse: flowers gathered for me in a cup by the bed, a birthday surprise trip to a carnival in Indianapolis, the time he helped me bury Chestnut after I found him stiff and cold in the woods behind the house, his gums crusted over with vomit.

When I left town, four days after my eighteenth birthday, and two days after graduation, I drove west to Chicago with my heart in my throat and two suitcases in the trunk, certain for every second past the city that God would strike me dead. *You're only safe in Barrens.* For more than half my life I thought I would be sent to hell if I jumped ship. Like leaving was the end-all sin. But then I realized hell was right here in Barrens, and that made leaving worth the risk.

Gravel crunches under my boots as I make my way up the path. There's the bird feeder I made when I was eight. There's a dirt patch where the grass never recovered from the kiddie swimming pool that sat there through many seasons. There's my mother's old wind chime clinking softly from the porch—I feel a pang at this—that she made herself out of tin and painted wood. A splintered cross is still tacked to the front door.

The air smells like charred logs, like summer. But behind the familiar smells of grass and dirt and char that I've always loved is another odor, thick and pungent. I know that smell. Reeds. Rot.

The smell of drought. The reservoir is less than a half mile from here, concealed from view just beyond the trees.

Inside, I find my father in the squat little living room, washed in bluish TV light that reminds me of being underwater.

My father looks small. Small, and old. The shock of seeing him nearly causes me to stumble. He was always a big guy, not tall but the kind of person who swallowed a room just by walking into it, and muscled from years of working outside: roofing, carpentry, excavating, work on the local farms. The few times a year we speak on the phone, that's who I imagine on the other end of the line.

Now his muscles seem to have melted into folds of skin, which is gray and thin and draped like a sheet over his bones. He looks like a powdered corpse, and when he turns toward me, it takes his eyes a second to focus.

For a moment, I'm terrified: he doesn't recognize me, either.

Then he begins to hoist himself up, gripping the arms of his easy chair.

"It's okay, Dad. Sit." I lean down and let him hug me. I can't remember the last time we hugged.

"Sweetheart." He pats my shoulder and brushes his dry lips against my cheek. His voice is faint, and his greeting—*sweetheart*—is one he hasn't used since I was a small child. "I hoped you were still coming."

"Of course, Dad. I told you I was," I say.

"It's been so long . . ." He closes his eyes, leaning back in his chair, as if even the small physical effort has exhausted him.

I resist the urge to apologize. He knows why I haven't come sooner. Everyone knows—about his temper, about his fits, about his dark moods. For weeks after my mother died, everything I did made him erupt in a fury. And then, just as quickly, he would withdraw into silence, would pretend I didn't exist at all. But everything he did was okay, because he'd "found the Lord." In town, he wore his religion like armor, and somehow that kept him untouchable. At home, he wielded it like a weapon.

Everyone knew, and at the same time, no one saw; no one said a thing. In the city, everyone is anonymous; but in a small town where everyone knows everyone, it takes real skill to look the other way when you're looking at a face you recognize.

Nothing has changed in here, aside from the addition of a single photo—one I sent from college graduation—tacked above the mantel. My mother's china on display in the hutch. The painting of Jesus on the cross in the corner of the dining room. An old box TV with a VCR—God, a *VCR*—just opposite my dad's easy chair. A fine layer of dust on everything. And my dad's slippers—the same slippers he had ten years ago—nearly worn through. It's as if time stopped when I left.

I didn't know what to expect coming here. My aunt Jen— Dad's sister, older by four years—sent me a note last Christmas after she'd passed through. She was the one who told me about Dad's decline. Alzheimer's, she thought, though of course my dad refused to go to the doctor.

It's just little things, she'd said. *Where his keys are. Mood swings. He falls down a lot. He still knows who we are, though.*

"How was the drive?" His voice sounds old, worn to thinness, and makes an unexpected swell of pity rise inside of me.

"Fine. Traffic stopped up on 83, but only for a half hour or so." Ten years and we're talking about traffic. There's a long, awkward silence and I fumble for something to say. What did we ever talk about? *Did* we talk?

Instinctually, I count the steps to the front door in my head: twenty-three. Thirteen to the door that leads through the kitchen to the backyard. Seventeen to the stairs, in case I need to flee to my room.

My *old* room. This isn't my house anymore. This isn't my life.

"I've made dinner," he says, almost proudly. This time he succeeds in pulling himself out of the chair and, leaning heavily on one hand, fumbles for his cane. "I need this thing now."

I don't really know what I'm supposed to say, so I just give him a tight-lipped half smile and follow him into the kitchen. He's slow, hunched over his cane, and seeing him like this is beyond confusing. That feeling again—sadness, pity, yearning to make it better—flares up in me, unbidden. I've prepared, but not for this. Suddenly I feel a new kind of fear—that I will have to learn all over again how to survive in the presence of this man, how to find myself. That he will make me love him again, and then disappoint me, and I will have to learn all over again how to unlove him.

My dad has made lasagna—"from scratch," he says, "not the frozen ones"—and I feel another pang when I imagine him stumping around the kitchen on his cane, cutting onions one-handed, layering the sauce and cheese. It's vegetarian, too. Although the signs of his illness are there—he forgets the word for potholders, and mentions my mother once in the present tense—he hasn't forgotten that I don't eat meat.

I suddenly wonder if he remembers the night we sat at the table and I asked if he knew what happened to Little Bubsy, the pet rabbit I kept as a kid. I was probably five. My mother stared down at her plate, her eyes milky from drugs and illness.

"You just ate him," my dad said. I haven't been able to stomach meat since.

I wash my hands in water so hot it sends billows of steam toward the ceiling.

We have our lasagna mostly in silence. It's only after dinner, when I'm washing the dishes by hand, that I realize we didn't say grace over our meal.

Did he forget?

Sweat gathers under my armpits.

He falls asleep in front of the TV while I clean. I grab a quilt—a quilt my mother made—and cover him in the chair. He rouses slightly and grabs my arm so hard I nearly gasp, unreasonably—afraid.

"I'm happy to have you back," he says. "I'm happy you're here."

Suddenly I want to cry. This is the worst trick of all.

"Only for a visit, Dad." I fight to keep my voice from breaking. After so many years. How *dare* he? Anger was the only thing I had, the only thing I've ever been able to depend on.

How dare he take that from me, too?

Chapter Six

Only the second day on the job and the potential civil suit is imploding: in the morning, I find out that two of our half dozen complainants, the Davies and the Ioccos, have now withdrawn their complaints. Rich Iocco is coach of the local Little League team, and funds for new uniforms and a bus to away games mysteriously dried up after Optimal learned he was planning to talk to us.

Which means that either we might be onto something or we might be running straight toward a brick wall.

Unfortunately, the two aren't mutually exclusive.

I send Portland out to speak to some local GP's, to swing by the hospitals and befriend the nurses—brutal, often fruitless work, but he's easy on the eyes and his beard should make people feel at ease. Portland and Flora will head up the door-to-door canvass to try to suss out potential support. A handful of farms top the list of water usage per acre, so I direct them to start there: if anyone should be worried about supply, it's the people whose livelihoods directly depend on it. Farmers don't get their subsidies from Optimal, and may be easier to persuade. It will be my job to track down Carolina Dawes, whose kid has been complaining of rashes.

Joe and Raj get to geek out on data: two years ago Optimal

subcontracted IBC Waste to deal with hazardous chemical disposal and environmental protocol.

In other words, they passed the buck, big time.

"Even if we prove Optimal is pumping goddamn uranium into the kiddie pools, they will just point the finger at IBC," Joe says.

It's not even nine thirty, and already, my mood is cracking. I take a deep breath. "So we'll have to show that Optimal had direct knowledge. We'll have to prove they're the ones behind the steering wheel."

Joe sighs. "Hooray. Two cases for the price of one. I always loved me a twofer."

CAROLINA DAWES LIVES in a converted hunter's cabin in what counts for a zoning error: just beyond it lies a now-defunct dump within shouting distance of the shore of the reservoir. The only car in the driveway is mounted on cinderblocks.

I have to wedge my car in behind a rust-eaten Geo Tracker so filmed with dirt the original color is impossible to measure. Someone has written *Wash Me* on the rear window with a finger. Real original.

When I step onto the porch, a Chihuahua starts freaking out, pressing its nose against the screen and yapping incessantly. A woman hushes it sharply.

"Chucky! Shut it!" she says. A second later she shoves open the door so hard I have to jump back. "Sorry. Damn thing's all swelled up." She is enormously fat, wearing teal polka-dot stretch pants and an oversized shirt with a Carhartt logo across the chest. Cigarette smoke rises off her like a mist.

"Ms. Dawes?" I ask.

"What do you want?" She says it not rudely, but as if she's genuinely curious.

"I'm Abby Williams. I work with the Center for Environmental Advocacy." This means nothing to her, obviously. "A few days ago, one of our team members was going door to door and you mentioned you'd had some kind of problems with your water . . ."

"I didn't say that." For a second, my heart drops, until she adds, "I said my kid Coop has been getting rashes. At first I thought it was ringworm like from one of the other kids but when I went to the clinic the doctor said no that wasn't it. Then he asked me about what kind of laundry detergent I use and where we get our water from, so I put two and two together."

"Does your son ever swim in the reservoir?" I ask her, and she nearly hacks up a lung.

"He don't know how." She pounds her chest, loosening whatever's rattling around there. "Sorry. I worked over at Optimal for fifteen years. That's why the cough." She lights a cigarette.

"Is that why you left?" I ask.

"Didn't leave. I got fired."

My heart sinks: any good defense lawyer will blow holes through her story, claim she's looking for revenge and a payday. Still, I persist. I kind of like Carolina Dawes and her polka-dot stretch pants.

"You have well water, don't you?" I ask her, and her expression folds up around her cigarette, like she's trying to suck herself down it, not the other way around.

"We *should*," she says. "But how things been going . . . this is the third year straight running with a drought . . ." She taps her ash angrily onto the porch. "So I figure why not take a little something free?"

Suddenly I understand. The PVC piping, the hoses rigged like laundry lines in the backyard: she's been tapping the reservoir.

"But that's when Coop started having all those problems, when we decided to try and give the well a rest . . ."

"Do you have pictures of his rash?" I ask her, and she grinds the cigarette out into the railing, exhaling a long plume of smoke.

"I can do you one better," she says, and then turns her head to shout. "Coop. Coop! I know you hear me, so get your little butt down here. He's a little shy," she adds, as someone moves in the darkness behind the screen door. "And all that itching and nonsense ain't helping none, let me tell you. Come on, Coop. It's all right. This nice lady's here to help."

A little boy, maybe five or six, edges carefully into the light. He is unexpectedly beautiful: big blue eyes, blond hair, perfect features. Cherubic. Half his face is still in shadow; half his face glows in the sun.

He steps right up to the door and places a hand to the screen. Then he turns and leans his cheek against it, and the sun catches the scabrous raw sores on his cheek and jaw and neck, the desperate marks where he has scratched his way through the skin.

"It itches," is all he says.

Chapter Seven

What do I remember?

—Kaycee Mitchell narrowing to a long dark shadow, moving down the road, whacking at the corn with a blunt stick, teasing out the rats, sending a blur of dark bodies across the road.

—Misha Dale, smile as wide as a fishbowl, standing by the bathroom sinks when I pushed out of a stall. How I almost crawled back into the toilet. How I wanted to flush myself away. *You know there's operations for ugly now*, she said, cocking her head. *I bet we could even raise donations.* Kaycee was putting on lipstick, drawing the lines in real thick. Unexpectedly, she turned around. *They've got operations for being dumb, too*, she said to Misha. *But once they can cure bitch I'll let you know.* A warning in her eyes when she looked at me, a subtle tic: *Go.*

—Kaycee leaning against a fence, smoking a cigarette, the dazzle of floodlights in the football stadium turning her to silhouette. The smoke, the way it curled, like it had questions to ask.

—*God doesn't exist, people made him up.* It flew out of Kaycee's mouth in the middle of senior year. History. Her fingernails were filed sharp, painted with Wite-Out. When I turned around to stare, I hardly recognized her.

—Kaycee alone in the art studio, after the final bell, working on an enormous canvas, slashing in broad strokes of red and black, painting like she was cutting, like the color was bleeding out.

—And finally: Kaycee, bent over a toilet in the fourth-floor bathroom. The stall door swinging open. A sour smell hanging heavy in the air. *Go away*, she said, when I reached for her. She turned; streaks of bright red blood ringed her mouth. Then I saw it: blood on her fingers, blood in the toilet. Vomit tangling her hair. *Leave me alone, you freak!* But instead I just stood there. She retched again, almost missing the toilet. This time when she looked at me, her eyes were wide and desperate, like open sores. *What's happening?* she whispered. *Please. What's happening to me?*

Chapter Eight

If there are chemical contaminants in the water now—blistering Cooper Dawes's skin, leaching bad smells from the taps—there might have been chemical contaminants in the water ten years ago, when Kaycee Mitchell first started collapsing in class. I return to the idea that maybe Kaycee Mitchell really *was* sick. That there was truth buried deep inside the lies.

If so, I could use Kaycee's testimony, especially now that the Davies and the Ioccos are backpedaling. A little thrill moves through me at the idea of finally having an excuse to reach out—but I have no idea where she is.

And for the first time in a decade, the full force of the question returns to me: Why did she run away? Misha didn't. None of the other girls did. Was Kaycee simply looking for an excuse to disappear?

I've looked for her before. How could I not? I found hundreds of Kaycee Mitchells on Facebook but never the real one. Once, late at night, my then roommate banged through the door, drunk, and caught me combing through pictures of strange blond girls. *Who's the hottie you're creeping?* she asked. I slammed the computer shut so hard I nearly snapped her nails off. After that she never walked around in a towel in front of me again; she brought her clothes into the bathroom and changed right after leaving the shower.

How could I explain it to her? I couldn't even explain it to myself. All I know is that Barrens broke something inside of me. It warped the needles on my compass and turned the south to north and lies to truth and vice versa. And what happened to Kaycee senior year—what happened to all her friends as they began falling, fainting, and forgetting—is the central magnet. If I have any hope of finding my way again, I have to figure out which way the truth was pointing all along.

Which way did you run, Kaycee Mitchell?

THERE ARE FOUR porn stores and six strip clubs named Temptations in Indiana, three of them in Gary alone. Luckily, only one is in Barrens.

I count the rings by primes. One. Three. Five.

Kaycee's mom ran off even before I became friends with her, back in first grade—that was a bad time for crank in Indiana, and her mom was a user. Her dad, a notorious drinker, owned the 99-cent store. I never liked being at Kaycee's house when her dad was home, and I got the sense that she didn't, either. That's why we were so close when we were kids: we met in the woods, and we practically lived there, toeing the edge of the reservoir, pretending the water was a mirror that would slip us into a different world.

When we were in middle school, Frank Mitchell opened a porn shop—the same one I passed on my way into town. Everybody was sure he sold weed there, too, and six-packs from a cooler concealed behind a wall of old *Playboy* magazines.

I'm about to hang up when he answers.

"Mitchell's." The site gives the official name of the store as Temptations, but we always called it Mitchell's, plain and simple. I guess he's picked up the habit.

"Hi, yes. Mr. Mitchell." That uneasy feeling hits me right in my chest. He's one of those men with a face like a *caution* sign, always on the edge of a bad mood, like he could snap at any moment.

His voice is harsh over the phone, like he just swallowed a handful of gravel. Still, I keep my voice sunny. "My name is Abby, and I'm an old friend of Kaycee's." As soon as I mention her name, his breathing hitches, then starts again. "I'm back in town for a bit and was just wondering if you knew how I could reach her? I would love to connect with her."

"No." The word is a short, explosive burst. Then silence for so long I check to see if he's hung up. "No idea where that girl is. Haven't talked to her in almost a decade."

"You don't have a number? An e-mail?"

"She ran off because she wanted to be alone, so I left her alone," he says—sharply, like he's daring me to say he did wrong. "If you were such good friends with Kaycee, why don't *you* know how to get ahold of her?"

"Mr. Mitchell, wait," I say, before he can hang up. I squint into the lowering sun. "Do you remember when Kaycee got sick, when she was in high school? Can you talk to me a little about that time?"

Another pause, and my pulse begins to climb. Nothing from the end of the line.

"What are you," he said, "some kinda journalist?"

"No," I say. "Just a friend."

"What'd you say your name was?"

"Abigail." I don't give my last name. "I'm from Barrens, like I said. I just had a few questions for Kaycee. I was hoping she'd be willing to talk to me."

There's another long stretch of silence.

"Mr. Mitchell?" I say. "Are you still there?"

"Still here." He clears his throat. "As far as I'm concerned, Abigail, you can talk to Kaycee in hell."

Chapter Nine

The house I rented is tucked behind a beauty salon in town, not far from where I once babysat as a girl. When I was a kid, the town was basically Main Street, which was also Route 205, and the three official streets that bisected it: First, Second, and Maple. Other than that, it was all nameless county roads that everyone called by the people and businesses that lived there—the Simmons' Farm Road, the Dump Route. Since Optimal arrived, however, the town has been spreading steadily, sweating new housing clusters and tackle stores and stop signs. The single real estate agent I could dig up told me glibly that Barrens was in the middle of a housing boom—as proof, she could find me only two places for rent, and the other was a converted shed at the back of a slaughterhouse.

As I get out of the car, the loud sound of crickets is broken by a kid laughing. Across the street, outside another nearly identical two-bedroom, a young girl hula-hoops in the driveway. Long-haired, pretty, giggling.

In the hiss of the wind I think I hear a whispered voice and turn around. A blond girl is just locking up the salon and for a second, I imagine that Kaycee Mitchell has come back after all, or that she never really left. She must feel me staring because she turns and glares, hitching her bag a little closer.

But Kaycee, I realize, has left her fingerprint on everything in Barrens; by disappearing, she ensured that she would never leave. She is a slick on the telephone poles once molting with flyers begging for information on her return. She is a shadow on the football stadium bleachers, where she once sat to watch Brent play, sucking on a Newport while Misha and Cora shimmied on the sidelines in their cheerleader costumes. She is in the reservoir and the sky, she wanders the halls at Barrens High, I bet, her face mascara streaked, holding a tissue soaked with blood.

Of all of them, Kaycee was the only one who ever showed me pity. Sometimes, she even showed me kindness. Almost as if brief flares of the past, of our friendship, would sometimes burst again into her memory.

But she could be cruel, too. I remember when she collapsed out of her chair at the desk next to mine, she nearly bit off my hand when I tried to help her. Not metaphorically: she actually almost snapped down on my fingers, like a dog.

And then there was Chestnut, and the collar she'd left in my locker. One of her last gestures. Twisted, cruel, incomprehensible.

Almost as bad as killing him in the first place.

THE HULA-HOOP SLIPS from the little girl's waist, and the noise of it startles me back to the present. She hops out to recover it with her arm, spinning it back up to her elbow.

As I lean over to get my bag out of the passenger seat, a male voice rings out: "Hannah! Time to get ready for bed."

I get out of the car again and almost can't believe it: it's Condor. He's silhouetted in the beam of light from the streetlamp.

"Abby?" He squints, and the girl—Hannah—turns to stare. A smile creeps over his face. "You following me?"

"Seems like it's the other way around." I slam my car door, and hitch the bag a little higher on my shoulder.

"I don't know." He gestures to the little girl. "Hannah and I have been living here for a long time." He puts a hand on Hannah's head when she tries to get behind him. "Small town." I can't tell if he means that as a good thing or a bad thing. "This is my daughter, Hannah. Go on," he says, when she doesn't greet me. Then he turns back to me. "She's shy," he says.

"That's all right," I say. "Looks like you've got some moves on that hula-hoop, Hannah. I'm impressed."

This earns me a cautious smile. "Thanks," she says.

"Hannah's in a big hula contest next week," Condor says, and she says "*Dad*," and glares at him.

"It's not a contest. It's a competition," she says with great disdain, and Condor gives me a *what-can-you-do-kids-these-days* kind of look. "There's a trophy and everything," Hannah goes on. "I could teach you, if you want."

"Uh-uh, no way. I'm wise to your tricks." He grabs Hannah by the shoulders and turns her in the direction of the house. "No more stalling. This hula girl is twirling off to bed. Run upstairs and I'll be up in a minute."

"Nice to meet you, Hannah." I give her a wave and she sprints upstairs, slamming the door behind her. "Cute kid," I say.

Condor shrugs. "She's a handful, but I'll probably keep her." He's wearing a T-shirt that shows off his tattoos, bare feet, jeans rolled up to the ankle. He looks like he smells good, like he feels good, and I suddenly imagine his hands all over me.

Dangerous.

"So we're neighbors, huh?" Condor says.

"For a little while," I say quickly. Before I can regret my tone of voice, I start for the door. I'm going to take my cue from Hannah. "Good night."

"I wouldn't have pegged you for the early-to-bed type," he says, before I can make it across the yard.

I hate it when people read me. I turn around to face him. "It was a long day."

"I'm right, aren't I?"

"You're cocky," I say.

"How was the wine, by the way?" he calls out again as I reach the door. "Did you like it?"

"No idea," I say, and then, before I can stop myself: "Want to find out?"

Just then, Hannah appears in an upstairs window and shouts: "Dad! I'm ready!"

"One minute, sweetheart." He smiles. "I'll come by after I tuck her in. Can't let a lady drink alone."

I bump into the low, plaid-upholstered couch as I enter the darkened living room, and curse at it, as though it is the idiot who just invited Condor over for a drink and not me. I'm used to tight spaces, rooms that open straight into other rooms, apartments too small to even need a hallway, but this house makes me uneasy, because it's not *my* space. And the disarray of items the owner has chosen to keep around are even worse—they should add up to form a picture of the people who once lived here but there's no story, just junk.

Quickly, I slip on a casual T-shirt, one that hangs off my shoulder a bit and shows the straps of my bra. Brush my teeth and wash my hands. Wash them again.

I head to the kitchen to dig up some glasses, but the cabinets are as disorganized as everything else. Mouse droppings along the back of one of them.

Condor knocks on my front door so lightly I almost miss it. He's carrying a box of Chik'n Biscuit crackers and a block of cheddar.

"Hannah's favorite," he says, gesturing to the box of crackers. "Don't tell her."

"Jars okay? Couldn't find actual wineglasses."

IN THE LIVING room, Condor takes the sofa. I grab a rickety chair and set it across from him. He pours us each some wine and tells me there's a way to open a bottle by using a shoe. He tells me about the store, about his favorite wines, about the garbage Hannah watches on TV, about how he likes to hunt on the weekends. Most of it is not very surprising. He brags about his great aim, then laughs.

The first glass makes me warm and the second glass makes me feel loose and the third, when we're nearly at the end of the bottle, brings him more strongly into focus: his jaw, the way his eyes crease when he smiles, the way he uses his hands. His lower lip, perfect for biting.

"What is it?" he says, and I realize I've been staring. "Why are you looking at me like that?"

"I'm not." I stand up quickly, so he won't see me blush, and pass into the kitchen. Of all the things the landlord left, one of them is a bottle of Johnnie Walker stashed beneath the sink. "I mean, I was just wondering what it's like to live here. That's all."

"Didn't you used to live here?" Condor asks. He doesn't blink when I set down the whiskey.

"I meant now," I say. I'm half-drunk and work will be a bitch tomorrow. But it's too late anyway. It was too late when he called out to me across the yard. "What's it like, living here *now*?"

Condor leans forward and tips the last drops of wine into my glass. He spins the empty bottle between his palms. "I haven't *only* lived here," he says, in a different tone. "I took Hannah and moved to the coast of Florida when her mom and I——" He breaks off suddenly, and a shadow moves across his face and takes the rest of his smile with it.

He uncaps the whiskey and pours us each a glass. When he looks up, his expression is unrecognizable.

And again, dimly, I remember the rumors: some trouble in high school, something Condor did.

"It's all right," he says with a shrug. "I'm still angry about it, I guess. Hannah's the best kid in the world, and her mother wants nothing to do with her. Drugs," he clarifies, in answer to a question I haven't asked. "She had an accident and then got hooked on the pain pills. She's in Indianapolis. Or she was. Went through rehab a few years ago. Still has visitation rights." Condor frowns into his glass.

"Sorry. For asking." Again, it isn't quite the right thing to say.

"I bet you are." Condor's crooked smile is back. I want to tell him that isn't how I meant it, but I can't——what's the point, anyway?

"It's better now that Hannah's old enough to understand. I'm very honest. She knows her mom's an addict, that she's sick, that it's not Hannah's fault." He looks away. "Ah, well. Mistakes of our youth, you know? You never really outrun them."

"I hope that isn't true," I say, which makes him laugh.

"What about you?" he asks, settling back again in the sofa. "What's it like coming home after all this time?"

"I'm not really coming home," I say, as if he's accused me of something. "I'm just here for a job."

"Still. Must be weird to see how things have changed . . ."

"And how they haven't," I say, and he raises his eyebrows. I'm more than a little drunk now, and it feels great. All the doubts and uncertainties are drowning. Condor is here and we both know how this goes, and until then there's nothing to do but keep going.

Condor sets down his glass. In the silence, he fingers the scar over his lip.

"What happened there?" I ask.

Condor just shrugs again. "Another childhood mistake."

I lift up my glass. "To childhood mistakes, then."

Slowly, he smiles. "And grown-up ones," Condor says.

"Sure," I say. "To grown-up ones, too."

He tastes like whiskey when he leans in to kiss me, and long after he leaves, my skin continues burning.

Chapter Ten

My sleep is restless, full of nightmares that feel more like memories, one bleeding into the other. Now I'm shivering yet drenched in sweat. All my life I've been like this—too hot or too cold, too conspicuous or too plain, too tall or too thin or too *something*. My mother used to say I was like Goldilocks, trying out Big Bear's and Little Bear's things. She used to call it "Middle Bear" when something was just right. I wake up and for a second the smell of my mother, her lotion, her hands, seems to float through the room.

In the bathroom I touch my lower lip, as if Condor might have left an impression. Instead, the Bordeaux has left a black stain. *Weak spots.* The words float suddenly to my mind. He kisses just how I thought he would, as if he needs it.

And yet it went no further than that. As soon as I started to take off his belt, he stopped me.

Wait, he said. *I should get home.*

I shower, and dress—the sky has turned gray and heavy, I notice—and as I wrangle with my hair I think about weak spots. Being a lawyer is a little like being a doctor in reverse: you look for the damage and try to grow it, try to push in, dig a little deeper, open up the festering places, like how I used to scout the woods for soft soil, spaces where I could easily bury my belongings—little things I didn't want my dad to find, like the cigarette stub Kaycee and I split in fifth grade, the one and only time I tried smoking, or the orange blush and shiny mirrored compact, obviously stolen, she gave me for my birthday.

Carolina Dawes has confirmed we're right about the water, but she isn't enough: she's not credible, and Optimal will no doubt be able to show that Coop comes in contact with a number of things that might have caused skin irritation. And Optimal's public image is as sturdy and slick as the plastics they make. Still, there must be a weak spot, a break, a place I can crack with a little bit of pressure.

Luckily, there's only one Brent O'Connell in Barrens, and it seems he's an early riser.

WOODY'S IS JUST clearing its breakfast rush when I arrive an hour later. I check my reflection in the rearview mirror one last time before getting out of the car. My dark waves—one good feature I inherited from my mother—have already expanded in the humidity, but I look alert and sharp and, shockingly, not at all hungover. If I'm not beautiful, I'm still nothing like the girl I was when he knew me.

The sky darkens overhead, and I wonder when the clouds will tire of holding back the rain and let go.

Before I get a chance to open the door, it swings open from the inside, and there's Brent O'Connell, smiling, motioning me inside. I was hoping he might have gotten fat, or lost some of his hair.

He looks just the same as he did in high school—blue eyes, blond hair, a boy-next-door, but all grown up. The only thing that's changed is his clothing. He has abandoned the ripped jeans and V-neck T-shirts of our high school years for khakis and a collared shirt.

And even though I'm wearing tailored jeans and a decent blazer, I have a brief flash of panic: It's an act, and he'll know it. All the seams will come apart.

I remember his skin, warm despite the chill of the lake water that dripped from his hair. I remember voices in the distance, the smell of house paint and wood smoke. How he reached for my hair, how he left me, wordlessly, lifting a finger to his lips. *Shhh.*

"Abby Williams," he says. "God. You look fantastic."

"It's hindsight," I say, and Brent laughs. "Looks good on every-one." I stop myself from saying that Brent looks good too—not because it isn't true, but because it is. Upon closer inspection, Brent *has* changed. He's just as handsome, but in a softer, more accessible way. His muscles have relaxed and he looks just tired enough to be real.

He shakes his head. "If I'd been smarter in high school . . ." Real, fake, fabricated. Maybe everyone in Barrens has trouble tell-ing the difference. "Come in, before it starts dumping on us."

I have to squeeze myself past him and for a second I smell his shampoo, and I remember that night in the woods and the water left on my skin from his hair after he kissed me.

I follow him to a booth in the corner and slide into my side, clutching a menu like it's a life preserver. In high school, Woody's was huge: when there were no parties, nowhere to go or no one to buy beer or no money to buy it with, everyone would go to Woody's for the free coffee refills, shouldering up next to old-timers playing cards in their usual booths and groups of giggly girls pitching in for a plate of curly fries. I used to come by myself, after everyone else had cleared out, just to avoid being at home. It smells like the fryer and maple syrup just like it always did.

"So?" Brent leans forward, as if he can't stand to leave any dis-tance between us. "How is it to be home after all these years? Just like you remember it?"

"Hard to say, since I've spent half my life trying not to remem-ber," I say, and Brent laughs. Of course, he has no way of knowing how hard I've tried to put Barrens behind me. And how badly I've failed.

The waitress shows up, and I can tell by the way she laughs that Brent is still the big fish in town. I duck my head and pretend to be absorbed by the menu.

"You like omelets? Best in town. Two Western omelets, please,"

Brent says. "And two coffees. You don't mind if I order for you, do you?" His voice is teasing, and friendly, and happy.

I snap my menu closed. "I'll just have scrambled eggs. No coffee. Tea would be great." As soon as she leaves, I'm not sure why I did it. Only that I don't want to make Brent so happy.

Or I do, which I can't allow, either.

If he senses a rebuttal, he doesn't act like it. "Strong choice," he says. "You know, I always liked that about you—how you did your own thing. You never ran with the pack."

I was too busy running from *them*, I nearly point out, but I don't. He's just being nice. But it's Brent.

"You must be wondering why I wanted to see you," I say.

"Come on, Abby. You haven't been gone *that* long. You know how this town works. You hadn't been back five minutes when Misha put out an all-points bulletin."

The idea stirs an old anxiety, the kind that comes from spending years as a bull's-eye in a field full of arrows. "You're still close with Misha, then?"

"We *became* close, after . . ." He trails off, fiddling with his coffee cup, spinning it between his hands. "I guess that kind of thing bonds you pretty good. You know Misha's vice principal at the school now?"

I still can't wrap my head around it, but I nod. "She told me."

"She's doin' good, too." Then he clears his throat, looking suddenly embarrassed. "Well, I know you didn't come back so we could take a stroll through memory lane. I know why you guys are here and I'm happy to help however I can. I figure I owe you that much, right?"

"Owe me?" My pulse picks up. "What do you mean?"

For a second, he falters. When he adjusts his position, the vinyl squeaks faintly again, like the sound of a new shoe. "Teenagers can be real assholes. I know we were. I know *I* was. And Misha, and Kaycee, and the others. Honestly, I have no idea why." He puts his hand through his hair and it falls easily back into place. "What I'm trying to say"—he looks hard at me, as though seeing me for the first time—"is that I'm sorry."

The apology is so plain, so straightforward, I'm left wordless.

He was with Kaycee, but he liked you, Misha had said at the Donut Hole. *All that long hair . . .*

"I don't need you to apologize," I say, feeling suddenly angry: Misha, my dad, Brent. They're all twisting my memories, making me doubt things I always counted on as true.

"I know. But I *want* to apologize."

He wants me to tell him it's okay—but I won't. I *refuse*. I decide to cut to the chase. "So you've been at Optimal since high school graduation?" I hate the idea he might think I've come here to work through my past—or, at least, *his* part in it.

"Well, you know my dad was there for years. I was already interning by senior year. Then I started loading trucks. Way fancier than it sounds. My cousin Byron had a buddy over there . . . kinda took me under his wing—and I've been moving up ever since." He stirs his coffee carefully, just the way Misha did, adding sugars one by one. "Optimal really saved my dad back when he left the carpenters union. I'm not sure what he would've done. I never forgot that. It saved his life. Men need good work."

"Women, too," I say, without missing a beat.

"Women, too, of course." It's hard to stay annoyed when he smiles like that.

"Optimal has done a lot of good for the town," I say carefully. "We're just here to make sure they haven't done bad."

He scoffs. "Gallagher's all fired up, I hear." When the waitress arrives with the food, he pretends not to notice how she stares at him. "Remember the time he shot Grant Haimes? Got him in the knee. He had to drop varsity." He shakes his head. "'Goddamn ky-oats!'" He does a decent imitation of old man Gallagher.

"I thought he nicked his ear. Grant, I mean."

Brent shrugs, like it's a minor detail. "Look. I'm telling you this because I actually give a shit. My grandpa was a farmer, and my dad loved absolutely nothing besides his .44 and his fishing rod. No one cares more about Barrens than I do." He shakes his head, picks over his omelet. "Gallagher's an anarchist looking for a reason. A conspiracy theorist. He'll take potshots at anything—literally. But he's misfired big this time. Optimal's clean. We've had plenty of audits and passed them all. Flying colors."

"But Optimal did settle a case—" I begin.

He interrupts me. "That was back in Tennessee."

I don't blink. "They've had plenty of bad press. Rumors of violations across the board—corruption, getting in bed with local politicians, paying people to look the other way."

"Bad press isn't a legal statute," he says. "And rumors aren't evidence. *Every* company has bad press, Abby, and you know it." It's a deft redirection, and he might actually believe it.

I decide to go all in—if we're going to remove the weeds, might as well get down to the roots. "I've been looking back at the Mitchell case." I watch his reaction carefully, but he barely blinks. "You were with Kaycee back then. You must have an opinion."

"Opinion." He repeats the word as if I've just asked him for money. "I don't have an *opinion*. They made it up. It was typical Kaycee: act first, think never. She was so desperate for attention. I felt bad for her."

I don't like how easy it was for Kaycee to slip away, and how willingly everyone in Barrens let her go—even if she was lying. *Especially* if she was lying.

"Have you talked to her?" I ask.

"No. She didn't even tell me she was leaving. I had no idea."

"So you didn't talk to her at *all* after she left?" Brent and Kaycee were together for nearly two years, which in high school is an eternity. And yet when she left, it was as if she stepped out of her old life completely, like shrugging out of a coat.

"Misha talked to her, once or twice," he says vaguely. His smile, this time, is very thin. "She made it obvious that her goal was to *avoid* speaking to any of us."

"Didn't she say why?" I ask. "I never understood what she was after. Why did she lie about being sick?"

He shakes his head and his voice turns unexpectedly hard. "I thought you were here to look at Optimal. Don't tell me you're a detective, too."

"She was Senior Queen. She painted her whole body for graduation." I remember our last day of school seeing a comet-streak of paint left by her hand against the wall when she stumbled. Even sick, she had to be painted and worshipped. "She didn't seem like she was on the verge of running away."

He folds his napkin carefully. When he looks up, he seems exhausted. "Everything she did was an act. Not just the getting sick but . . . other things, too." He stares into the distance. "I don't think she ever said a single thing that wasn't a lie."

I think of the way she looked at me, the day I found Chestnut in the woods and knew what Kaycee had done to him. *That's sick*, she'd said, lifting her chin, as if I were the rotten thing. *How could you even think something as sick as that?*

I think of the day years later, when I found her hugging a toilet seat, with blood unspooling in the water behind her. *What's happening to me?* Truly afraid. I would have sworn it.

Brent clears his throat and leans back. "You want to look for the real violations around here? Check out the old construction, not the new. Can you believe the high school was basically crawling in asbestos when we were there? Optimal wanted to donate a new gym and convert the old into an auditorium, but abatement was half a million dollars. Made more sense to build out the new community center instead."

"Asbestos isn't what we're looking for," I say.

"I'm just saying, it's the *old* Barrens that's screwed up." Brent holds up his hands as if in surrender. "Optimal turned this town around. Gallagher is just angry his way of life is going down the tubes. He wants someone to blame."

Brent O'Connell is certainly good at what he does: he's a natural-born salesman.

"You might be right," I say. I keep my voice light, casual. "Or you might be wrong. That's why I'm here. To figure out which."

"And I thought you just wanted to see me," Brent teases. "Just do me a favor and don't let Gallagher take off an ear—you're too pretty for that."

Ten years ago I would have died if he said I was pretty; now I'm surprised to find that it irritates me.

"I'm from here too, remember," I say. "I know how to shoot back."

The bill comes. Brent pulls out his card, but I get to it first. "On me. Please. For taking up your time."

"You'll have to let me make it up to you," Brent says, just as the first rain drums against the window. "Will you?"

It takes me a second to understand that he's asking me on a date. "I'm not sure—" I start to say, but he cuts me off.

"Please, Abby. It's really nice to see you again." He sounds like he means it. I was prepared for deflections. Prepared, even, for his charm. But the apology, the compliments, the flirting, and now this . . .

Memories of last night do a quick-shuffle through my head: Condor's smile, the way he drums his thigh when he's thinking, his hands, brown from the sun, pulling me closer to him. Brent's hands are pale and well kept. I realize the difference between Condor and Brent. With Condor, the person I don't trust is myself.

"All right, screw it," I say. Brent O'Connell, the Golden Child, football quarterback, hometown hero, wants to take me on a date. "Sure. Why not."

Brent smiles. "Welcome home, Abby Williams."

Chapter Eleven

Barrens High School, a squat concrete-and-brick building, is smaller than I remembered and strikes me as surprisingly quiet. I guess I was expecting the raw energy and noise of restless teenagers to be oozing out through the windows and walls, to see kids perched on the hoods of their cars smoking pot, shoving each other into the Dumpsters, shouting to each other in the halls. But of course, it's still raining, and everyone's inside.

Freak! I think I hear someone call out from far away. But there's no one. The windshield wiper whines and snaps, whines and snaps. I shut off the engine, wondering if I have it in me to get out of the car. But there's something drawing me here, one of those instincts. A hunch.

I cover my head and hurry across the lot to the main entrance; the strangled cry of the front doors rips through me, feels like an old cut torn open.

Survival instinct—that deep, anxious burn I practically subsisted on in high school—shoots adrenaline through my veins.

But all is quiet and still inside, too. They say smell is the sense most closely linked to memory—this place smells like a hundred-year-old stairwell with no ventilation. I'm immediately transported back in time. I peer down the long empty hallway. First period classes must still be in session. The inside looks smaller than I remembered, too—why is that always the case? The ceiling seems lower, but I've been five foot nine since I was in the eighth grade so I know it isn't because of a sudden growth spurt. The walls are still beige, but there is also a faint smell of paint. They must have attempted a makeover. It was a waste of time. The strangle of memories lessens somewhat as my wet boots slap against the tile floors; still, my whole body's alert, ready to flatten itself against the rusted metal lockers in the event of a stampede, to perform its old magic trick and become invisible.

Only a few days after I swore to myself I would never ask Misha for help, I've arrived to do exactly that.

At the main office, I am told that Vice Principal Jennings is in with a parent. I still can't reconcile the Misha who used to bring vodka to school in a water bottle during Spirit Week with the woman nominally in charge of the students' education, and I can't help but wonder what Kaycee would have thought.

I remember the day Chestnut's collar turned up in my locker, the sudden rage that overtook me, the way Misha slammed me against the lockers after I'd tackled her in the halls.

Did you know what she did? I was practically choking on my own rage. *Did you know all along? Did you think it would be funny to remind me?*

I'll never forget how she looked then: scared. Truly scared, maybe for the first time ever.

I have no idea what you're talking about, she whispered.

Is it at all possible that Misha was a victim, too?

A bored-looking secretary shows me to a folding chair and hands me a copy of the school handbook. I flip through it—anything to keep my hands busy. Nothing seems to have changed: it's all no drinking, no smoking on the premises, stuff like that. A zero-tolerance policy that I doubt is ever, or was ever, enforced.

Finally the visiting parent storms off, clutching her pocketbook to her chest, and the secretary shows me in. Here among the clean angles of the modest office, surrounded by towers of paperwork, is Misha.

"Thanks for seeing me on such short notice," I say.

When she stands up to give me a quick hug, I see that she's wearing a skirt suit just a tiny bit too small for her. I focus on that visible flaw to counteract a surge of panic.

"Please. You're doing me a favor. At least now I have a break from the usual rotation of parents. They don't see why their precious Jeremy is flunking out of school when he shows up at *least* once a week."

I take the chair pulled up close to her desk. Maybe it's meant for students—it is noticeably lower than hers, and suddenly I feel like a kid, like I should be apologizing for something.

"I see the school has expanded," I say, directly.

"Sure has. We had to absorb the kids in Basher Falls after the town lines got redrawn."

"That must have been a strain on the teachers." I've stolen this technique from Joe: Start with some softballs, some light chitchat, the conversational equivalent of a sedative. Then, once they're relaxed, strike hard and get out quick.

Misha smiles brightly. The sun shining through the window makes a good impression of a halo around her head. "Luckily, we were able to bring in some new hires. And we've been working with local donors on a scholarship fund to improve extracurricular involvement."

Somehow, even though I can see her speak the words, they still seem as though they're coming from someone else's mouth. Rehearsed. "Let me guess. Optimal is one of the local donors?"

"The biggest." She spreads her hands. She doesn't look sorry. "Like I said, they've been great partners. They've really helped turn this town around. How was seeing Brent, by the way? You know there's nothing to do in Barrens but mind everybody else's business," Misha says teasingly.

Time to go in for the kill. "That's good to hear," I say, "because I actually have some questions for you about what happened to Kaycee Mitchell back then."

I might as well have slapped her. The smile drops right off her face. After a long second, she forces a laugh. "I could have saved you the trouble," she says. "I haven't heard from Kaycee since three weeks after she left."

"Where was she?" I ask.

"Why do you care so much? I thought you were here to look at the water."

"We are. I thought Kaycee's perspective could be valuable."

"Here we go. I thought that stupidity had gone to the grave." Misha is much better at controlling her temper now. "It was a *lie*. I've put that whole episode behind me."

"But you must have gotten the idea to lie from somewhere," I say. "There was a case back in Tennessee, before Optimal changed names—"

"It was Kaycee's idea. And you know as well as I do, Kaycee never needed a reason for anything." Misha's voice turns hard, like the old Misha, the one whose first instinct was to attack. "Last I heard she was on her way to New York. Honestly, I was relieved. It sounds awful, but I was sick of all her little games. I was sick of playing along. You know how it was."

I do. But again, I resent her for reminding me. "Is it possible she had another reason for running away?" I ask, and Misha sighs, as if she's realized I won't be easily distracted.

"No," she says. "She knew that I wanted to come clean about making the whole thing up. Cora and Annie, too. We never expected it to get that out of control. I mean, Cora's mom went on the news . . ." She shakes her head. "Kaycee ran off before everyone could call her a liar. Best day of my life, God's truth."

For a second, I'm left speechless. Did anyone actually like Kaycee Mitchell? Was *anyone* sorry to see her go? But before I can ask Misha anything else, the secretary pokes her head in.

"Mrs. Danning brought in another cell phone. Jessica Moore again. She's on her way in for detention."

Misha stands up so quickly she bangs a hip against the desk, sending several pens rolling to the floor. "I'll take it," she says. Turning back to me, she adds, "No-cell-phone policy. We give them back. But during school hours it keeps the kids from getting distracted. Cuts down on cyberbullying, too, although I swear some of these kids spend more time in detention than they do in class."

For the first time, I think I see the appeal of the job to a person like Misha. It must make her feel powerful to mete out punishments and rewards. And for that part of the gig, at least, she's a natural.

An ear-splitting bell signals the end of first period, a pitch identical to the one that used to hack up my days into periods of forty-five minutes.

When Misha remains on her feet, I realize the meeting is over.

"*So* good to see you, Abby," she says, embracing me again. While her lips are still very close to my ear, she whispers, "It's just like old times, isn't it?"

I half expect to feel her teeth sink into my jugular, vampire-style.

But she just releases me and laughs. "Next time, I say we meet for a *drink*."

AS I WEAVE my way through the hall, navigating the throngs of students pouring out of classrooms, a memory needles in the back of my mind, begging for attention. We had our own version of bullying, back in the early days of Facebook, before Snapchat, Instagram, and trolls. I haven't thought about the Game in years, or the rumors that spread like a toxic fume, the girls who were targeted moving through the halls, white-faced, humiliated, trailed by a faint snake-hiss. *Slut. Slut. Slut.*

There was Kelsey Waters, in the blue light of a basement, with her underwear around her knees and mascara ringed around her eyes. There was Riley Simmons, passed out drunk on the bathroom floor during a party. Jonathan Elders took off her bra and photographed her. The next day at school all the boys were huddled around looking at the photos and laughing. He told everyone she was too ugly to have sex with and she cried in the lunchroom when she heard.

And then there was what happened to Becky Sarinelli. That was even worse.

Chapter Twelve

It started at a pep rally, early senior year, just before the sickness, the hysteria, the allegations, the confessions—or at least that's when I became aware of it, of the Game.

High school rallies were mandatory. Never mind the kids who didn't have a group to sit with, who didn't care about the rally—or the bonfire that would come later—because no one would ask us to go or notice if we were there. Still we were forced into the football stadium bleachers, to cheer for the players and watch the cheerleaders shimmy in their short skirts, while the boys shouted *pussy* from behind cupped hands.

Bradley Roberts, the class VP, droned on at the microphone about school pride, the importance of unity, the Barrens Tigers, rah-rah-rah.

And then: a shout, high-pitched and strangled. The crowd shifted, and for a second I imagined flames racing up the bleachers, consuming us all. A real bonfire.

Some of my classmates rose from their seats. Their excitement was thick; it made my stomach curl. Still, I turned with the rest of them.

I saw Becky Sarinelli moving through the bleachers, tripping over book bags and risers, desperate, obviously panicked. She was reaching for pieces of paper—they looked like flyers. Snatching them wildly and hurrying on to the next. But there were too many: dozens, floating hand to hand as though drawn on an invisible current. Some people were laughing; some looked sick.

Bradley cleared his throat a couple of times, but no one cared anymore what he had to say about school spirit. Mr. Davis was heading toward the podium.

"Quiet!" he said. "Everyone, be quiet. Sit down." But no one listened.

The flyers were making their way toward me. One floated to the floor in the aisle, faceup. Only then did I see it wasn't a flyer at all.

It was a photograph, blown up and pixelated. Clear enough, though, to see what it was.

Becky.

My heart went still.

She was lying on a bed. Her eyes were half-mast, her makeup smeary. Her skirt had been pushed above her waist, and her large white thighs glared bright in the flash, so bright she looked like a plastic doll. Her shirt was unbuttoned and she wasn't wearing a bra. Her underwear was twisted somewhere around her knees. The murmurs came together, gelling in the same way our school song might have, if things had gone the right way.

Slut. Slut. Slut, they said.

Stop, I wanted to scream. *Stop. It wasn't her fault.* But I couldn't open my mouth, couldn't say a word.

Slut. Slut. Slut.

Eight days later, her father found her in the toolshed.

She didn't leave a note to tell us why. She didn't need to.

Chapter Thirteen

For the rest of the week I avoid both Brent and Condor: Brent, because I'm not sure I actually do want to see him again, even though I said I would; Condor, because I want nothing more.

Even as a kid I was drawn to the animals that bit. I once tried to save a raccoon that had somehow made its way into our basement, and it nearly took off a pinkie—I still have the scar. But even then I cried not for the blood or the rabies shots that came afterward, but when my dad, hearing me shout, came running downstairs with a rifle and plugged the raccoon between the eyes.

I always want the things that hurt most.

Instead, I throw myself wholeheartedly into the case. What we really need are Optimal's books. Everything always boils down to money: corners cut, pipes improperly cared for, testing fudged once the results start coming in wonky, and people paid to keep quiet about it. Because it gets incentives from the state to keep business in Indiana, Optimal's quarterly reports are available to the public. But we need to go deeper. We need their General Ledger, checks received and dispatched.

Some people pay. Other people collect.

I do what I do best: paperwork, numbers, patterns and disruptions that might mean everything or nothing at all. Barrens

Township has had the water tested every year—the results are filed according to the Indiana Access to Public Records Act—and that surprises me, given the fact that much of the infrastructure is seventy-five years old.

They're trying too hard to seem clean.

FRIDAY NIGHT, INDIANA, dusk: the sky is blue and pink, and the rains earlier in the week have left the fields looking fresh. The crows silhouetted on the telephone wires are too numerous to count.

I'm only half a mile away from my rental behind the beauty salon when my cell phone rings: Indiana area code, a number I don't recognize. I nearly silence it but at the last second decide to pick up.

"Yeah?"

"Is this Abigail Williams?" The voice is male and unfamiliar.

"Speaking," I say, already pulling over, reaching for my note-book and a pen. "Who's this?"

"It's Sheriff Kahn. We've got your father down here at the station—"

My stomach drops.

"—Picked him up on Main Street. Seems he was confused, kept insisting there should be a honky-tonk there. He had your number written down in his wallet. I heard you were in town?"

I close my eyes and see, in the darkness behind my eyelids, the old Dusty Chap line-dancing hall. The loud country music, the smell of fries and beer, my mom tush-pushing to Wynonna or Travis Tritt beside me with her cowboy boots and her hair piled high on top of her head in a scrunchie. It was one of the most fun things I would do with my mother before she died. It went out of business years ago, when I was in middle school.

"Yes, I am. I'll be right there," I say, wheeling the car around.

. . .

MY FATHER HAS calmed down by the time I get there and doesn't seem to understand why he's sitting in the sheriff's office at all.

"Shame on you," he says to Sheriff Kahn, even as I'm trying to wrangle him into the passenger seat. Somehow, he's lost his cane. "Shame on you, roughing up an old man like that. I wasn't doing anything but minding my own business, and you come around and talk nonsense about the dancing hall—"

"That place closed, Dad," I say, shooting Sheriff Kahn an apologetic look.

"I know that, Abigail," he snaps, sounding, for a second, more like the dad I remember. *Don't talk back to your elders. Watch that filthy mouth of yours. I'm your father and you'll do what I say.* "Closed right after your mother died."

Back home, I find his cane propped near the door. Who knows how he made it anywhere without it. I suspect one of his neighbors gave him a lift, not realizing how bad my dad has gotten. He slaps my hands away when I try to make him take his medicine, but finally he calms down and lets me put the pills on his tongue myself, sitting there meekly, watery-eyed, as if trapped beneath the thin liver-spotted skin and the stale breath is a child in need of attention. I leave him sleeping and promise to call in the morning.

I am gutted by his need, and by my desire to fix him. I should be relieved. He's too pathetic now to hate. I never truly planned to confront him. I never really expected to reconcile any of it. Seeing this version of him, I know in my whole body that none of those things will ever even become an option. It is too much.

In the bathroom I wash my hands, splash water on my face, and wash my hands again. I yank open the cabinet, palming a few Valium from a bottle made out to his name. But I'm still too shaky to drive, and when I step outside, the smell of fire reaches me across the distance and touches old memories: lake parties that never included me. Kids dragging coolers and beach towels into the woods. My father hitting me hard and open-palmed across the face the one time I tried to sneak out.

Distantly, I hear the shrieks of laughter and the thud of music. I know that sound. Someone is having a bonfire.

Memories are like fire, and need only a little oxygen to grow. I remember now how I used to see the far-off light of bonfires from just a little farther than my back porch. I remember that sometimes my father would find crumpled beer cans in the woods near the toolshed, how the braver kids would get close enough to pelt the house with empties—just because they could, because it was there—until my father took his rifle and fired blind into the dark.

I was never invited. The bonfires were for the party crowd— for the *crowd*, period. Still, I would sit outside sometimes and swear that the smoke touched the back of my throat, even from that distance.

Impulsively, I grip my sweater tight and set out across the fields to the forest, and, beyond it, the reservoir—the reservoir, the start of it all—even while yearning for Chicago and the blessed anonymity of the high-rise where I live. I miss being several hundred miles away from my dad, from all this.

The woods are cold and very dark and I instantly regret not bringing a flashlight. The sun will set any minute. But soon I can see the far-off flicker of the bonfire and the silver wink of the reservoir. It was here, in these woods, that Brent kissed me.

Don't tell anyone, he whispered, touching his thumb to my lower lip. I remember the smell of paint and the noise of crickets.

And then, as I approach the beach, past and present merge. Like shadows silhouetted by the fire, breaking apart and re-forming, the Brent of my memories transforms into real Brent, hailing me from a distance.

"Abby!" He breaks loose from a knot of his friends. I catch Misha's eye a split-second before she, too, calls up a smile. Then Brent engulfs me in a hug and I lose sight of her. "You are like a surprise from the heavens."

"You are obviously drunk," I say, pulling away.

He laughs. "Only a little." Then: "Seriously, I was just thinking about you."

As everyone down by the bonfire turns to stare, I recognize various people from high school I'd hoped never to see again. Already, I regret coming. But it's too late now.

"Meeting of the secret society?" I ask.

"Nothing secret about it," Brent says, smiling. Today he's in a polo shirt, khakis, and loafers. He looks like a Ralph Lauren ad made flesh. "I tried to invite you, but you don't return my calls."

"Sorry," I say. "Busy week."

Brent shrugs as if he knows it's an excuse. "It doesn't matter. You came anyway. See? It's a sign." He loops an arm around my shoulders. He's definitely wasted.

"You smell like the beach," I say, even though what I mean is that he smells like a booze factory.

"I smell *great*. I just went swimming."

"In the reservoir? Brave man."

"It's one hundred percent safe. You'll see. Pure as Iceland." He wheels me around toward the fire and begins piloting me through the crowd. "Come on, city slicker. Let's get you something to drink. All work and no play never did anybody good."

If it weren't for the thinning hairlines and paunch bellies, I might think we'd traveled back in time: I recognize everyone, football and basketball players, cheerleaders and dance squad girls, all of them eyeing me now with a special brand of curiosity and suspicion. I haven't seen any of them since graduation.

I remember Kaycee painted in school colors, standing and trembling, blinking in the sunlight, as the girls began to fall down like a wave.

She must have been lonely, although it's funny to think of her that way. She always seemed to have everything, even though, in retrospect, she didn't have much at all: her mom gone, no money, her dad in his porn shop and spending all weekend at the bar.

Kaycee was the only one who dreamed of going to art school, who dreamed of doing *anything* besides getting married and staying right here to have babies and start the cycle all over again. Even as a kid, she would talk about all the places she would go someday, half of them made up. In a way, what's surprising isn't that she ran, but maybe that she waited so long.

"I don't believe it." A stranger shoves out of the crowd, teetering on wedges that would be dangerous even if she was sober.

"Abby. Fucking. Williams. Holy shit. I seriously didn't believe it when Misha told me you'd come back."

She sways where she stands, shaking her head as if hoping it will help her focus. But her eyes keep sliding away from mine, landing somewhere over my shoulder. And I have absolutely no idea who she is.

"You don't remember me." Her words slur into laughter. She swings to Brent, sloshing some of her drink, so he has to quickstep backward to avoid it. "She doesn't remember me? It's because I got fat." Then she's back to me again, gnawing the rim of her cup, looking suddenly like a kid. "Isn't it? It's because I'm fat."

"Of course I remember you," I say quickly.

"What's my name, then?" She staggers a bit, regains her balance, and smiles at me hazily.

Brent breaks in before I have to reply. "Come on, Annie. Let's get you some water."

Now, at last, I recognize Annie Baum. The former head cheerleader, once miniature and muscled, is soft from drinking, prematurely old.

She pulls away from Brent as soon as he takes her arm. "Don't touch me," she says sharply. But when Brent holds up both hands, a wordless apology, she turns cheerful again. "It's a party, isn't it? So let's party."

She wastes more alcohol than she lands in her cup. Before I can stop her, she has pressed a shot into my hand. The liquid is already sweating through the flimsy paper cup, like the kind you see in dentists' offices.

"How about you, Brent? A drink, for old times' sake?" Annie seems to find this idea hilarious, and says, "Old friends, old memories, old. We're old, now."

Before she can drink, Misha materializes, neatly snatching the cup from Annie's hand.

"You need to slow down," she says lightly. For a second, Annie looks like she might argue.

But in the end, she only shrugs and turns back to me. "She

always could tell me what to do," she says. "Both of them." I assume she means Kaycee, too. Then she wheels off abruptly into the crowd.

"Three times in one week! How did I get so lucky?" Misha manages to level off directly between sincere and sarcastic. She touches her cup to mine. "Cheers. Go on. You deserve it."

Deserve—maybe. I need it, for sure. I almost never take shots and am thankful, at least, that Annie poured out whiskey and not rum. Still, it's cheap liquor, and it burns going down.

Brent must notice my grimace, because he laughs.

"Let me make you a real drink. No—don't tell me." He pretends to size me up. "Now let me see. Vodka cran? No. Too sweet. Definitely not gin. Too suburban."

"You think you can guess?"

"I don't *think*. I *know*." He holds my gaze for just a beat longer than necessary before turning to Misha. "You want something? Gin and tonic?"

Her smile tightens. "Gin and soda," she corrects him.

"Coming up. Don't go head to head with this one," he says, turning back to me and jerking his head in Misha's direction. "She'll drink you under the table. Or under the reservoir, as the case may be."

He says it lightly, but for some reason, Misha flinches. Once, I told my mother I wanted to be a mermaid, and she told me that real mermaids were the drowned souls of broken-hearted women; I don't know why I remember that now. I blink as if it will help clear out the memory.

Brent turns and shoves his way toward the makeshift bar: a litter of alcohol bottles and mixers spread out on a blanket. Already, I can feel the whiskey doing its work, spreading warmth to my chest, softening the glow of the fire. Misha tonight looks more like the Misha I remember, in jeans and a Barrens Tigers T-shirt.

"Brent was so worried you wouldn't come," she says brightly, without preamble. "I told him you wouldn't miss the chance to relive the glory days. Isn't that what going home is all about?"

I can feel her watching me for a reaction—but what kind of reaction, I'm not sure. It occurs to me that Misha never had a boy-friend in high school. She had plenty of *boys*—but no boyfriend. I wonder if she was jealous of what Kaycee had. Another question I'll never ask her.

"Maybe for some. In my glory days, I would never have been invited. And they weren't so glorious. But I'm sure you remember."

It's a cheap shot, but hey, at least now we're even.

But when Misha says, "I deserve that," it makes me wish I hadn't said anything.

As I scan the crowd, it occurs to me that I don't see Cora Allen. She used to stick to Misha like a shadow. "Do you ever see Cora anymore?" I ask, partly to change the topic.

Misha tries to arrange her face into a look of concern. But somehow it doesn't quite land. "She doesn't come around," she says shortly. Then: "She got all messed up, honestly. Drugs."

Before I can ask her anything else, Brent returns, balancing three cups. He passes one to Misha and presents mine with a flour-ish. "Cheers."

I take an experimental sniff. "Vodka soda?"

"Did I guess right?"

"Trick question." I can't help but smile. He looks so damn pleased with himself. "I drink it all."

"Even better. That way, I'm always right." He touches his cup to mine and holds my eyes while we drink. By the time I think to include Misha, she has vanished.

Things are blurring, and my body feels warm and loose, as if the coil that keeps it responding to my brain has slowly begun to unwind.

"Whoa, there. Easy," Brent says, and catches me when I stum-ble on a log half-buried in the grass.

"I'm not drunk," I say.

"I'm not judging," he replies, and pulls me closer. I feel his belt against my stomach. I pull away because the world is turning now.

"Do you remember Dave Condor?" I ask, before I can think better of it.

"Sure," Brent says, but looks away. "He's still around. Works at the liquor store. Once a burnout, always a burnout." He tugs on the collar of his shirt. "Why?"

"Just curious," I downplay. "I ran into him, that's all."

"Keep your distance." Brent's voice sounds as if it's coming from far away. "He's not the guy you want to keep running into."

"What happened with him in high school?" I ask. "Why did you and your friends jump him?"

His blue eyes lock with mine again, hard to read in the darkness. "You remember Becky Sarinelli?" he asks. "That's why."

Of all the things he could have said, this might be the least expected of all. "Condor was the one who passed around her photos?"

Brent shakes his head. "He was the one who took them."

TIME SHREDS INTO ribbons. Hours fracture into quick-cut images:

I'm sitting on the ground with Brent's arms around me in front of the fire, laughing without knowing why.

"You're going *hard* tonight." Brent's voice meanders through my fog. "I like it."

"I like it," I repeat, and laugh. I'm fucked up. Too far gone to hide it. I lean against Brent's chest. He's so solid and warm. He is comfortable. Brent tilts my chin back toward his to ask me something; and then we are leaning into each other. Kissing. But I'm too drunk to know whether I like it or not.

I pull away. Brent's eyes hold a look I can't read.

"Isn't this funny?" I ask. "We're kissing. I thought we kissed in high school, and this whole time I haven't been sure, and we're kissing now, and I don't even know whether I made it up."

"I wanted to. I wanted so badly to kiss you in high school," Brent whispers. Does this mean he did or he didn't?

My mind slides to Dave Condor, his mouth hot on my skin . . .

Dark. Light. Dark. Light.

Becky Sarinelli's thighs, blazing in the glare of the flash.

The laughter of the crowd in the stands. Her photo fluttering up toward me.

Then:

The faces around the fire are no longer familiar: they are huge, bloated like balloons. Brent's voice is somewhere in the background, talking incessantly. He won't be quiet.

I'm sleeping. This is a dream. I lie down, but the ground won't stop moving. It feels as if I'm on a boat. I try to open my eyes.

"You're okay," says Brent's voice. "You're okay." His voice is a separate thing. Listening to it makes me feel tired. And sleepy.

No. Wait. Something is wrong.

I try to sit up. Time is thick and slow, like a clear gel. I wonder if I've been drugged, but the idea itself feels unreal, like something I've only dreamed. Then I remember: the Valium, and more drinks than I can count. I never even checked to see how much was in each pill.

The beach is empty. The bonfire has vanished. Not burned out—vanished. There is no trace of it on the beach, no mound of charred logs, no smoke.

And then: a scream. I look around. There's a dark shape on the water. A rowboat. I know that voice.

Kaycee.

I stumble to my feet. My head feels like a bowling ball about to roll off my neck.

She's under, she's under.

She won't stay down.

Flashlight beams crisscross the water and I see Kaycee, her beautiful hair fanned out over the water, her mouth distorted in a scream.

No. Wait. Not Kaycee. Kaycee ran away.

But someone *is* in the water. A girl. No—more than one girl. One of them is screaming for help . . .

I try and shout but I can't. My vision splits and re-forms like a kaleidoscope.

We have to make sure . . .

She's not breathing . . .

We have to make sure she's not breathing . . .

Confusion and horror war within me. I sway on my feet. My arms and legs feel leaden. I try and shout but my voice splinters through my skull. I'm on my knees again.

The girl's screams echo over the reservoir. She's going to drown.

They're going to drown her.

Darkness bubbles up around me, and when I open my mouth to scream again, a wet terror rushes into my lungs like water, and pulls me under.

Chapter Fourteen

Sleep is a heavy blanket I peel back slowly, climbing out beneath a suffocating fog. I stay like that for a moment, suspended between sleeping and waking. For a second, I don't know where I am. Everything is unfamiliar, down to the suitcase spilling its guts in the corner.

I sit up and a raging headache comes to life; my body is stiff, my heart is palpitating, my mouth feels like cotton, and I'm so nauseous I have to close my eyes and wait for the room to stop swinging. I've been hungover before but this feels different: like the hangover is everywhere, in my skin, even.

Finally, the world clicks into place: the suitcase is mine, the stained carpet and wobbly furniture redraw themselves into the silhouette of my rental house. Sun slants hard through the windows—it must be ten or later. My feet are killing me; they're bleeding. I must have cut them on something, maybe gravel or broken glass. Sweeps of red in the sheets show me running in my sleep.

I try to climb back through the hours, retrace my moves, but all I get is a kind of panic that overwhelms my memories. What happened?

Think.

My shirt is wrinkled, and damp, and smells like sweat. My

jeans—the same ones I wore last night—pinch in a thousand places and are caked in dirt and sand. My boots are gone. Next to the bed is a pair of dirty pink flats that I don't recognize.

Think. Breathe. Try to remember.

A jump cut; Brent cradling my foot in his lap, asking if it hurts, and splinters of broken beer bottles glowing emerald in a dying fire.

The beach. The bonfire. Did Brent take me home last night?

A sudden punch of nausea, and I hobble into the bathroom, barely making it to the toilet in time, to throw up mostly bile. I feel a little better, but just a little and it's fleeting. It was the Valium that did it—that, and drinking too quickly, continuing to drink even after things turned watery and warped.

Why did I do that? I've never been big on pills, not since a flirtation with Adderall in my first year at CEAW that landed me in therapy and nearly lost me the job. Still, I've taken Valium before, but it never worked like it did last night: like a saw to the brain, cutting out everything important.

Why can't I remember?

Think.

The shower water runs freezing at first while I strip down to my underwear, throwing my dirty clothes in a ball on the floor. I gasp in the cold, and the shock dislodges another memory: Brent's lips, cold and mossy-tasting, like the reservoir. Shouting.

Hold her down. Hold her down. I'm pinning her wrists . . .

No. That can't be right. That's an old memory—a memory of my father trying to get my mother to swallow the pills she was refusing. *Hold her*, he told me. *Hold her down.* I grabbed her wrists and felt all the way down to her bones, as he forced open her jaw, shoved his fingers down her throat so far she couldn't do anything but swallow.

I scrub hard with soap everywhere—in between my toes, under my fingernails, between my legs. I shampoo my hair, and rinse, and shampoo again.

Still, the anxiety and panic stay.

I turn the water as cold as it will go, close my eyes, and stand shivering as long as I can bear it. Images bob like ice cubes to the surface: the lullaby sway of a boat on the water; someone saying, "You shouldn't have come," beer bottles arcing into the water, hurled by hands that belong to no one I can see.

No. Someone is definitely screaming. *No. Stop. No.*

SATURDAY. ONE P.M.

Without the rest of the team, our makeshift headquarters more closely resembles its former life as a functional barn. The smells of hay, old wood that's been wet and dried a million times, and corn feed waft through the open air. Outside, crows caw in the fields, and a tractor revs to life.

I was hoping that work would help me focus and would pull me back to whatever it is I've forgotten—about Kaycee, about what happened last night, about the reservoir. But memories of Brent, pulling me close as the smoke curled around us, keep interfering. Brent pressing his lips against mine. Voices laughing and joking in the background and the gentle sloshing of lake water against the pebbled shore.

After my third cup of coffee and seventh Advil, my headache eases, finally, and so does my hangover—chased back to hell, or wherever bad hangovers come from.

Work has always centered me, especially the early stages, the research, the reading, the note-taking. Like unwinding a braid made out of a thousand strings, and tacking each one down into place.

When Optimal was called Associated Polymer and headquartered in Tennessee, the company settled a complaint against them by a group of two hundred plaintiffs claiming runoff from their plant was causing bad smells, skin irritations, headaches. Unfortunately, because the case didn't ever make it to court, public information is limited. But it stands to reason that they settled because they knew the claims were valid. Why else?

Even if Kaycee, Misha, Cora, and Annie did pretend to be poisoned, pretend to have the same symptoms as the complainants in

Tennessee because they were hoping for a payout, it also stands to reason that they may have unconsciously hit on the truth. If you throw a dart enough times, eventually you'll hit the bull's-eye.

But five years of safety audits and public records yield nothing: Optimal has never even gotten a ticket. From the very beginning, the mayor and eight-person city council all but showed up for Optimal greased up and naked with a bow.

Before Optimal Plastics, the town was on the verge of collapse. The vast majority of the residents were over the age of seventy-five, not working, on disability, or just not in a position to move. Optimal has brought jobs, and young people, back to Barrens. They helped reconstruct the high school after it was damaged in a bad storm. They've poured money into roads and infrastructure. They've inspired new businesses, new house construction, new life.

But it's possible they've done it at the expense of the poorest people, the ones who always suffer the most: the people who live closest to the reservoir, or farmers like Gallagher who depend on public water supply for their livelihoods.

Even if we do find something on Optimal, litigation will be a nightmare—like going after the most popular boy in school for stealing money from the church donation box. Optimal has been busy courting locals and state politicians up the chain. The contributions, if not the amounts, are listed proudly on the company's Corporate Sponsorship page, beneath Barrens Little League and the Veterans Health Fund.

I dig up an old interview with a guy named Aaron Pulaski, the old Monroe County prosecuting attorney. The interview, published by a regional newspaper with a circulation of maybe a few thousand, if they're lucky, focuses on Pulaski's determination to clean up corrupt business interests in the county, and to make sure that Indiana tax dollars were flowing back to homegrown businesses.

He mentions Optimal by name—not for environmental violations, but for skirting labor union laws and hiring mostly foreign workers in its distribution centers throughout the Northeast.

Still, it's something.

But if his office conducted an investigation, it has disappeared down an online sinkhole. That bothers me. It's standard practice for the county prosecutor's office to announce criminal investigations against major public figures—or against corporations. And announce it big.

An idea takes shape.

Weak spots.

After a little more digging, I learn that only six months ago, Aaron Pulaski hopped from the county prosecutor's office to a state congressional seat, running on an anticorruption, antiestablishment platform that easily handed him the vote. And though Pulaski doesn't appear on Optimal's list of corporate donations, a quick visit to the financial disclosure section of the Indiana state legislature confirms my suspicion.

Only a few months after Pulaski was quoted in a newspaper saying he would investigate Optimal for labor violations, and a few short months before he landed his congressional seat, Associated Polymer, Optimal's parent company, wrote a $100,000 check to his campaign.

A bribe.

Has to be.

But more important: a way in. We'll need help, and luck, and a really friendly circuit court. But Optimal might turn over their finances to us even before we've filed if the alternative is turning them over in a criminal case.

It's a long shot—but at least it's a shot. Finally. *Something.*

My whole body is humming with *something something something* by the time Joe throws open the door with his shoulder. I've almost forgotten the nagging doubt that tailed me all morning, that something terrible happened at the bonfire.

"It's a Saturday." Joe smiles at me.

"Exactly. What are you doing here? Couldn't resist the Barrens social scene?" I say. A joke—until I realize, from his just-got-laid grin, that he probably spent the day with Raj. Joe can't do one-night stands. The sex always unrolls into brunch dates and trips to the farmers' market, Saturday-night Netflix binges on the couch. Joe is one of those people who can be around other people all the time. He doesn't need solitude to recharge, like I do.

He's just easy and malleable and he can make a home everywhere he goes.

Some of us are out of place even when we *are* home.

"I figured I'd have a better shot at going door-to-door on a Saturday." He shook his head. "But it seems we've already overstayed our welcome."

"What do you mean?"

"Most people wouldn't even open their damn doors. Not used to a queer black man showing up on a weekend, apparently! One asshole—Paul Jennings, I think? Or Peter?—came to the door with a shotgun. I kid you not. He apologized and said he was jumpy because his wife never came home last night. I wouldn't, either, if I was married to him. And then a woman named Joanne Farley tried to convince me that—"

"Wait." In the flow of his complaints washing over me, alarm bells have started going off. Misha. "What did you say?"

My pulse is so hot in my ears, I miss Joe's reply.

"More important," he's saying, "the guy slammed the screen door in my face—my tie almost didn't make it out alive. So much for small-town hospitality." He stops when he takes in the expression on my face. "Are you okay?"

Wrong, wrong, wrong.

Inside, fear sharpens.

Misha Jennings didn't come home last night.

But I did.

Wearing her pink shoes.

Chapter Fifteen

Brent lives on the opposite side of town, past the Westlink Fertilizer & Feed store and the new community center that's going up, past the newer area that's been built up to accommodate for what Barrens counts as a population explosion. Ten years ago this was rural open countryside and now it's all new construction, contemporaries slotted onto pancake-flat plots of land. The houses are bigger and upscale by Barrens standards: two-story, generous lawns, U-shape driveways.

Brent opens the door almost immediately. Even in slippers and jeans, he looks put together, well rested, and not hungover at all. He's standing there as if the doorbell has summoned him out of some J.Crew catalog.

"Hey, Abby. You survived." He grins at me, but not quickly enough—for a split second, I thought I saw him wince. I think again of the body in the water . . . a nightmare. Has to be. Surely, if anything bad had happened, if something awful went wrong at the party, there would be signs of it—chaos, tension, maybe even police.

Unless I'm the only one who knows.

"What happened last night?" I ask him. My voice sounds distant, as if it's coming from someone else's throat.

"What *didn't* happen?" He leans the door open a little wider. "I think I'm off vodka for the rest of my life. Come on in."

His ease, his flirtation, the way his eyes sparkle: all of it confuses me. His hallway is clean. Light-filled. Running shoes laced neatly by the door, a key dangling from a peg on the wall, beneath framed photographs of Brent at various stages of his life: Brent trout fishing with his dad, Brent suited up in his football uniform giving a thumbs-up to the camera, Brent getting head-knuckled by a curly-haired guy dressed in a flashy suit against a backdrop of cornfields.

"I don't remember getting home," I say. I meant to ask straight away about Misha, but fear closes my throat. Brent speaks before I can.

"Really? You weren't even weaving." He glances over his shoulder to smile—a slay-them-where-they-stand look I remember from high school, though then it was never directed at me. "Erickson drove us both. He's on the wagon. I asked you if you wanted help getting inside but you seemed to know what you were doing."

It's a small relief. I hate the idea of Brent seeing all my clothes disemboweled from my suitcase, my mess in the kitchen, the unmade bed. That amount of vulnerability is just too much to bear.

"This way." Brent gestures for me to follow him. I take in the muted colors of his house, the orderly lines and the faint medicinal smell of the air conditioner. It's a grown-up house, nicer even than my condo in Chicago, which looks clean only by virtue of having hardly anything in it. "Misha's in the back."

"Misha . . . ?"

"Yeah. It was a rough night. We were taking care of Annie until four in the morning. So Misha needed to crash." Seeing my look of confusion, he adds, "Annie nearly got herself drowned last night. Don't you remember?"

"Things are pretty fuzzy." An understatement.

Brent's whole face darkens. He's almost never so serious, and for a split second, he looks like a different person. "She got it into her head to go swimming. But she was too drunk to make it back to shore. Misha was a hero. She charged straight into the reservoir."

Annie. Misha. The girl screaming for help. Relief washes over me. I was all wrong—Misha was trying to help Annie, not hurt her.

"Annie needs to quit drinking. But we've tried to tell her a thousand times . . ."

Brent waves me out onto the screened-in patio. There, sitting on the couch in a robe that's hanging off her shoulder, is Misha Jennings.

"Abby. Hi." She looks tired, and while she recovers quickly, she seems momentarily annoyed to see me. "How are you hanging in?"

"Better than Annie," I say.

She sighs. "Brent just drove her home." Despite the fact that it must be nearly six, she's wearing a bathrobe, and there's a towel turbaning her hair. She must know what I'm thinking—Misha and Brent, here together, and both with wet hair—because she unconsciously cinches the bathrobe tighter. "I finally took a shower. I actually feel human again."

"Take a seat." Brent doesn't sit, though, even when I perch awkwardly on one of the armchairs, wishing almost immediately I hadn't. "You want a soda or something? I'd offer you a drink but if I ever touch alcohol again, shoot me."

"A tranquilizer, if you have one," I say. Brent laughs first. Then Misha joins in. I quickly add, "I'm joking."

"I hope we didn't scare you away for good." Misha leans forward and puts a hand on my knee. I clock right away that two of her nails are broken. "I'm glad you came last night. Did you have fun?"

"From what I can remember," I say carefully, but I don't know why I still feel uneasy. "I heard your husband is worried because you didn't go home last night."

Misha's eyes flick to Brent. A wordless communication passes between them. I'm surprised that I feel a little jealous. Not of them, exactly, but of the easy intimacy, the way they're playing house. Like Joe spending a lazy Saturday morning with Raj. It seems as if everyone but me can trip and fall into comfortable relationships.

For the first time it occurs to me that maybe Barrens isn't

rotten. Maybe the problem is me. Maybe the problem has been me all along.

"Peter and I had a fight and, well . . . I wasn't exactly sober," she says carefully. "Brent was nice enough to offer up his couch." She emphasizes the last word very slightly. "Me and Peter fight like rabid dogs sometimes. It's probably my fault . . ."

"It's not your fault," Brent says quietly. He takes a seat and puts a hand on her leg. That bothers me; I'm ashamed to feel so little sympathy for her. She looks upset—and much younger without any makeup—but I still feel like she's faking.

"You must think I'm a mess," Misha says. I'm not sure whether she's speaking to me or to Brent, but he gives her knee another squeeze.

Then Brent turns back to me. "I told her not to marry Peter," he says. He keeps a hand on her knee. "She never listens."

Misha inhales a laugh. But when I look again, she's swiping a tear with the back of her hand. "Lies," she says, half laughing, half crying. "I always listen to you."

Suddenly I know what's bothering me about their pose: I've seen it before. Senior year, I stumbled on Misha and Brent sitting together in a knot of woods behind the administration building where I went to eat my lunch sometimes, rather than brave the cafeteria. The Dell, people called it—the smokers went there to get high between classes, and someone had even set up an old table and chair between the felled logs to serve as furniture. But at noon it was usually deserted.

Not that day, though. As I crashed through the underbrush I remember seeing Brent and Misha just that way. He had his hand on her knee. She looked as if she was about to cry. But when she spotted me, her expression transformed in an instant into one of slick hatred.

Are you spying on us, pervert? she spat out.

Leave her alone, Misha, Brent said. And then: *She didn't hear anything.*

Only now does it occur to me it was a funny thing to say.

"Sorry," Misha says. Once again, something has changed—an invisible current, a communication between them I haven't heard. "God, I can't imagine what you think of us. You must be dying to go back to Chicago."

"I'm just glad everyone's okay. Last night, I thought—" I break off. I can't understand why I was so scared. Then I realize Brent and Misha are watching me, waiting for me to continue. "I just—I don't usually get that drunk. It's not like me. When I woke up and realized I had taken your shoes . . ."

This, finally, gets a smile out of her. "Oh, thank goodness," she says. "We must have swapped. I thought I lost them when I went in after Annie."

"Are *you* okay?" Brent squints at me. "You want a water or something?"

"No. I'm fine." But I stand up too quickly and a head rush darkens my vision.

"Actually, I *will* take the water. Don't get up," I say, when he starts to stand. "I can get it."

In the kitchen, I wash my hands, using up the last of Brent's hand soap. I count my breaths, listening to the murmur of conversation from the other room. But their words are too muted to make out.

Here, too, everything is clean, pristine, almost unused. Brent has installed a water purifier to the tap, but his sink is perfectly dry and I wonder whether he's ever run it. Curious, I ease open the refrigerator: the upper two shelves are crammed with pallets of bottled water.

"Leftovers from a corporate picnic last week. You should see all the Sprite I got stacked in my garage."

I spin around at the sound of his voice, closing the refrigerator door; I hadn't realized he had followed me into the kitchen. But if he notices my discomfort, he doesn't appear to.

"If you want ice, it's in the door," he offers brightly.

"Just water's fine," I say.

He crosses to the cupboard, takes down two glasses, and fills them from the tap. He downs his and watches me carefully as I drink, as if my reaction will bring a final and definitive end to our investigation. The water tastes fine.

Brent's refrigerator door is cluttered with magnets, and before we leave the kitchen, I notice that one of them bears Aaron Pulaski's name. He sees me looking at it.

"Local guy," he says. "Or as local as he can be. He comes from over in Hanover. I did some work on his campaign." He says it casually enough, but I'm sure I'm not imagining the new tension in the way he's standing. "I thought he'd do some good for the district. Turns out he's just as incompetent as the rest of the pack." He shrugs. "Oh, well. We all make mistakes, right?"

"We sure do," I say. When he turns his back to me, I slip the magnet into my pocket. *Weak spots.*

Chapter Sixteen

Monday morning, Joe and I strategize. We've got one chance in a thousand that a circuit court will take our slipshod suspicions for evidence, but all we need to do is file the suit—and hope Optimal is frightened into giving us *actual* evidence.

We can't get a court appointment until Wednesday afternoon, which gives me a few days to put together a cohesive picture and try to find a prosecutor's office willing to work the criminal side of the investigation.

Flora and Portland head down to greet the ETL lab techs; they've arrived to draw samples from the reservoir and from the filtration plant it feeds to, and I want to be sure no one bothers them while they work. Maybe I'm being paranoid, but given Optimal's long tentacles, and its grip on Barrens, I can just see some local townies trying to chase them off with pitchforks—or, more likely, .22s.

I put in a message to the county prosecutor's office where Aaron Pulaski worked until recently, and kill a few hours researching the bioaccumulation of a variety of types of heavy metals, detailing the evidence found in plants and seedlings—at least we know the foliage can't be paid to keep quiet.

Just before lunch my phone blows up, and a woman with the

kind of chirpy voice that immediately suggests a pantsuit introduces herself as Dani Briggs, junior prosecutor. "I got your message," she says. "But I'm afraid we can't help out. There was a personnel sweep after Mr. Pulaski left."

One skill I've learned as a lawyer: to make a *no* into an opportunity. "Why so much turnover?"

She hesitates for just a fraction of a second. "When Mr. Agerwal"—the new county prosecuting attorney, and a board member of the Indiana Prosecuting Attorneys Council—"took the job, he promised to take all the politics out of the justice system."

"Like what? Bribery? Corruption? That *is* politics."

Her laugh is surprising—deep and rich and swallowed just as quickly as it comes. "Maybe. But not our kind of politics."

"So he purged the old guard."

"I wouldn't call it a purge," she says. "Given all the scrutiny around police departments and prosecuting offices throughout the country, he felt the MCPO needed a clean start."

This is how lawyers confess: by edging just close enough to the issue that you can take a hop-skip-jump to the truth yourself. "Here's the thing: I'm looking into a donation to Pulaski's state congressional campaign by a company he had threatened to go after for labor violations. Does that sound like *his* kind of politics?"

Another momentary hesitation. Now I understand her silence is code for *yes*. "I really can't speak to that," she says. "What our predecessors do is, unfortunately, kind of a black box." Maybe she can sense my hesitation over the phone, because she adds, "Let me take your contact info. I'll talk to Mr. Agerwal when he comes back."

I put my head down on my desk, against the cool wood, willing the pulse of so many strains of information to finally hit a rhythm that I can latch on to. Will any of this get me closer to understanding what happened to Kaycee? Will any of it get me closer to answering the question that drove me out of Barrens and to Chicago in the first place? I thought if I could prove that Optimal was making people sick, I could cure Barrens of what had poisoned it—and then Barrens would finally let me go.

But now, I'm not so sure.

"Ms. Williams?"

I nearly punch out of my skin: Portland has returned, soundlessly.

"For fuck's sake. We need to install a bell on you or something." Then, I notice he has the strangest look on his face.

"You said she was faking it," he says.

He slides a photo across the desk, and I'm shocked to recognize Kaycee, painted up in school colors. Graduation day.

Her arms are what strike me first. They're skinny—as skinny as a child's. It could be an effect of the paint or maybe the angle, but her cheekbones are blunt, like two axes that meet in the center of her face. Her clavicle emerges prominently from her neckline. She looks . . . sick. *Really* sick.

It may be the first time I've ever felt truly sorry for Kaycee Mitchell. I nearly reach out to touch her face, then remember Portland is watching me.

"Where did you get this?" I ask him.

"I went to the high school," he says—so casually I nearly wince. I don't know why, but it disturbs me to think of Portland walking those too-familiar halls—it is further proof that two sections of my life are collapsing. "I figured small town, the nurse would probably be the same a decade later. I was right."

It was a brilliant move. Nurses at public schools aren't bound by laws of confidentiality.

"Good thinking," I say. "Why the hell didn't I think of that?"

"Kaycee wasn't lying," he says simply.

"The girls admitted it," I say, but even *I* hear it as a question.

"The *other* girls admitted it," he says, in the same soft cadence, as if he knows he's breaking news I don't want to hear. "But she was sick. You can see it. The nurse saw it."

Just hearing the words like that is like the hard stun of a wave you've been watching get closer. It takes my breath away momentarily. Right away I know that this, this photograph right here, is the whole reason I came back. It's why I could never entirely leave it all behind.

Another Kaycee surfaces in my mind: the creamy, seamless

skin, the curve of her mouth rearranging itself into a wolfish smile—or sneer. Perfect. Suddenly, I realize after all I don't *want* it to be true. If it's true, it means Kaycee is just another one I got all wrong. Not a predator—a victim.

FRANK MITCHELL GAVE up the trailer Kaycee grew up in and now lives only half a mile from his shop. God knows why I felt compelled to bring Portland—it's highly doubtful that Mitchell will find the sight of a guy who looks like he could be the singer of an indie-rock band reassuring. Maybe I'm the one who needed reassuring.

The garage door of number 217 is half open. I'm betting that Frank's one of those guys who drinks five to midnight. It's only noon, which means he might be sober enough to be reasonable, or hungover enough to be irritable.

We find him bent over a motorcycle, his back bony beneath a stained white shirt.

"Mr. Mitchell?" When he turns around, I see he's aged considerably. Yellow-stained wrinkles falling into his salt-and-pepper mustache. His T-shirt's emblazoned with a hunting rifle and the slogan *Guns don't kill people, I do.* "Hope we aren't catching you at a bad time. Abby Williams. You and I spoke briefly on the phone . . . ?"

"I remember. I remember you from back when, too." He sizes me up, sweeps his eyes over Portland, and turns back to his motorcycle. "I thought I told you I didn't have anything to say."

The years haven't softened his personality. But he hasn't ordered us to get out yet. That's a start.

"I'm still having trouble tracking Kaycee down," I say. "I really think it would be helpful to speak to her." The Internet is proving to be no help. So far, all I know is she might have settled in New York or San Francisco or anywhere in between.

"Like I said on the phone, you're barking up the wrong tree. I haven't talked to her since she ran off—with five hundred dollars of my money, too." He doesn't look up, just keeps working the rag.

"You're a Harley man, Mr. Mitchell?" Portland asks, casually reaching for the matte black helmet that's sitting on the workbench next to a pile of bolts.

"Yup." Mitchell spits. "You know anything about bikes?" He asks as if he highly doubts it.

Even I'm surprised when Portland shrugs. "A little. My dad taught me to ride when I was a kid. I used to have a 2009 custom Ultra Classic. Sold it to help pay for law school."

Frank Mitchell actually does a decent impression of a normal human being. "An Ultra Classic, huh?" He looks at me. "Those are built for long rides—nine, ten hours at a stretch. Bet he thought he was gonna go cross-country."

To my utter shock, Portland nods and looks at the floor, sheepish. Frank Miller laughs. "I'm working on a Fat Boy out back. I'll show it to you, if you want."

I make a mental note to kiss Portland as soon as possible.

"Can I use your bathroom?" I blurt out, with fake desperation. "Sorry. I had two coffees this morning . . ."

Mitchell's eyes barely flick in my direction. "Through the kitchen in back."

The back porch is cluttered with old machine parts. The downstairs is blocky and functional and contains a bedroom pungent with the smell of old sweat and alcohol; the kitchen, buzzy with flies; and a grimy bathroom where the toilet seat wears a pink furry cover that matches the rug beneath it. I wonder briefly who picked it out, and when. Mr. Mitchell's voice comes through a partially open window—soft but crisp, like I'm listening to a ham radio. Portland's still got him talking.

The last room's a sort of office, or maybe junk room is a better description. In addition to a desk and a relatively new desktop computer, the room is cluttered with random furniture, a tangle of holiday lights, old electronics, a toaster still in its box, stacks of old hunting magazines. But there's no trace of Kaycee here.

I rifle through a massive stack of old mail Frank Mitchell has cordoned off in a massive wicker basket, thinking that she might be the letter-writing type. I slip my fingers into the accordion of gutted envelopes: promotional offers from fishing magazines, inserts, slick torn-away pages with glossy photos of lures and other tackle, bills, faded bank statements, and what looks like a greeting card from a relative—the last name "Mitchell" is scrawled above the eviscerated return address. Inside, a cold greeting: BEST WISHES ON YOUR SPECIAL DAY. No signature. Why did he keep all this stuff? Years-old ads, outstanding bills, promotional coupons long expired.

Maybe after losing his daughter, he can't bear to let anything go.

Maybe that's why he hates Kaycee. She wouldn't let him hold on to her.

I land on a smooth envelope, unopened. The return address is for a local storage company, U-Pack. With one finger, I slice the envelope open and pull out a single piece of paper, folded in thirds. There's a comfort in crossing this line. Outside, something metal hits concrete—maybe on purpose, I think, a warning from Portland.

Footsteps creak across the porch. The screen door opens. My hands begin to sweat. I quickly find the date, and my chest tightens: the account's been active for exactly ten years.

Meaning Frank Mitchell rented a storage space only a few weeks after Kaycee disappeared.

I commit the membership number to memory and slip the folded bill back into the mess just before Mr. Mitchell shoves open the door.

"What the hell do you think you're doing in here?" He seems to swell. Or maybe I shrink, funneling back to the little kid I was when just the sight of him would make me cross the street.

"I guess I got turned around." My smile feels sticky, as if it's congealing at the edges.

"Get out." His voice is a growl. Now his T-shirt looks like a direct threat. Guns don't kill people. I do. "Now."

I have to push by him, and for a second he gets in my way, and I have a quick flash of physical fear, a terror he won't let me leave. But at the last second he turns, angling his body and giving me room to pass.

I practically sprint to the door; only after I'm standing on the porch, gulping air, do I realize I was holding my breath. As if a monster were about to get me. As if the house were a graveyard.

As if I were afraid to raise the dead.

Chapter Seventeen

I still haven't heard back from the county prosecutor, Dev Agerwal, so I leave a message with his office, and, in desperation, send a follow-up e-mail through a contact form I find on his website. But I don't hold out much hope. Agerwal has reason to be protective of his office, even if he did clean house when he took the position.

I leave the office early, while Joe is on the phone, to avoid having to give a blow-by-blow of our trip to Frank Mitchell's house—I know he thinks we should be focusing on rooting out people who've had problems with their water and are willing to say so.

The cloud cover has burned off, and the evening sky has transformed into stripes of gold and auburn. Instead of turning right on County Route 12, which will lead me down past Sunny Jay's where Condor works, the Elks Club, and, finally, the hair salon that conceals my rental house behind it, I turn left. I need to know what Frank Mitchell, whose home is halfway to hoarder, dumped in a storage space only a week after Kaycee disappeared.

U-Pack is a depressing sling of buildings ineffectively roped off by a sagging chain-link fence. I've always said that if you haven't touched something for two years, then you don't need it. But I've always hated junk and clutter. I don't like *stuff* weighing me down.

I would never need a storage locker; in fact, when people come to my condo in Chicago they ask if I've just moved in.

A cheerful bell *tings* when I open the door. The clerk, a man in his sixties, looks up from a magazine.

I can see the nicotine stain on his fingernails from where I'm standing. Smell it on his breath, too. "How can I help you?" He manages to say it as if he very much hopes he can't.

I put on a smile. "Hi, I'm here for a friend—Frank Mitchell?" He doesn't blink, doesn't give any reaction to the name. "He's drowning in stuff, honestly drowning. Total packrat and just can't bring himself to toss any damn thing."

"That's why we're here," he says. I can't tell if he's making a joke or not.

"He can hardly find his couch nowadays, and of course he's gone and lost the key to his unit." I'm rambling and I know it. Less is more. "So I offered to come down and get a replacement, maybe take some stuff off his hands."

He shakes his head. "Can't let no one in besides the owner. He'll have to come down here himself, give ID and his account number and put in for a new key."

"That's just exactly what I told him," I say, making a big show of amazement, as if we've arrived together at the solution to a major physics problem. "He gave me his account number and told me to give it a shot anyway. I have his number, too—you can call him if you want."

He looks at the phone on his desk as if it's a dead mouse he hasn't yet cleared away. I hold my breath. Finally, he just shakes his head. "You said you got the account number?"

I recite it to him. He turns to the ancient computer on his desk and spends a few labored minutes trying to get it to do whatever he needs it to do. Then, with a heavy sigh, he stands and disappears into the back office, returning a few seconds later with a key. But before I can grab it from the counter, he nudges a heavy leather-bound security log in my direction.

"Sign, date, and print your name clear," he says. "Name of the unit owner, too."

Not until then do I fully register the cameras winking at us from the ceiling. And for a split second, I have a feeling like waking up abruptly from a dream and seeing the real world rush at you.

But what rushes at me now is the gravity of what I'm doing. I don't remember enough of criminal law code to know exactly what law I'm breaking—false pretenses, maybe, or larceny-by-trick, but only if I remove something—but either way, a violation of this size could get me disbarred.

I nearly leave the key where it is. I nearly mumble an excuse, turn, and hurry back to the car.

But I don't. I scrawl a fake name into the ledger. The key—a new one—is very small and extremely light. Cheap keys for cheap locks for a cheap storage facility filled with cheap belongings. A no-man's land of possessions: sufficiently disposable to be locked away, but too dearly loved, or at least too familiar, to be abandoned. I wonder how many storage rooms are built out of broken hearts and broken relationships, dead fathers and brothers and wives. I also wonder how many of them are just meth labs.

Standing in front of unit 34, I could swear there's a low hum radiating down the long metal alleys. And I wonder whether in fact the keys and locks were meant to keep these old memories and broken objects safe—or if they are really meant to keep them from getting out.

THE UNIT IS full of art.

The storage space is roughly 10 x 20, but so packed with canvases and old art supplies I still have trouble squeezing inside. Many of the paintings are wrapped in tarp and duct tape and garbage bags while a few are left exposed. Not all of them are finished, although it's difficult to tell: there's an image of a woman's face that seems to simply explode or disappear into white space, even though her clothing is painstakingly detailed. They're Kaycee's.

Some paintings are better than others. But all of them are good. I can tell that much without knowing a thing about art. I move as carefully as I can, afraid to touch or disturb anything. I peer through the clear garbage bags to puzzle out the shapes she pinned down with her brush: cornfields, the football stadium, even the Donut Hole. All familiar and deeply ordinary—and yet somehow, in her frenzy of brushstrokes and colors, they all light up with a strange and terrifying beauty. The football field opens like the jaws of a shark to consume the sky. The Donut Hole glows against dusk, and its sign casts a fluorescent halo into the clouds, but in the parking lot a figure lies curled in the fetal position.

There are portraits, too: I recognize a young Misha in one, a shadow splitting her face. The next painting, distorted through plastic, looks at first like a collage of random shapes. Then I find a pair of eyes buried deep in the thickness of the paint, and another, and another. It's like one of those visual deceptions where a vase is buried in a woman's hair—in a millisecond the jigsaw of random shapes becomes instead a series of faces staring out at me from the paint.

Some glower, others appear to weep. All of them are Kaycee. It's a self-portrait, an explosion of her—or versions of her—again and again on canvas. One has hair the color of blood. In all of them, her features are obscured, cut up, or erased, some imagined in negative space.

Even when we were little, she had that gift: she could study something I'd seen every day, take it apart and make it new. I labored over line drawings while she made flowers ripple on the page. She spent hours one day in the sun drawing the same enormous mushroom, over and over, until she was satisfied she'd got it right. When she asked if I liked it, I asked her to show me the actual mushroom she'd been staring at all day, but there wasn't one. Just a scattering of shattered beer bottles in the middle of the field.

It amazed and scared me, the way her unseen world could seem more vibrant and alive than the real one. There was a time when I loved her imagination, would follow her anywhere. And yet even then, I hated the way she could make me question things that were obvious facts, things that were right there before my eyes.

I suddenly feel bad. I shouldn't be here. Whatever Mr. Mitchell says about Kaycee now, he loved her and he still does. Why else would he be so careful to preserve her art? Kaycee's paintings feel like live things, bits of skin and bone strapped down beneath their protective covering: but still bleeding, invisibly, all over. Even after I'm back in the car, I imagine the smell of paint, and keep checking my fingers and clothes for residue. Kaycee transmuted into oil paint looks different from the Kaycee I remember: lonelier, deeper, even desperate. I remember what Kaycee said to me that day, the day she turned beer bottles into a mushroom that seemed to be growing right out of the page. *You know the problem, Abby, isn't that you can't draw*, she said, out of nowhere. *It's that you can't* see.

I'm beginning to think she was right.

Chapter Eighteen

On Tuesday morning, my ass has barely touched the chair before my phone rings: an upbeat clerk announces that Dev Agerwal, the county prosecutor, is on the line for me.

I unroll the same song and dance I gave when I spoke to his junior prosecutor Dani Briggs just a few days before, and he listens patiently and without interruption before politely telling me that Ms. Briggs had already filled him in. I like him for that; he's the type who likes to get the same story from different angles, more journalist than lawyer.

"But I don't know how much help I can be," he says carefully, and though it's exactly what I expected him to say, my chest deflates. "My predecessor never announced a formal investigation into Optimal's business practices."

"But he spoke about it in interviews," I counter.

"Off the cuff, sure." He sighs. "Look, Ms. Williams, I've built my career on trying to take big business and big money out of local politics. But unfortunately, it's mostly a gray area. Optimal has done a neat job of blurring the line. And corruption has to be provable."

"Only if you plan to prosecute," I say. "We just need a reason to open up the books. A subpoena would be a slam dunk, but right now, you're the one with the best shot at a case."

Agerwal is quiet for a while. Then, abruptly: "Have you thought of speaking to Lilian McMann?"

I scribble the name on the back of a coffee receipt. "Never heard of her."

"She might have some things to tell you about Optimal, and about their relationship to the . . . political climate. She used to work at the Indiana Department of Environmental Management. She was at the Office of Water Quality."

That, I have definitely heard of: IDEM works directly with both local monitors *and* the feds. Just my kind of girl.

Dev Agerwal hangs up after taking down my e-mail address, with a promise to send me Lilian McMann's contact information. And a few minutes later he makes good.

Actually, he makes great. The e-mail, sent from a personal e-mail address—not the state government server—also includes several attachments and a short note.

Hope this is helpful.

When I open the attachments, I nearly fall out of my chair. He's included a copy of the check stub written from Associated Polymer, Optimal's parent company, to the Campaign for Pulaski, as well as several e-mail exchanges between an Optimal employee and a campaign aide. The e-mails are carefully crafted, but the subtext is clear.

The most damning of them, sent from someone in Gifts, expresses hope "that our support will spark a new era of cooperation and mutual support between the nominee and one of Indiana's most successful homegrown businesses."

On Wednesday, Joe, the snake charmer, works his magic on the local superior court. Unbelievably, our petition passes, and after we nudge Optimal's legal counsel by dangling the threat of a much bigger problem down the line, we float an unofficial list of document requests. Now that we've gone ahead and filed, a deposition will be coming soon enough. After some hemming and hawing, Optimal agrees via their ancient-sounding lawyer to provide five years of financial records related to any third-party payments before the week is out.

Not totally ideal. I was hoping to go back further, ten years, to the complaint the Mitchells, Allens, Baums, and Dales dropped, and for bigger scope—investments, subsidiaries, the whole deal. But I know better than to say so to Joe. Still, he reads it on my face.

"You should be kissing my feet right now," he says.

"I'll let Raj do that for you," I say, and he smirks in a way that doesn't quite hide a genuine look of happiness. I feel a sharp stab of jealousy, and then another of disgust. When did other people's happiness start feeling like assault?

But the answer comes quickly, and brings a bad taste to my mouth. Always. I didn't ever stop feeling excluded. I just started to wear it and pretend it was my choice. Maybe that's why I was drawn to the law of poisoned things, and hurt people, and scabby chemical earth. Maybe *toxic* is the only thing I really understand.

MORE GOOD LUCK: that very afternoon, less than twenty-four hours after Agerwal directed me to her, Lilian McMann returns my call. I get out a hello and half of an introduction before she interrupts to suggest we meet in person.

Her office is about forty-five minutes out of town. Locals call this "uptown," even though there's nothing "up" about it. This is Anytown, strip malls and chain stores, and as a kid this is where we would come to hit the big grocery store when we wanted to buy in bulk. The storefronts have turned over but the structure is the same.

I get lost, circling several times around the address she provided before giving up and phoning again.

"There's nothing here but a sports equipment store and a Chinese restaurant," I say. "I must have written the address wrong . . ."

"You didn't. We're behind the restaurant. Just circle around to the back and you'll see a sign."

Inside, she's done everything she can to smooth the cheap edges into something elegant and professional. She's almost succeeded.

Lilian comes to greet me herself. The secretary, if there is one, has abandoned her post. There is no other word for Lilian than *manicured*. She is practically uniformed in an earth-tone pencil skirt, blazer, and kitten heels. Her makeup is flawless, albeit a little heavy on the eyeshadow, her nails are done, and her hair is sleek despite the heavy must of the office, which is chasing the heat by means of a whimpering window A/C unit.

Her office is small but very orderly. She takes a seat across from me and I look for something to compliment—a kid, a husband, a dog—but find nothing personal at all. It's bare.

"Thank you for seeing me," I say. "I know you must be busy." This is so obviously untrue, to both of us, I feel immediately embarrassed.

"You're looking at Optimal?" she says, with careful politeness. And with those simple words, I understand she has given me permission to short circuit at least a half hour of painstaking bullshit.

I could kiss *her* feet.

"I'm with the Center for Environmental Advocacy Work, based in Illinois," I tell her, and explain what brought us into town in the first place. "Before Optimal moved to Indiana, the company had to settle a case that involved chemical leaching. It seems to us like they've bought their way out of trouble several times—and not just to skirt environmental regulations, either." She doesn't blink. "The county prosecutor's office dropped an investigation they were planning—for labor violations—after Optimal cut a check. I don't like the pattern."

Still, she says nothing. She doesn't act surprised, either. I can't tell how much of this she already knew.

I clear my throat. "You were the compliance branch chief at IDEM, is that right?"

"Co-chief," she corrects me immediately. Then she smiles. Even her smile is deliberate. "There were two of us. Colin Danner was my partner."

I can tell she has more to say. But again she just sits there. I try a different tack. "What brings you to the private sector?" I ask. "That's quite a shift—going from public policy to contracting for the private sector."

"You mean quite a downgrade," she says calmly—and though that is exactly what I meant, I feel another rush of embarrassment. "It's all right," she says. "I'm happy enough." She uncrosses her legs and leans forward, practically pouring her words in my direction. "Look, I didn't choose to leave. I was forced out. I'll say it, and they would say it, too, though not for the same reasons. One day I was co-head, and the next day I couldn't take a step that wasn't crossing some kind of line or violating public policy or abusing my position. They buried me under an internal audit—I had to dig up duplicate receipts for all my expenses for the tenure of my time with IDEM. Random monitoring, they said. Bad luck." She shakes her head and allows a look of rage to surface before she harnesses it. "I got shut out of all the big projects. Then, when I missed deadlines— deadlines I didn't know existed—I was threatened with termination. I left instead."

"What happened?" I say.

"Colin sold me out," she says matter-of-factly. "I'm not sure exactly what he said, or what complaints he filed, but I'm sure he was the one who launched the audit."

"Why would he do that?"

Now she looks at me as if the answer is so obvious she hates to have to point it out. "Optimal," she says. "Of course."

A buzz of excitement notches up my pulse.

"We butted heads almost from the start on how and when the environmental review should take place. I thought it was just his usual shit. He didn't like that they appointed a co-head. He especially didn't like that they appointed a woman." She says this with no inflection at all, not even a catch of anger in her voice, as if it had nothing at all to do with her. A true pro.

"So he steamrolled you?"

"That's what I thought at first—he always challenged my recommendations, questioned my reports. But this was different. It was as if he didn't want to look at all. But that didn't make sense. The compliance branch of OWQ had done an inspection, several years earlier, before I arrived. An inspection every two years is standard, unless issues of permitting or expansion make it necessary to test even more. So he wasn't against it in principle. But when I checked the report, I knew something was wrong. Plastics manufacturing uses some of the most toxic chemicals in the world—and a lot of them. But there wasn't a single fine. Not a single notice, zero safety concerns. No infractions at all. That *never* happens." Her voice hangs there, climbing toward a peak. "There's *always* something. I've never seen a report that clean, in my whole career. It isn't possible."

My pulse has turned into a joyful shout. *Yes, yes, yes.* "You think Colin was ignoring whatever he'd found in the inspections? Only one inspection was submitted into ICIS from your office," I say. I've read through the same stack of briefs so many times I could probably tell her exact dates. "The other two inspections were subcontracted."

She shakes her head. "Sure. But we depend on a third party to input reports into the system. A liaison who flows state information back to the federal level."

"You're saying even if the inspections were originally legit, they might have been *changed* afterward?"

"Maybe. Maybe not. Both reports were actually entered by the same person. An agency coordinator named Michael Phillips. Lives in Indianapolis now." Her eyes flare with a warning. "But he's from just outside Barrens originally. I looked him up. He and Colin were together at the University of Indiana."

Click. Another piece comes together. But it's not enough—not nearly enough. Everything I learn makes the picture clearer, but also bigger—like climbing out of a ditch only to find myself at the bottom of the Grand Canyon. "I don't understand why you didn't report him."

"The fact that they went to school at the same place at the same time doesn't necessarily mean anything," she says. "IU is a big school. And a popular one. Besides, their education wasn't a secret. It obviously hadn't raised flags before."

"Sure. But in combination with the inspections, it looks suspicious. It *is* suspicious. If regulations are as strict as you say, you had more than enough, at least to launch an audit."

She looks away again. She's silent for so long I start to get uncomfortable. And then, finally, just as I'm about to thank her for her time, a shock rolls through her and she begins to laugh. Little bursts of sound, like hiccups—like she's choking on the laughter.

"Sometimes I think I went crazy," she says, and when she finally turns in my direction I see she's crying and I'm so shocked I can't say anything. "Do you have any children, Ms. Williams?"

I shake my head. She gets control of herself, finally, stands up and moves to the desk. She comes back with her phone and passes it to me: on the home screen, a beautiful girl, a teenager—as dark as her mother, with the same large eyes and bone structure.

"That's Amy," she says. "She's a junior in high school this year."

"She's pretty," I say, after a quick look, and hand back the phone. I feel oddly resentful of her for unraveling in front of me. That's the agreement we make with strangers, that we'll pretend, and they'll pretend, so we can slide away from each other quickly and with no guilt.

"She's doing great now." She slides the phone into the pocket of her jacket. "During the audit, I was stressed. Working all the time. Trying to keep my head above water. She was on her own a lot. Her father only has her on the weekends." She closes her eyes and opens them again.

"I see," I say, even though I don't.

"She was a freshman," she goes on. "Sneaking around, drinking, nothing crazy, but she needed attention and I wasn't there. She spent a lot of time online, talking to people she'd never met. I didn't know any of it, of course. I only found out . . . after."

"After what?"

"One of her online *friends* . . ." Her voice breaks and she takes a breath. "He asked her to send some pictures. She did. Like I said, she wanted attention."

The image comes to me again of a girl, calling for help, floundering in the water, her voice nearly buried by the pitch of laughter.

"The next day, the pictures were all over school. Sent through a class e-mail blast. Even her teachers got them. Even the principal. I—" But she stops, overwhelmed.

"I'm sorry," I say, and I really am. "That's awful. Teenagers can be awful. Believe me." I try and force everything I know, everything I've carried, into those two words. "But you can't blame yourself. It wasn't your fault."

She looks up sharply. "I know that," she says. "It was Colin's fault."

"You're not serious."

"Colin's son is in school in Crossville. They play against Barrens all the time. They share friends on Facebook."

"That's hardly evidence of . . ." I trail off, unsure exactly of what she believes. That Colin pressured his son into getting pictures from Lilian's daughter? All to keep her from pushing on his connection to Optimal? "What you're talking about . . . I mean, that's a felony. She was—what? Fifteen at the time?"

"Fourteen. I know it sounds insane. It is insane. I never would have made the connection. But then . . ." She stands up abruptly and moves to her desk. Slides open a drawer and fumbles for something out of sight.

"In the pictures, Amy was wearing socks. Nothing else. They were argyle. Pink and green. I always buy her at least one pair for Christmas."

She straightens up. Comes around the desk. Suddenly I don't want to know, and wish I hadn't asked, hadn't come, hadn't ever heard of Lilian McMann.

Mutely, she extends her hand, letting the socks hang loose as if they're a corpse that might still come alive. Argyle. Pink and green. Unworn, and still tagged.

"He gave them to me when I left," she says. "He left them on my desk with a note. *Great socks make a great outfit. Hope these keep you warm through cold nights ahead.*"

Her words trigger a long-buried memory: Jake Erickson, one of Brent's friends, elbowing into my lab space during senior year chemistry. He was always messing with me, switching my chemicals, knocking over my test tubes, turning off my Bunsen burner so I could never finish in time, but that day he was too busy bragging about feeling up a sophomore behind the Dumpsters between classes.

She's totally fucked in the head, he said, and I could tell he knew I was listening. *The crazy ones are always the easiest. They just open up for business the second you even look at them.*

"He wanted me to know." Now her voice leaps to a note of high anguish. "Not just that he'd seen the photos. But that he'd gotten them from her in the first place."

We can do anything we want with them. Jake Erickson's voice fills up my head. *They* let *us. And why not? It's not like they're going to complain afterward.*

I stand up, suddenly dizzy. "I'm sorry," I say, without knowing exactly what I'm sorry for.

For her daughter, for her job, for that sophomore behind the Dumpsters, men who get to do anything they want, and the people who are taken advantage of.

Because isn't that, ultimately, what the case comes down to?

There are the people of the world who squeeze and the ones who suffocate.

Chapter Nineteen

The closest bar isn't nearly close enough. Ray's Tavern—a dump that shares a parking lot with a Fireworks Emporium—is already half full, despite the fact that it's only four P.M. Some of the customers look like they may have been crusted on those same stools since the beginning of time. They appear to be grown into the décor, like alcoholic barnacles. I can't stop scraping my palms with a cocktail napkin, as if Lilian McMann's story has embedded itself in my skin.

I don't know that I can believe her: not because she's lying, but because she might simply be wrong. The problem with spending a lifetime looking for patterns is that it teaches you to see them everywhere; but coincidences happen. Colin Danner might simply have known about the pictures through his son, and decided to give one final twist of the knife before Lilian left. In all likelihood, that *is* what happened.

But her story has left me with a bad feeling, like I've just swum through oily water, and the sink in the bathroom is so filthy that washing my hands only makes me feel dirtier. My first whiskey-soda does little to help and the second only makes me sad. I can't help but think of Becky Sarinelli, and of that poor fluttering photo that landed in the aisle at that pep rally: her skin a glare in the camera flash, her exposed body. And that was before photos could be instantly shared the way they are now.

Thinking of Becky Sarinelli gets me back to thinking about Condor, and wondering why and how he could have done that to her.

Old mistakes, he'd said, about Hannah's mother. But old mistakes are never old. We relive them again and again. We repeat them, and hope this time things will turn out differently.

I don't want Condor to be a mistake.

Or maybe I just don't want to be alone. Being in Barrens is reminding me of how lonely I was here. It's reminding me I've never really stopped being lonely.

That was what drew Kaycee and me together as kids: we were the two loneliest best friends in the history of the world. My father was lost in his religion, and hers lost in his alcohol, his rages, his black-market economy and the people who bought and sold from him. My mother was dying. Hers might as well have been dead.

But being best friends with Kaycee could be just as lonely as having no friends at all. She was so unpredictable, even back then. She could be cruel and distant, explosive. She could hit you and then stroke the bruise, promising to make it better. Either way, I soaked up the attention. I remember building forts with her in the woods, and how I would always turn tree stumps into crowds of friends, into imaginary siblings who comforted me and cheered me on. Kaycee wouldn't invent friends, but subjects. That way, she said, they would never disobey her when she ordered them to stay.

Sometimes I think Chestnut—a stray, just like me, skinny and desperate and fearful until I managed to coax him to me with a handful of shredded chicken—was the only real friend I ever had.

In a sick way, it made sense that Kaycee had to kill him.

BY THE START of my third drink I know that calling is a very bad idea, but by the bottom of it, I don't care.

Pick up, I think. And: *Don't pick up*.

He does, on the second ring. He sounds clean, even over the phone.

"Abby," Brent says, and I try to pretend that he's the one I wanted to call all along. "So crazy. I was just thinking of you. What's up?"

I shred the damp napkin beneath my now empty drink and eye the clock over the bar. Four forty-nine. "I'm just leaving the office," I say. "How about a drink?"

"HOW DID YOU even find this place?" Brent asks, as he fumbles onto the stool next to mine. In his collared shirt and suit jacket, he looks out of place.

"A friend recommended it," I say. No one in their right mind would recommend this place.

"I like it." He makes it sound convincing. But rather than feel reassured, I feel a quick pulse of anxiety. Brent is a good liar.

He orders a tequila and I get another whiskey-soda, pretending it's my first, and the bartender, with a face worn from hard living, doesn't comment.

"I was gonna call you," he says. "When you saw Misha at my place . . . I didn't want you to get the wrong idea . . ."

"What idea is that?"

"Misha always had a thing for me," he says bluntly. Somehow, hearing the words out loud is a relief. Because, of course, thinking back on it, I see that he's right, that it was always so obvious.

"For a little while, after Kaycee disappeared, she pushed us to . . ." He trails off, shaking his head. "But I never thought of her that way." He adds, a little more quietly, "I like you. A lot."

"I like you, too," I say. But as soon as I say it, I know it's not true. In high school, I would have said I loved him. I dreamed of all the improbable ways I might find myself alone with him—a sudden fire that forced just the two of us into one portion of the school, waiting for the fire department to reach us; a flat tire that might leave me stranded only a few yards from his street. But it occurs to me now for the first time that I'm not sure how much of that feeling was simply because Brent belonged to Kaycee. Maybe I always intended revenge. Maybe I wanted to take from her, like she had taken from me.

Or maybe, in a weird way, I thought that if Brent could love me, Kaycee would have to love me, too.

"Why did you kiss me that day in the woods?" I blurt out.

"It was the last day of school," he says. I can tell I've surprised him. "I guess . . . when I saw you there, in the woods, like you'd just *appeared* . . ." He smiles. "It felt like a sign."

That's what he said the other night, at the bonfire: that my arrival was a sign. "You were my first kiss." Immediately, I could punch myself for telling him this. My tongue is slipping. I set down my drink.

Brent smiles, big-wattage. The smile that used to knock the wind out of me in the cafeteria. "You know, back then it seemed like we were really at the end of something. All those girls getting sick, and no one could explain it. It was like Kaycee turned a lie into an actual infection. Like we might all catch it eventually." He brings his hand to my face, just like he did that night at the bonfire. "Not you, though. I always knew you were just beginning."

I shift away from him. Does he really believe that? Does he really think *I* can believe it? "You really never tried to find her, after she left?"

He sighs, as if I've disappointed him. "I tried calling her, obviously," he says. "She never picked up. Misha said she didn't want to talk to anyone." This gets my attention. Maybe Misha was more attuned to her former best friend than she claims. Turning back to the bar, Brent fiddles with a damp cocktail napkin. "The funny thing is, Misha and I weren't even close until Kaycee ran off." He takes a long pull of his drink. "Tragedies do that, I guess. Bond you with people. I think she was hoping it would do more than bond us."

I think of surprising Brent and Misha together at the Dell. Brent was either comforting her or pleading with her—I couldn't tell which. They looked close then. But even then I had the impression that Kaycee was with them; that she was hovering, unseen, outside the circle of their bodies. That they'd been talking *about* her.

"Is that what it was, when Kaycee left? A tragedy? At the diner, you seemed happy about it."

"Never stop being a lawyer, do you?" He says it jokingly, but I can hear the reprimand. "Can't it be both? I was . . . happy, to be free of her. But it was tragic that it got to that point. She . . . destroyed things. Do you know what I mean?"

For a moment I imagine Kaycee coaxing Chestnut toward her with treats. How furious she was when Chestnut began to snap and growl. *There's something wrong with that dog. It's probably rabid. Someone should shoot it.*

"Yes," I say simply. Then, without thinking: "Did you ever love her?"

Brent is quiet for a while. He stirs his drink and then empties it in one swallow. Finally he looks at me.

"What did I know? I was young." Now his smile has left behind a lingering exhaustion. "Can you love someone who isn't capable of loving you back?"

Funnily enough, it's my father who comes to mind. *Do dogs go to heaven?* I asked him once, my throat raw from crying after Chestnut died.

No, he replied shortly. But afterward he took a plastic garbage bag from the toolshed and bundled Chestnut's body inside of it, and told me to get the shovel. We walked down to the lip of the reservoir, and in silence he made a grave and lowered Chestnut into it. *Heaven is for redeemed sinners*, he said, after hours of silence. *Dogs don't need it. They live their whole lives in heaven.*

And I loved him more then than I've ever loved anyone.

"Oh, sure," I say. My drink tastes like hair spray. I've let it sit too long. "I think that's probably the realest love of all."

OUTSIDE, THE SUN is just setting, and a golden glow lingers over the parked cars.

"Listen, Abby." Brent seizes my hand when I've already said good-bye—embarrassed, in the sudden light, that I've said anything or called him at all. He takes a step closer to me, and for a second, I'm sure he's going to kiss me. "I know you're here for blood, okay? You're not going to find anything."

"I'm not here for blood, Brent." We're standing so close I can see the veins of color in his eyes. "I'm here for the truth."

He frowns as if he doesn't believe it. "I know it sounds crazy, but this town loves Optimal. *I* love Optimal." He's searching my face as if for signs that I believe him. "They've done a lot of good. You should see the new community center—you should see the theater they've built, a whole arts wing for the school to use. They've given *life* to this town."

He talks like the converted do about church.

I extricate my hand from his. "If they've done nothing wrong, there's nothing to worry about."

He shakes his head. "I'm not worried about them. I'm worried about *you*. I just . . . don't want anything to change between us, okay?" he says at last, though I'm almost positive that isn't what he originally intended. "After all these years . . ." He sucks in a breath. "I always wanted to see you. I always hoped I would."

Then he does kiss me. His lips are cold and taste like cheap tequila. A little like metal, too.

Like he's the one who's out for blood.

Chapter Twenty

$\mathbf{M}$y rental house is dark and humming with recycled air. I punch off the window units and shove open a window in the kitchen and my bedroom, even though I'll regret it when I wake up sweating. Immediately the sound of country relaxes me. Emptiness punctuated by crickets chirping and the hoot of an owl. For eighteen summers, I fell asleep to that same sound.

It pulls me back to the past, to riding my bike—a salvaged thing my dad found behind one of his job sites and hammered into shape—down the rock-studded path that led to the reservoir. It pulls me back to stripping with Kaycee down to our underwear to swim out in the reservoir, competing to see how long we could hold our breath underwater, and of how she used to float on her belly, letting her hair fan out around her, pretending she was dead.

It was the summer after sixth grade when I found Chestnut—or, rather, he found me. Kaycee got a bad flu, and for a week straight I didn't see her. I spent hours alone in the woods. I was lying on the ground counting clouds when I heard the whine of something behind me and sat up imagining a bobcat, a bear, or I don't know what. Instead, a wiry, half-starved dog was eyeing me through the branches in the woods. Crying and wagging its tail all at once.

One of the only things I bothered unpacking is an old wooden jewelry box that used to belong to my mother and still, I imagine, every so often, releases a bit of her smell.

On top of the stained velvet lining that's peeling away from the wood is a plain red collar, faded with age.

Chestnut Williams, it reads, next to the home phone number my dad still uses.

I begged my dad to take me to the pet store to buy it; he told me I was stupid for trying to put a collar on a stray, that Chestnut was just after a free meal, that he'd disappear soon enough, that I was wasting my money buying him toys and a collar he'd never wear. But when I slipped the collar over his head, his tail perked up. Like he was proud to finally belong to somebody. My dad thought Chestnut would be a burden on us both. But it didn't take long for my dad to come around and let him sleep at the foot of my bed.

Kaycee couldn't believe what she'd missed. She'd had the flu for seven days, she said, and I'd replaced her with a mangy animal. She sulked about it, and I thought she was only joking. I told her she would love Chestnut when she got to know him. I told her how he would eat right from my palm, how his leg would play a fiddle when you scratched his belly just right. I told her Chestnut could be *our* dog.

I've always wanted a dog, she confessed to me, in a whisper.

Once she got into the idea, she couldn't stop talking about Chestnut and all the fun we'd have together, how we could teach him tricks and at Christmas we could dress him like a reindeer and tie him to a sled.

I don't know what went wrong, exactly. Maybe he was sick. Maybe we'd startled him. Maybe he just took one sniff of Kaycee and knew. But Chestnut started growling at her, really growling, his back arched, all the teeth showing in his gums. I'd never seen him growl like that. I called his name, I tried to soothe him, as Kaycee stood there terrified.

"He hates me." And that was the first time ever that I'd seen her cry. Two tears—that was it.

"He doesn't hate you. He's only scared because you're a

stranger," I said, even though I knew it wasn't true. In an instant, Chestnut lunged for her, snapping an inch from her fingers.

"He tried to bite me!" She was screaming.

I'd never seen her look like that. It was rage, pure rage, like I'd only ever seen on my dad.

"What's wrong with that stupid dog?"

"There's nothing wrong with him."

She looked at me. "Oh, yeah? So you think it's normal to try and bite somebody's hand off?"

And then, because I was angry: "Maybe there's something wrong with *you*."

Right away, I wished I hadn't said it. Kaycee froze. A normal twelve-year-old kid would have cried, or shouted, or insulted me back.

But not Kaycee. She just stood there, very still.

"Maybe," she said finally. She turned away. Then she added, almost as an afterthought, "Dogs like that should be put down."

NOW I BALL the collar in my hand. I aim for the trash can, knowing, of course, I won't do it. For years I've threatened to get rid of the collar. For years I've pretended that I keep it only to remember him. But I've kept it to remember *her*, and to remember what she did.

She didn't poison Chestnut right away. I'm not sure why. Maybe she thought that way she'd get away with it.

When I accused her she barely blinked.

He's so dumb, he probably got into the rat poison all on his own, she said.

Except, she had stolen his collar. So I would know it wasn't an accident. Even way back then, she liked to turn the truth inside out, to make it look like a lie and vice versa, until you couldn't know the difference.

The craziest part was that she actually blamed *me* when I said I would never speak to her again. She actually seemed hurt, like she couldn't understand why I was being so mean to her.

For the next six years, after she'd grown, after she'd gathered all the subjects she had ever imagined for herself, she never once admitted to touching Chestnut.

And then, on the last day of school, I went to clean out my locker and found Chestnut's collar hanging neatly from a hook.

She kept it.

All those years, she kept it.

A few hours later, she asked Misha for a ride to Indianapolis, saying she wanted to scout for bartending jobs and would take a bus home later. But she never took the bus home. She never came home at all.

Why did she do it? Why was it the *last* thing she did?

I drop the collar back into my mom's jewelry box and latch the whole thing shut.

Sometimes, I think, in her crazy way, Kaycee left me that collar because she knew it would hurt, and hurt was how she knew that I would never forget her.

Other times, I think that maybe she was just saying good-bye.

Chapter Twenty-One

The next day, Thursday, I'm up at an hour even my father couldn't criticize.

I make my coffee so strong it tastes like mud. I might have gotten four or five hours of sleep max, even though I was home before eight o'clock. I spent the night sweating out cheap alcohol, staring at the ceiling, and twisting between different memories and half-formed ideas.

I slug my mud-coffee and watch Barrens shake off its nighttime mist. I try to see Barrens as a stranger might, and in the early light it looks beautiful. Maybe Brent was right and I am on some kind of witch-hunt. Maybe I want Optimal to be crooked, just so I have something, anything, to straighten out.

Maybe my obsession is all a fantasy.

Or maybe not. But this morning, I'm going to follow Brent's advice: it's time for a tour of some of Optimal's good works.

THE BARRENS-OPI COMMUNITY CENTER is halfway between the high school and the gates of the Optimal Plastics Complex, directly across the road from the Westlink Fertilizer & Feed store. The theater that Brent mentioned is complete; it's a modern, steel-and-glass exterior completely at odds with the squat brick shoeboxes that otherwise define architecture in Barrens. It's not even nine A.M. and there are already cars in the newly poured lot, and though the doors are locked, when I press my face to the glass I can make out a blur of movement inside. I'm surprised to see Misha in the lobby, pacing, phone pressed between shoulder and cheek.

When she spots me, she hangs up without saying good-bye and slips the phone into a pocket. She hesitates for a fraction of a second before unlocking the door.

"Abby." Today, she is dressed the part of vice principal, in a cheap pantsuit and a lavender blouse. "You pop up everywhere, don't you? I'm starting to think you might be following me."

"Small town. You said it yourself—there's nothing else to do but be in everybody's business. Besides, it isn't every day Barrens gets a community center."

"True enough. But we're not actually open yet. Can I help you with something?"

Last night, Brent told me that after Kaycee left, Misha had told him that she'd wanted a clean break. But if Kaycee confessed her desire to disappear, she might have confessed other things.

"I was supposed to meet somebody from Optimal for a tour before opening," I lie, seizing the opportunity to talk to her. "I made an appointment, but I'm afraid she thought I said yesterday. No wonder she's not picking up my phone calls."

She hesitates again, then bumps the door open a little wider with her hip. "Come on," she says. "Although there isn't much to see. Only the first phase is complete."

"I was so curious. What an ambitious project."

"Oh, this isn't half of it. Eventually, we'll have a reception venue, plus a gym for after-school sports programs. Classrooms for alternative education, too."

The building is expansive, open, and airy, and sunlight filters through the skylights.

"Wow. It's . . ." Ugly. The kind of ugliness only a shit ton of money can produce. But of course I won't say that. "Ambitious. Doesn't even feel like Barrens in here, does it? Must be costing a fortune," I say brightly.

Her eyes slide to mine only briefly. "Optimal is financing most of the project," she says. "We've got government grants as well. Taxes pay for the rest."

"You seem very . . . passionate." What I actually mean is: very *involved*.

"Principal Andrews and I both pushed for it. Before, our students had nowhere to go and nothing to do after school," she says. "Often their home lives are a big part of the problem. When there's nothing else to do . . . Idle hands find trouble." She reaches a door that points the way to the theater stage, and again she holds the door open for me.

"Have you ever thought it might be a problem that so many people depend on one company?" I keep my voice casual, as if I'm just thinking the question myself.

She glances at me. "Why would it be a problem?"

"For years Optimal has been dogged by rumors of pollution, of corruption, cover-ups."

"Rumors aren't facts, Abby. Thank God. Otherwise we *all* would have been in trouble in high school. You especially."

That's another point to Misha. I smile as sweetly as possible. "True. And smoke isn't fire. But sometimes where there's one, there's the other . . . No one wants to hold Optimal accountable. In fact, no one will even entertain it."

"We're proud of Optimal here," Misha says pointedly. "I don't see how that's a *problem*."

I pick my words carefully. "They've bought a lot of love, is all I'm saying."

I'm worried she'll get angry. Or maybe I'm hoping for it—a crack in her veneer. But this only seems to amuse her. "Last time I checked, that wasn't a crime."

"Well, that depends on who's buying," I say.

"The problem is that people think in black and white. They think they can have the good without the bad. But everything that's good for one person is probably bad for someone else. Life isn't like the Bible says it is. It isn't a choice between good and evil. It's about choosing which evils you can stand."

"So you admit Optimal is evil."

That, at least, gets her to smile. "All I'm saying is that if Optimal has made mistakes, do a few rashes here or there mean we should shut down the biggest employer in the area?"

"We're not just talking about rashes, and you know it. We're talking about chemicals that cause major damage. People aren't disposable. People shouldn't have to sacrifice their lives and their health to put food on the table."

"Oh, Abby." She sighs. "I envy you. It must be nice to know you're right so much of the time."

A knot of anger rises in my chest. "I don't know I'm right. But I know what's *not* right."

"Do you?" She tilts her head to squint at me. "Take Frank Mitchell as an example. He makes his living selling *pornography*." The way she says it, the word has about a hundred syllables.

"Pornography isn't illegal," I say.

She raises an eyebrow. "Fine. Sure. But let's say he has a customer, a normal man, husband and father, who keeps a little porn stash on the sly, nothing serious. And then, let's say, at some point he says what he's really after are the younger girls. *Much* younger. And it turns out this nice, upstanding man, with his nice, upstanding family, has a fetish for schoolgirls." She says all of this calmly, with immense self-control, as if we're still talking about plans for the auditorium. All the hairs lift on the back of my neck. "Now let's say Frank Mitchell sells him a magazine where the girls look much younger than they actually are. But of course they are of age. Paid professionals. The man goes home happy. If he doesn't, the man will just go out and find the real thing."

I am so stunned I just stare at her.

She spreads her hands. Innocent. "You see, some people would think Frank Mitchell had done a terrible thing by selling that kind of magazine. But it would still be the *right* thing."

"Or," I say, trying to keep the tremor from my voice, "he could simply call the police."

"The man would just deny it." Misha shrugs, as if the point is so obvious it barely needs to be stated. Then: "Should we continue the tour?"

I want nothing more than to run—from Misha, from this cold palace built on Optimal money to save the kids it might be pumping full of poison, from the crazy economy of sacrifice that Misha believes in. But I follow her mutely through another swinging door.

Misha raises the lights and the hallway takes shape in front of us: dark-painted walls, and a row of student photographs framed on both sides, surrounded by constellations of paper stars.

"These are our Optimal Stars," she says brightly. "The recipients of the Optimal Scholarship. Remember the scholarship program I mentioned? For several years now, we've worked with Optimal to grant full or partial scholarships to a handful of students who show academic promise. Most of them struggle with difficult home lives. Some have had disciplinary problems. But the program really turns them around." She sounds like she's reciting from a brochure. For all I know, she might be. "The first was Mackenzie Brown. She was a ballroom dancer. Don't get that much around here."

She indicates a girl with a beauty-queen smile. Actually, all the girls have beauty-queen smiles—and out of eighteen scholarship recipients, only two are boys. One portrait in particular stops me. The girl looks distractingly like Kaycee: a waterfall of blond hair, wide-spaced blue eyes. According to the little brass nametag, her name is Sophie Nantes.

"Why so many girls?" I can't help but ask.

"Well, we keep *need* in mind as much as we do talent," Misha says. "Plenty of colleges offer their own sports scholarships, but most of the money is for the male teams, so there's that. And there are more local opportunities for our male students who don't want to go to college. Farming, construction is making a comeback, entry-level jobs at Optimal. That kind of thing."

The door at the end of the corridor leads us to the auditorium.

"Next year, we'll mount our first musical production," she says. Her voice is swallowed by the vast space. Tiers of seats climb into darkness. "And we have forty students already signed up for a two-week music camp in August. Half of them will be playing on donated instruments. Can you imagine? For years, the marching band had to meet in the back parking lot while the cheer team got the cafeteria after school. Now they'll rehearse here." She opens her arms to the silent stage. For the first time, she seems happy. Not just happy, but joyful, alive with energy and pride. She turns to me. "And do you know what was here before?"

I shake my head.

"Nothing." There's a dark satisfaction in her eyes. "Absolutely nothing at all."

Chapter Twenty-Two

Joe is on me as soon as I walk in the door.

"I've been calling you for an hour," he says. "Where were you?"

I put down my bag, nice and slow. "Good morning to you, too." I reach for my computer but he's too fast and snaps it shut.

"You ducked out yesterday, too." He gives me a funny look. "Do you need a refresher course in *teamwork*?"

He's right; I've never had a problem sharing strategy with Joe before. But weirdly, I just feel resentful of him for asking. Optimal is mine—my mess, my mystery, my case.

It has to be. Otherwise, the magic won't work, and finding the truth won't help me forget what happened.

But Joe is watching me, and there's no reason to lie. "I took a tour of the community center," I say. "It seems more and more like Optimal's determined to buy their way into the town's good graces."

"And ours," Joe says. He pivots and goes to his desk, returning with several binders so stuffed with paper they could double as bludgeons. When he dumps them on my desk, I have to reach for my bag to keep it from skipping straight off the table.

"What is this stuff?" I ask. But as soon as I fan open one of the binders, even before I make sense of the 1099s, I know. "Optimal delivered."

"They didn't deliver," Joe says. "They dumped. Most of it is still boxed up in the basement of the courthouse."

I stare at him. "There's more?" Each binder is five inches thick, and packed with data. It will take weeks for us to make a picture of expenditures, even if the whole team did nothing else.

All the humor has vanished from his face. Joe hates mistakes—especially his own. "One hundred and seventeen binders in all. And in no order, from what we can tell."

"They buried us."

"They did what we asked them to do," Joe says, through gritted teeth. He just manages a smile. "But yes, they buried us."

"And we have no idea where to start," Flora adds.

Thanks, Flora.

Flipping through pages and pages of expenditure reports and 1099s, I feel increasingly hopeless. Of course it's our fault. I don't know what I was expecting. Big red arrows, some helpful Post-its flagging payments to the EPA, maybe a few expenses politely filed under "Bribes."

WE SPEND THE day trying to piece a thousand pages of data into some kind of story—or the beginning of one, at least. It's too hot to think—by noon, it reaches ninety-eight degrees outside—and more and more I get the feeling that the answer I want can't be found in any numbers.

At six I give up and pack the boxes of documents into the trunk of my car, swearing to myself I'll look at them later. I've promised to see my father for dinner, and although I can't think of anything I want to do less, I've run out of ways to put him off. I swing home to take a shower as cold as I can stand it, soaping hard, as if I can wash away some of the day's frustration.

I'm surprised to find the garage door open when I arrive, and my dad's car is running, although the driver's-side door is open. I can almost hear my heart slamming against my chest.

"Dad?" As I step into the shadow of the garage, fear falls on me like the pressure of a hand. I reach into the car to shut off the engine. "Dad?" I keep calling for him, even though he's clearly not here.

The house is open, and I go from room to room still shouting for him. Nothing.

The basement is dark, and there's no sign he's been down here in ages—the junk is undisturbed, and impassable.

Then I remember: the toolshed.

I sprint up the stairs again. Before I'm even out the door, I spot him—not at the toolshed, but a dozen yards away, lying motionless on the grass.

"Dad!" I rocket off the porch. Dropping to my knees, I put my hands on his chest. His eyes flutter. "Dad! Can you hear me? *Dad.*"

He opens his eyes. His face is sunburned. His lips are peeling. He must have been out here for hours.

"Abby?" He blinks once, twice, and finally his eyes find focus.

"How long have you been out here?" I'm scared to touch him, to move him—I remember that you aren't supposed to move people who have fallen. Or maybe that's people who have been in an accident. I can't think straight. A dumb animal panic is grinding my thoughts into uselessness. "What happened? Are you hurt?"

His eyes drift past me and land again. "I—I think I fell."

"You think?"

"I don't remember." He frowns. "It's the squirrels. There are squirrels in the attic again. I thought I'd patch the roof . . ."

"There's no attic, Dad," I tell him. "That was in the old house, remember?" We moved when I was five from the other side of Plantation Road because of problems with the neighbor: my dad became convinced he was spying on us, then accused him of doing hell's work, then became the one spying so that he could prove it. I haven't thought of the squirrels in years.

"I can hear them moving around."

"That was the old house, remember? Back when Mom was alive."

He closes his eyes. The skin of his eyelids is so thin it shows the movement beneath them. "I remember," he says. Barely audible.

Then, a little louder: "It's my back. That's why I couldn't get up. I must have thrown it."

I hook him beneath the shoulders but hardly manage to lift him before he seizes up in pain, crying out so loudly I nearly drop him.

"Dad, please." My voice sounds frail. Desperate. Young. Not more than a week back in this place and the old Abby is emerging from the dark shadows like a skeleton. "I'm trying to help!"

The second time I try to lift him he only seems heavier. Sweat slicks my underarms. Pain has turned his skin waxy, and when I say his name again he barely shakes his head.

I stand up and the ground swings beneath me, like it wants to buck me off. A shadow circles high overhead. An owl, maybe, or a hawk. Bad omens. My legs feel strangely wooden, like a puppet's, pulled by phantom strings.

In the kitchen I find my purse where I dropped it and rifle through it for my phone, shaking so hard I mistype the code twice before I manage it.

Condor picks up on the first ring.

I'M WITH MY father, holding his hand, trying to comfort him, when Condor arrives, quietly and without comment. Together we move at a crawl, supporting my father between us to his car.

It doesn't even occur to me to tell Condor that it's okay, that I can drive my father to the emergency clinic in Dougsville, that he can go home now, and he doesn't suggest it. In the car, I don't say a word, although my father revives enough to rant against doctors, to claim they're all quacks after our money. I'm too tired even to be embarrassed.

X-rays show what is likely a broken rib: a painful injury, but one that has to heal itself. The doctor writes a prescription for painkillers and tells my father sternly that he'll have to take it easy.

In private, he asks me when my dad last had a physical. Immediately, my skin heats up.

"Not long ago," I say, convinced that the doctor can tell that

I'm lying, that I have no idea, that I'm a terrible daughter. "A year or two, maybe."

"His blood pressure is pretty high," he says. "And he was confused by some of my questions. Has he complained to you about headaches?"

I feel like I'm back in high school in front of a quiz I haven't studied for. "No," I say.

The doctor folds his mouth into a thin line. "He gets headaches." Then: "Take him to his regular doctor for an exam. Soon."

It's nearly midnight when we return my dad to his house. As soon as I try to loop an arm around my dad's waist, he says, "I got it, I got it." Instead, he leans on Condor's arm, and I trail behind them. Condor raises his eyes to hold mine and I read the sympathy there. I have to swallow the urge to cry.

Finally, when my dad is sleeping, after I slide behind the wheel of my car again, I find that only a few hours have passed since I first pulled into the driveway.

I follow Condor back to my rental house, guided by his taillights. We go slowly, as if in a processional. Condor pulls into his driveway, but emerges immediately to cross the browning yard to my car, getting a hand around the door to open it for me even before I've cut the engine. The surge of the crickets is so loud it sounds like an ocean.

"Thank you," I say. My whole body is heavy with exhaustion. The porch light activates. I can feel his eyes searching me all over.

"All in a night's work." He keeps his voice light, but he isn't smiling. "Are you going to be okay?"

I nod. I can hardly stand to be so close to him. It makes my body ache for entirely different reasons.

"You want to come over for a drink or something?" he asks me.

I don't risk looking at him. If I do, I'll say yes.

Condor picked up on the first ring. He helped my limping father into bed. And ten years ago, he took those photographs of poor Becky Sarinelli, and passed them around to everyone as a joke.

True or false? Good or evil? I'm beginning to think Misha was onto something. Maybe the line isn't so clear after all.

"I should get some sleep," I tell him.

But as I turn away, he skims my shoulder with a hand, and just that touch freezes me in place.

"Listen." He licks his lips. I imagine following the line of his teeth with my tongue. "I don't mean to overstep—I mean, you're obviously dealing with a lot. I read things wrong . . ." He looks uncertain, and momentarily young. "*Did* I read things wrong?"

My whole body burns from standing so close to him. I can feel the rhythm of my heart beating in my ears. "You told me you made a lot of mistakes back when you were younger. Was Becky Sarinelli one of them?"

The change is immediate. It's like a gate slams down behind his eyes.

"Where did that come from? Who did you talk to?" Even his voice sounds different. For a moment, I'm afraid of him. Of his bigness. Of the darkness. Of the fact that no one is around to witness whatever happens next.

I lift my chin. "Just answer the question."

For a long time, he stands there, staring at me. The long look of his hatred hooks me right in the stomach, makes me dizzy with guilt and regret.

Finally, he laughs. But there's no humor in it. "Yeah," he says. "Yeah, you got me there. Becky Sarinelli was one of those mistakes."

I turn, stumbling on the grass, and hurry for the door. I'm not sure why, but my throat feels raw and I'm suddenly sure I'll be sick. I drop the keys on the porch, snatch them up again, and shove them in the lock.

"Why did you really call me tonight, Abby?" he shouts after me. Taunting me.

"I don't know," I tell him. I slip inside, close the door and lock it. For a long time, I'm afraid to look outside, afraid to see him there. But when I finally work up the courage to check the window, there is nothing outside but the night.

Chapter Twenty-Three

The phone yanks me awake just before dawn.

It goes silent before I can find it—still buried at the bottom of my bed, under a pile of yesterday's balled-up socks and under-wear, gum wrappers, and wrinkled receipts. It's almost dead, of course—but starts ringing again right away.

Joe. For God's sake. I almost hit ignore.

"You don't get to be a pain in the ass until after nine A.M.," I say.

"There's been a fire," Joe says. Nothing else. No details. No panic. Just: there's been a fire.

I stand up and sway slightly, lightheaded. "Where?" I say, although I already know.

"Gallagher's," he says. "Get here." He hangs up.

BY THE TIME I get to the farm the volunteer firefighters have cordoned off the blaze, spraying it down from different angles, like it's some monstrous animal they're trying to tether in place. The fields are all tinder, brittle from lack of rain, just waiting to go up.

The barn is gone. Little evidence is even left of what happened. It's just a flat portion of foundation and a tunnel of ash whirling hot to the sky. Gallagher's house got scorched, too, but not as bad. The damage is contained mostly to the paint job, although part of the east side has succumbed to the heat and crumbled away, leaving a view into his kitchen. The noise sounds like violent messy eating, like something giant snapping its jaws. The dogs are freaking, too, and for a terrible second I think of the cows and the donkey Gallagher keeps around.

Joe must know what I'm thinking, because the first thing he says is, "None of the animals were hurt." He adds, almost as an afterthought, "Gallagher's fine, too. It was the barn they were after."

That's all he has to say. Whoever did it, it was a stupid, desperate, clumsy move. Maybe the fire was meant to scare us off. Maybe it was somebody who is worried about having a job and a brand-new community center and plastic swing sets in the park.

Standing there in the smoke-choked morning, staring at the ghost silhouette of our makeshift office, now nothing more than ash and rubble, I feel almost giddy. This fire proves we're right. It proves that we're getting closer to the center of the maze. There will be answers in Optimal's records. I'm sure of that now. And those records are sitting in the trunk of my car. Perfectly intact.

By noon the fire has been extinguished completely, and we waste an hour picking through the remains. It's just something to do, a way to shove the day back into some kind of order while we wait for the men from the sheriff's office to finish poking around, like they might find a can of gasoline with an address and a signature. Joe answers some questions, all the same way (Seen anything? No. Know anything? Nope. Anybody giving you trouble? No.), until the conversation finally lands on Optimal.

Now they want to know what we're doing, what we've heard, what ridiculous stories Gallagher's been feeding us, and do we know he got busted back in the day with enough illegal fireworks to blow the whole town apart, and do we know that Optimal employs sixty percent of Barrens half- or full-time, not counting the locals who run the bars and grocery and post office, all of them busy again after the town was nearly dead, if you thought about it that way you couldn't count the people in Barrens who weren't on payroll one way or the other . . .

And *if there is something in the water it sure as hell ain't running out of Optimal.*

And *do you know what you're getting yourself into?*

In the afternoon we lump the whole team into the tiny living room at my place until we can figure out a better solution. We divide twenty binders between us and get to work. Except for the rhythmic hiss of turning paper, we work mostly in silence, and un-expectedly I feel a sense of ease that I haven't felt in I don't know how long.

It's Flora who first spots the discrepancy: not money going missing, but *too much* money accounted for. Optimal has been pay-ing Clean Solutions Management, a firm they subcontracted to deal with chemical disposal, massive sums almost quarterly.

Clean Solutions Management's website is all low-tech and full of meaningless jargon.

It always pays to follow the money.

I remember what Lilian McMann told me about the too-clean evaluations entered into the federal system on their behalf. There must have been a bribe in it somewhere. "Could Optimal be redi-recting money through a company like Clean Solutions?"

Joe squints at me. "What do you mean, redirecting?"

"I don't know. Think of what they did for Aaron Pulaski. Op-timal's parent company paid off Pulaski so he wouldn't come after them for labor violations, didn't they? Maybe one of their subcon-tractors is cutting checks, too."

"That would be a lot of effort."

"Well, maybe it's a lot of pockets."

Joe's eyes are like razors—I can feel them trying to dive straight down into my thoughts. "Like whose?"

Like Colin Danner's, I think. And maybe his buddy Michael Phillips, who cleaned up the reports he put into ICIS. Maybe the entire goddamn town.

"I don't know," I say instead. I haven't told him about what I learned from Lilian McMann except in general terms. "I'm just throwing it out there."

He doesn't seem convinced. For a long time, he stares at me. "On the off chance you've forgotten, we're working this case together," he says.

"I haven't forgotten," I say. "I don't have anything we can use." My heartbeat picks up. The room has gone silent, and the comfortable feeling I had earlier has vanished. "Look, if we knew where Kaycee Mitchell went—if we could just get her side of the story—"

But Joe doesn't let me finish. "If the Kaycee Mitchell case was legit, if she got sick, it only confirms what we *think*. We can't prove it because we can't ask her, and we can't ask her because we don't know where she is, and we can't find her because that's not why we're here. Abby, we need to focus on what Optimal is doing *now*—not what they did ten years ago."

"Don't tell me how to do my job," I snap. Joe doesn't understand that in Barrens, you can't just peel away the present from the past. It's like trying to get gum out of your hair: the more you try to separate it, the more strands get caught up.

"This isn't about Kaycee Mitchell," he tells me in a low voice. "This isn't about what happened back then." Then: "We might be able to save some people, Abby. But not her. You understand that, right?"

Despite the absurdity of storming out of my own rental, I'm out in the sunshine before I realize I have nowhere to go.

The same thing that makes Joe a good lawyer makes him a crappy friend: he's right almost all of the time.

Chapter Twenty-Four

I've got four voicemails from my dad's home line and half a dozen texts from TJ, a thirty-three-year-old war vet who lives down the road and spends all his time going house to house, checking the trees for signs of insect rot. TJ is the closest thing my dad has to a friend.

His texts are borderline incoherent, all abbreviations and shattered punctuation, but I get the message clear enough: I'm late to pick up my dad for his doctor's appointment.

TJ is still humping around in the yard when I arrive. He lifts a hand to wave, and then turns back to his inspection, sifting the leaves of one of our crabapple trees. His left arm swings useless when he moves.

There's nothing wrong with TJ's arm except, thanks to a case of PTSD, he doesn't know it's there.

"Waste of time, waste of money, these so-called doctors," my father grumbles, as he eases into the passenger seat. "All they do is take your money and fumble with a lot of doodads and in the end, what? They send you home with a prayer, a bill for five hundred dollars, and a prescription to see another doctor."

He stops my hand when I try to belt him in. "I can do it, dammit. I throw my back out and you act like I'm a cripple."

But I notice it takes him several times to work the seatbelt home. His hand is shaking.

When I was a kid we didn't go to the doctor. My dad said all we needed was God's love, and when I had my first visit—nine years old, my mom whittled by sickness—I thought the doctor's office was the cleanest, brightest place I'd ever been. By then I knew not going to the doctor was one of the things that made me a freak, so the waiting room felt like the heaven my dad always talked about, a place where nothing existed but quiet and a blinding whiteness that struck down every shadow. I got a lollipop from the receptionist, and when my mom and dad were with the doctor, I paged through magazines, rubbing perfume samples on my wrists and my shirt.

Then it was the oncology wing of a hospital in Indianapolis, although to me it was a doctor's office only bigger, even more miraculous. More magazines. More cold air faintly tinged with the smell of Winterfresh gum. More people in clean white coats, like angels with their wings folded around them.

Dr. Aster spends a long time examining my dad. I make it through every magazine in the waiting room: two months-old copies of *People*, a *Home & Garden* full of smiling housewives, copies of *Outdoor* and *Fishing*. I wonder how many people are sitting here, in this waiting room, reading about smallmouth bass just before they get news that changes them forever.

"Are you from Barrens, too?"

I look up to see the only other woman in the waiting room watching me, rocking a quiet baby in her arms.

"Chicago," I say forcefully.

"Oh. My bad. I thought I recognized you is all." If she notices that the question has annoyed me, she doesn't let it bother her for long. She shrugs.

"I went to Barrens High," I say, without elaborating or explaining that I also went to Barrens elementary and middle schools.

"I thought so! You were two years above me! My name's Shariah Dobbs," she says. Then, indicating the baby in her arms, "I would stand up, but . . ."

"That's all right. Abby." I'm suddenly ashamed of my bag sitting on the seat next to me—four hundred dollars, bought at Neiman Marcus with my first paycheck and way more than I could afford, but still—and of my boots and jeans. All of it is chosen to armor me precisely against the question she first asked. *Are you from Barrens, too?*

But seeing her moon-shaped face, her cheap skirt and knockoff sneakers, and the unselfconscious way she looks me over—both cheerful and sympathetic, as if she knows exactly what I think of her and doesn't hold it against me—makes me curdle with guilt.

I stand up and come closer to coo over her baby, so swaddled that from a distance it might be a folded T-shirt. "Boy or girl? How old?"

"Boy. His name is Grayson. Twelve months." She starts to peel the blanket back from his face and then, unexpectedly, her face clouds. "The doctors at the clinic have been so helpful. At first everyone told me he would just grow into it . . ."

I'm about to ask her what she means when she flips back the blanket and I suck in a breath. The baby is small, way too small, and his skull looks soft and malformed. His forehead is barely there at all. It's as if his eyebrows run straight into his scalp.

"No one knows if he'll be able to talk, even," she says, in a quiet voice. "Bad luck, I guess. But he's a good baby," she adds quickly. "He's my baby boy, and I don't care what anyone says. I did everything like they told me to, I quit smoking and even took those vitamins they gave me . . ." She covers his face again and looks at me sideways, as if she expects me to accuse her of something.

"You still live in Barrens?" I ask, and she nods.

"Over in Creekside." Her face flushes. Creekside is a trailer park—directly on the lip of the reservoir, within sight of the plant. "I'm still with my mom. My sister and her husband just moved back, right next door, so they help a lot." Her face clears and she smiles. "My sister's pregnant, too. So Grayson'll have a little cousin soon enough."

Before I can respond, the door opens and Dr. Aster appears

149

with one hand hooked around my father's elbow. My dad stumps forward, digging his cane into the carpet, looking more like his old self than at any time since I've been home.

"Sorry for the delay," Dr. Aster says. "It's been a while. I thought we should do the whole detail."

"Tests, tests, and more tests," my father says. "Is that all you people know how to do?" The best measure of my dad's health is how rude he is.

"Is everything okay?" I ask, turning away from Shariah.

Dr. Aster's eyes flicker.

"We'll know in a few days, when all the test results come back," he says. "Meantime, he should take it easy. Rest. Using a heating pad and ibuprofen should be fine."

My father shakes his head, rolls his eyes to the ceiling. "Five hundred dollars," he mumbles, "and a prayer."

Even as I help my father toward the door, Shariah Dobbs calls out to me, "Nice to see you, Abby. Take care of yourself."

"You too," I say. I can't bring myself to meet her eyes, though. I can't breathe through a burst of sudden fear at the thought of babies with soft skulls and brains that won't grow. *Weak spots.*

Chapter Twenty-Five

A sleek Lincoln Town Car is parked at the curb by the time I get home—I've kept it waiting. A crow is pecking in the dirt. I can't stop seeing little baby Grayson, his furry eyebrows and the scalp drawn too close.

One for sorrow.

Hannah is kneeling on the sidewalk in front of Condor's place, shading a gigantic chalk flower, which blooms next to a clutter of smiley faces, all of them pink or green. She has only two nubs of chalk left. I wave. She sits back on her heels to stare, wrapping her arms around her legs.

"Is that your car?" she asks.

"Just for the night. Pretty sweet, huh?"

Her eyes go from me, to the driver, back to me. "Are you famous?"

That makes me laugh. "Not even close."

"I'm going to be famous someday." She returns to her drawing, pushing hard on the chalk to scrape color onto the sidewalk.

"Oh yeah? For what?"

She shrugs. "Maybe dancing," she says. "Or drawing. Or maybe for discovering aliens."

"Aliens, huh?" In the house, Condor is framed perfectly in the window. It looks like he's singing along to something on the radio. He's shirtless. His hair is finger-combed; I imagine it still wet from a shower. I remember the pull of his lips, the way his hands felt holding on to my waist. "So long as you keep them away from me."

"Aliens don't hurt people, silly!" she says. She looks up at me serenely. "Only people hurt people."

That's the thing with kids: they're way smarter than you think.

PEOPLE DO AND say lots of crazy things in cabs, and private car services are no exception. Something about the division between the front seat and the back makes passengers think they're invisible. And for that reason, drivers are gold mines of information. Prestige Limo shows up again and again in Optimal's tax records. It's a shot in the dark, but if Lilian McMann is right—if Optimal is wining, dining, and bribing politicians for favors—there must be evidence somewhere, and chances are the drivers have witnessed it, whether they realize it or not.

The driver is a woman, which I wasn't expecting. I'm hoping that will make her more inclined to talk, but for the first half an hour I get nothing out of her but standard, monosyllabic answers.

You get a lot of customers back and forth to Indianapolis? *Sometimes, ma'am.* Where do you live? *Not far, ma'am.* How long have you been working the job? *Four years, ma'am.* You like it? *Yes, ma'am.* She might be a robot programmed with only a dozen replies.

I try again to land on something, anything, that will inspire her to talk. "Are you full-time with Prestige?"

On the subject of schedules, she warms up right away. "I do forty hours, sometimes more. But my schedule's mine. That's the good thing. I have a four-year-old and a six-year-old. I used to work at the Target but the day I had to leave my family on Thanksgiving to open was the day I quit."

"And you never feel unsafe, driving late at night?"

"Oh, no," she says quickly. "We don't get *that* kind of customer, not at Prestige. It's mostly repeats, especially this leg, between Optimal and Indianapolis. Can't imagine making the commute every day myself . . ."

"Big tippers, at least?"

Finally, I've landed: she snorts. "Hardly. Corporate guys. You ever noticed the fatter a wallet, the less it opens?"

"Oh, I know. I used to be a waitress," I play along. This is sort of true. I did spend a record two months working as a hostess at a hotel bar in Chicago before I got fired for going home with one of the regulars. It wouldn't have been a problem, except for the fact that I *wasn't* going home with the manager.

"Then you know. Some of these guys, they're top, you know? I'm saying Washington, real movers-and-shakers, think their shit don't stink."

My pulse leaps. "Anyone famous?" I ask, trying not to sound too eager. But I've overstepped.

"I can't say, ma'am." She catches herself. "I do my job like everybody else. I get in the car, and I drive."

I know I won't get anything else from her, so I turn to the window, watching the fields run into a geometry of roads and housing and strip malls that announces the outskirts of Indianapolis. Half the evil in the world, I think, must be someone just doing their job.

Maybe it's paranoia, but I have the driver drop me a good ten blocks from my destination and instruct her to wait. The neighborhood is nondescript, and well outside the central business district. I pass more than a handful of shuttered warehouses and storefronts boasting *Available for Lease* signs. A homeless woman roots around in a trash can.

Clean Solutions Management is wedged in the dingy second floor above an office-supply warehouse, and next to a vacant office that seems to have housed a divorce attorney at one point. It has no sign, nothing to announce its presence, other than a sticker peeling from above a buzzer that goes unanswered no matter how many times I ring.

"No one's ever there."

I turn and see a goateed guy smoking in the open door of the office supply. He looks, ironically, like he's never seen the inside of any office: you can count the patches on his skin that *aren't* tattooed.

"You know what they do up there?" I ask him.

He shrugs. His eyes sweep over my whole body, head to toe and back again, so slowly it's like he's making a point. "Imports-exports, or some shit like that," he says.

"Imports-exports," I say, as sweetly as I can. "Or some shit like that? Which is it?"

His cigarette hovers halfway to his lips. "It's like that, huh?" He smiles as if we've been sharing a joke, then takes one long pull, directing the smoke away from my face like he's doing me a favor. "Dude told me imports-exports. So I guess that's what they do."

"Dude?"

He shrugs. "Some douchebag in a suit." He smiles again. His teeth are bad. "Is he your ex or something?"

I give him a look and his smile withers. "All right, look. He gave me his number, in case of delivery. To call when he gets a package, that kind of thing."

"Does he? Ever get a package?"

"Sure," he says. "I got one in the back right now. Haven't brought it upstairs yet."

He rolls his eyes when I just stand there expectantly. "Ah, shit. You ain't a cop, are you?"

"Worse," I say. I give him my best pretty-girl smile. "I'm a lawyer."

Chapter Twenty-Six

Barrens at just after eight o'clock on a Saturday is as close to hopping as it ever gets. I straighten up as we pass the Donut Hole: a handful of picketers are gathered in the parking lot, holding signs.

WHAT'S IN OUR WATER?

OPTIMAL POISONS, INC.

We're past the protest almost before I've had time to register it, but it gives me a small lift of confidence. Optimal hasn't bought everybody, at least—not yet.

Mel's and the VFW bar spill patrons into the parking lot, keeping their doors propped open so the music flows out and the smoke flows in. A girl and her boyfriend are making out on the hood of the car. Her jean shorts hitched up where he's grabbing her. Her arms wrapped around his neck. Laughing like crazy while their friends pelt them with bottle caps.

Had things turned out differently, I might be standing at the bar next to Kaycee Mitchell, bitching about work and kids and husbands, slugging down a couple of vodka crans and sneaking a cigarette when we got drunk enough.

Wherever she is now, I wonder, does she ever miss Barrens? Does she regret any of what she left behind? Somehow, I doubt it. I'm beginning to think Kaycee Mitchell may have gotten her payday after all. Maybe she did get sick. Maybe she was paid to disappear, and her family—and even her friends—was paid to lie about it.

Leaving the VFW behind, the silence seems to flow into the car like dark water. Saturday, eight P.M., and nowhere to be, nothing to do, no one missing me, even in Chicago.

Condor's car is in the driveway, and the lights are on. For a second I debate going to knock on his door to apologize—but for what? And I can't forget the way his face hardened into anger, and the sudden leap of terror in my chest.

A jump rope is coiled on the front stoop, and for some reason it fills me with dread. As if Hannah might have been spirited away from the middle of her game.

Then Condor passes in front of the kitchen window and I turn away quickly, realizing I've been staring.

Inside, I punch on the air conditioner and listen to it grind to life in the dark.

Round trip, the ride to Indianapolis has taken three hours, not counting the fifteen or so minutes I spent chatting up the goateed guy. The bill from Prestige is close to two hundred and fifty dollars—nearly triple my weekly expense allowance.

And every single dollar worth it.

I pull out the card from Goatee and run a search for Byron Grafton.

His LinkedIn profile lists him as a consultant and his Facebook profile mentions investment management and real estate. Nowhere is he listed as associated with Clean Solutions, or Optimal, or waste.

But it's the picture that nearly punches my heart through my chest.

Byron Grafton is curly-haired, and in the handful of photos Google kicks back, dressed in the same kind of cheap, flashy suit that attracted my attention to the photograph I saw back in Brent's house. And now I remember—Brent told me he had a cousin, Byron, who had a buddy at Optimal that took him under his wing.

I land on a picture of Byron in the University of Indiana newspaper. Long out of college, he's nonetheless dressed in school colors, and tailgating outside of his alma mater with a bunch of other aging frat boys. Ten to fifteen pounds overweight, thinning hair, paunchy with money, they might all be identical twins.

Except that one of them, I recognize.

I punch in Joe's number, forgetting all about our fight this morning, and curse when it goes straight to voicemail.

"Call me back," I say. "I think I have something."

My phone rings almost immediately after I've hung up, and I pick it up without checking the number.

"Hope I'm not disturbing date night," I say.

There's a pause.

"Is this Abby Williams?" The caller has the gravelly drawl of a pack-a-day smoker.

I straighten up instinctively, I snap my laptop shut—as if someone might be looking at me through the windows. "You got her. Who's this?"

"This is Sheriff Kahn. I spoke to a Joe Pabon this morning about the fire. He listed you as the point of contact." Sheriff Kahn has been around since I was a little kid. Big-ass mustache straight from the seventies, yellow fingernails, Chiclet teeth. Kahn is the kind of person you'd expect to see wearing cowboy boots and spurs, but instead, every day that I recall, he wore a spotless pair of white high-top Nike sneakers. "I wanted to let you know we've made an arrest. Local kid. Been in trouble before. Made some threats against Gallagher last Halloween. I doubt he meant to do as much damage as he did, though. You know how kids are."

"Does this kid have a name?" I grab a pen and the first piece of paper I can get my hands on: Optimal check stubs, itemized, about two thousand of them, fanned out on my floor.

"Monty Devue," he says, and I freeze. I used to babysit for Monty back when he was a stringy goofball, all knees and elbows, who wanted to be a freight train operator or Bill Gates when he grew up. A good kid—gentle, softhearted. Slow to learn, but tenacious and curious.

"There must be a mistake," I say. Monty would never light a fire in the middle of a drought on Gallagher's property, if only because of the animals. Monty always loved animals, used to rescue snails and turtles from the road.

"There isn't," Kahn says, and hangs up.

For a long time I sit there. Monty. The fire. Lilian McMann, and her daughter in those argyle socks, and Becky Sarinelli with her skirt cinched at her waist.

I open my computer again. The results page emerges from the darkened screen.

Wallace Rush, the CFO of Optimal, with Byron Grafton at a pledge event.

Wallace Rush and Byron Grafton, as undergraduates, shirtless and painted with the same fraternity symbol.

Wallace Rush and Byron Grafton, suited up at an alumni dinner for their fraternity. With them is Colin Danner.

And finally: a formal reprimand of Wallace Rush, Byron Grafton, and Colin Danner issued by the University of Indiana for "abusing the position of power they assume as representatives of their fraternity."

Old habits, it seems, die hard.

I WON'T SLEEP, not unless I drink, and if I drink I know I'll be tempted by the closeness of Condor's house, by his bright windows lit against the darkness like some kind of sign.

Before I realize it I'm in my car and I'm heading for Frank Mitchell's storage space, as if I'm pulled there involuntarily by gravity.

Security is even shittier than last time: a secondary gate is wide-open, so I drive straight around to unit 34 without even blowing a kiss to the manager lumped over his phone in the main office. The whole place is a jigsaw of locked cells, a miniature postapocalyptic city with no people left in it.

The lock opens a little easier this time and I roll open the door, wincing at the way the sound makes crashing waves over the silence. But still no one comes, and I remind myself that I am here legally, sort of, that I've been given permission to enter legally, even if I got permission by lying. The lights blink on after a short delay, and I roll the door down behind me, once again wishing there was ventilation. The whole place carries a faintly chemical smell that tingles my nostrils and tastes sweet in the back of my throat. As I move toward Kaycee's artwork I imagine that the paintings themselves are sweating acrylic, that the wet, slick look of the paint isn't a trick of the light but because she was only recently here.

I'M ONLY A few miles from home when an SUV pulls out behind me and nearly blinds me with its high beams. The brights bounce off my windshield and gobble up the road in front of me. I put a hand out the window, signaling. But the driver doesn't take the hint.

Frustrated, I make a right on a ribbon of concrete that will loop me back to County Route 12 on the far side of the gas station.

A second later, the SUV turns, too.

My heart speeds up. I hit the gas, and the SUV accelerates to keep pace. It can't be a coincidence.

There are no lights here, nothing but fields stretching blackly on either side of us. It was stupid to make the turn. The SUV nudges closer. I can hardly see. The windshield is all glare. My tires hit a rut and the wheel jumps out of my hands before I realize I've drifted and jerk back onto the road.

I spin a left at a dirt road and have a brief moment of relief: the SUV misses the turn. But a second later, it screeches to a halt, guns backward, and spins around the turn. It's coming fast now.

Forty feet. Twenty. A scream knots in my throat.

Just as I spin the wheel and bump off the gutter and into the *thwack-thwack* of new corn, the SUV swerves around me. It's going sixty, seventy miles an hour, far too fast for me to make out who's driving. I jam hard on the brakes. Leaves churn up from my grill, smacking my windshield, and I bounce over stubbly ground.

Finally I get the car back on the road. By then the SUV is nothing but a pair of taillights swallowed into the night.

Chapter Twenty-Seven

When Becky Sarinelli died, Sheriff Kahn came down to speak to the students.

I remember we were herded into the gym and the windows beaded with the condensation of all that body heat; outside, it was a cold October. I don't know why they asked Sheriff Kahn to break the news—not like any of us hadn't heard it already, anyway.

"Certain tragedies can't be explained," he said. I remember that because it was so obviously a lie. We all knew why Becky had killed herself. It wasn't inexplicable at all. It was because of the photos. "Ms. Sarinelli was in a lot of pain. And I'm here to tell you that you got options. If you're in trouble, you can talk to your parents. You can talk to your teachers." They had him using a microphone and I remember that felt wrong. "You can come down to Blyck Road and talk to me."

Sunday morning, that's exactly where I find myself. Then, same as now, Sheriff Kahn looked like the last person in the world you'd ever want to talk to if you were in trouble. His whole mouth droops along with the line of his mustache, and the blunt furrows of his forehead read like a billboard for *shut up and bear it*. He's tanner than I remember, and blingier, too: in addition to his big class ring, a gold necklace is nested beneath his uniform, and he checks a thick gold watch just often enough for me to know he finds me an inconvenience.

"I'm telling you," he says, with a heavy sigh, after gesturing me into a seat across from his desk. "Got home just a few days ago, and I wish I could turn around and head right back on vacation."

"Where were you?" I ask.

"Sarasota. Got a condo down there. Swampy as hell right about now, but I like it when tourist season's over. Besides, all I do's sit in front of a pool anyway." His teeth are whiter than I remember, too. I can just see him in Sarasota, greased up and mahogany-colored, tanning oil quivering in his chest hair. "Now, what can I do you for?"

"I came about Monty Devue." This is at least half true.

"Oh, sure." Sheriff Kahn's expression turns even sourer. "Sorry, but I can't help you there. Turned the whole thing over to the county prosecutor."

I think of Monty when he was six or seven, bending over to scoop a caterpillar from the asphalt, holding it carefully in his palm. "Do you know if they plan to charge him?"

Kahn settles back in his chair, crossing his hands on his stomach, so his watch catches the light. "Arson's a serious business, especially in drought time."

Behind him, a bulletin board is pinned with memorabilia, ancient municipal notices, five-year-old local newspaper clippings about the police department's latest successes, and a flyer advertising the date of the Monroe County Police Department cookout. No surprise, Optimal is listed as one of the sponsors.

The air in the office is so dry it feels like trying to inhale sawdust. "He says he didn't do it," I point out.

"What do you expect him to say?"

"All your evidence is circumstantial."

"He boasted about getting revenge. The kid's a firebug, too. He's got all sorts of disciplinary problems." Kahn's losing patience. He leans forward again. "Listen, Abigail—"

"Miss Williams," I correct him, and he smiles like I've just told him the name of my doll at a tea party.

"You used to know Monty as a kid. But kids change. And even their own parents don't know the difference." He leaned forward. "Did you know Monty got in trouble last September for threatening a classmate?"

He grins when I react. "You *didn't* know? Tatum Klauss. Cheerleader, straight A-student. Nice kid."

"Threatening her how?" I say.

"Hanging around too much. Following her after school. Showing up when he wasn't invited." Sheriff Kahn is obviously enjoying himself. "One time she came home from a party and found him waiting for her."

I want to believe it isn't true. At the same time, I know Monty, and remember how he would fixate on things. I once spent forty-five minutes trying to coax a dead turtle out of his arms. He just kept clinging to it, trying to make it come back to life.

"I never said he didn't have problems," I say. "But that doesn't mean he started the fire. Look. You said it yourself. Monty's been threatening to get revenge on Gallagher since the fall. But we only recently came down to investigate Optimal. Don't you think that's a big coincidence? We could have lost a key paper trail."

If he gets what I'm implying, he doesn't seem to—which makes him either very dumb or very smart. He doesn't even blink. "So you of all people should appreciate how serious this is."

I'm tempted to tell Sheriff Kahn about the car tailing me last night, but I'm sure he's the type to chalk it up to female hormones.

I switch tactics. "You were sheriff back when I was in high school," I say, "back when Kaycee Mitchell disappeared."

This time, he's not quick enough to repress a slight ripple that moves his expression into one of distaste. "Oh sure. Biggest to-do this town's ever had. Hysteria. Teenage girls going cuckoo." He smiles thinly. "You weren't one of them, were you? One of the . . . ?" He holds out both hands, mimics a small seizure, the wild flapping of the hands.

"No. I wasn't." I'd seen what real sickness looked like. I knew that being sick didn't make you special. It just made you sick. "I just wanted to know whether you ever considered the possibility that she wasn't making it up."

"No," he says shortly. "It was all for attention. Everyone knows that. The other girls copped to it afterward."

"You mentioned hysteria. That spreads by copying, emulation. It doesn't mean there wasn't some truth in it."

He smiles again. "That's just like a lawyer," he says. "Always trying to make the plain facts more complicated. Kaycee lied and got embarrassed when it all blew up."

Every single person who talks about Kaycee mentions that she was a liar. But if she really was sick, she was the only one who wasn't lying. At least, not about that.

"Running away because she didn't want to admit she'd been faking it seems pretty extreme. Especially if she was as good a liar as everyone says."

He waves away the distinction. "That's old business, anyway. Can't see why it matters to you."

A memory surfaces: sophomore or junior year, I was passing Misha and Kaycee in the hall when Misha began to bark. That was her newest cruelty—I was ugly as a dog, she said, and she had started growling whenever I passed.

But that day Kaycee was with her. She turned to Misha and slapped her hard, once, in the face, so quickly and unexpectedly I almost missed it. And for a moment all three of us froze, stunned— Kaycee, lit up with fury and something else, something I couldn't name. Misha, shocked, her face slowly flushing with color.

I hate dogs, was all Kaycee said.

"Do you know where she is now?" I ask him.

"No idea." He's watching me closely. "She rang me up maybe a few weeks after she left. Told me she was in Chicago then. But that was ten years ago."

"She called you? Here?" This surprises me. "Why?"

He shrugs again. "Must've heard I was looking for her. Her friend Misha talked to her a few times."

I wonder if there's a possibility that even now, Misha is covering for Kaycee—and knows exactly where she is. "What did she say?"

"That was ten years ago, Ms. Williams." His voice turns flinty. "Things dead and buried are best left that way." He peels his lips back from his long teeth into a smile. "They don't look none too pretty when they come up."

Chapter Twenty-Eight

Even before Optimal came to town, there was one place we never cut corners: for more than thirty years, the Barrens Tigers have always played in a two-thousand-seater stadium donated by the great-great-grandson of the town's original founder. Barrens loves its football. And the team was always really good, too, competing against bigger schools in the state and putting Barrens on the map. More energy went into football and the team than anything else. From a distance, it looks like a gigantic spaceship landed in the middle of a plowed field. It dwarfs the high school next to it, and when I was in school it sometimes doubled up as an auditorium for assemblies.

The whole of Barrens has turned out for the end-of-year PowerHouse game, a tradition that mixes JV and varsity and pits the teams against each other, and includes all the swagger, name-calling, and end zone dancing typically barred at real games. The teams paint their faces and wear costumes over their padding. One person, typically the quarterback, wears a dingy set of fairy wings passed down from class to class.

When I was in high school, I would have killed to walk into the PowerHouse with Brent O'Connell. Now I feel almost embarrassed—as if I'm squeezing into clothes that don't quite fit anymore.

My hands are raw, sore from scrubbing them too hard before I left home.

Ever since I came home to Barrens, I can't shake the sensation of dirt embedded beneath my fingernails. Handling Optimal's documents just makes it worse. It's like they're covered with a chemical film that leaves me raw and itching.

When Brent reaches for my hand, I pretend not to notice and stuff my fists deep into my pockets.

Five hundred people, all funneled into the stadium seating, drum their feet along to the rhythm of the marching band—but the crazy thing is I spot Misha right away, or she spots us, one or the other. At the exact same second my eyes pick her out of the crowd, she lifts a hand to wave—a quick spasm that could be either an invitation or a desire to ward us off. Only when I see Annie Baum sitting next to her do I realize she's sitting exactly where she always sat, four bleachers up, right next to the aisle. There's even a little gap, a break in the arrangement of people, right next to her—as if an invisible Kaycee is still occupying her spot. A stranger has taken Cora Allen's place.

For a second, we lock eyes. She gives me a funny little smile.

I'm afraid Brent will want to go and sit with them—Misha converts her wave into a frantic, two-handed *come here* gesture—but he only lifts a hand and, placing one hand on my lower back, steers me toward an entirely different section of bleachers. I feel a rush of relief.

The game kicks off: a blur of green and white bodied players collide on the field. I find Monty and lose him again in a scrum of players. I know little about football except what I've absorbed from years of living in Indiana and from watching *Friday Night Lights*, and he seems like a more than decent player, although after he fumbles a pass from the quarterback his coach benches him for a quarter. High school cheerleaders shimmy with their pom-poms, and every time they leap or backflip, they seem to remain suspended momentarily in the air, hung like Christmas ornaments on a dark backdrop of sky. I always think about what will happen if they twist a few inches in the wrong direction; I see them landing on their necks, breaking like porcelain dolls.

"We weren't that small when we were in high school, were we?" Brent leans in to speak to me over the roar of the crowd and the stamping. "Do you think they're shrinking? I definitely think they're shrinking."

That makes me laugh. I never knew that Brent was funny, but he is. He tells me that when he played football, he invented a technique so he wouldn't be nervous: he'd pick a random guardian angel from the crowd, a stranger, the weirder the better, and name him or her. If he ever got nervous he'd just find the Angel of Lost '90s Hats or the Patron Saint of Handlebar Mustaches and say a quick prayer.

"Did it work?" I ask him.

He winks. "We were undefeated our senior year."

Weirdly, I find that I'm almost enjoying myself. With Brent. At a football game. In Barrens.

I have to remind myself again and again that I'm here for information. And yet the first quarter slips by, then the second, and then the third, and though we've talked almost continuously, the closest we've come to discussing the investigation is to debate the best junk food for powering through a long work night. Brent swears by Skittles. I'm a peanut M&M's girl. Protein and caffeine—can't beat it.

It's not until the fourth quarter, when the conversation turns to our families, that I see an opening. And by then, I'm almost sorry to take it.

"You told me you have a cousin at Optimal, too, right?" I ask, as casually as I can. "Byron Grafton?"

"You *are* good." Brent looks at me with either admiration or exasperation or a little bit of both. "Byron's not at Optimal, though. He's a subcontractor. But I bet you know that. Byron's the one who got me in with the CFO, Wally Rush. They went to college together."

Of course, I know this, too. "Byron's a good guy deep down. He had some problems back when he was drinking. Married, divorced, married again, had a kid, made some bad business decisions. Pie-in-the-sky kind of things, too much ambition and too little sense. Wally helped push him in a new direction."

And promised him a fluffed-up contract for waste disposal services that, as far as I can tell, never took place: a cozy arrangement. "So Optimal is a real family kind of operation, huh?"

Brent doesn't answer right away and I can feel his gears shifting. Then he leans in to me, voice hushed. "I'm beginning to think you're right about Optimal. Not about the waste. But there's something funny going on in accounting. Now, this has to be confidential . . ."

"Of course," I say.

"Optimal has been thinking of going public. It might be important. I'm trusting you."

"Thank you," I say, and mean it.

If Optimal is going public, why risk violating compliance laws, why risk investigation and censure? There must be something bigger at stake. More and more, I'm convinced that Optimal's been using its power and connections to bully, silence, and sway—and to keep everyone who might investigate them looking the other way.

The thunderous noise of cheering and stamping shakes the stadium and sends a vibration all the way to my chest: it's the end of another school year, the start of a long, brown summer. Brent turns and kisses me without warning. Today his lips are warm, and his chest is warm, and he smells like soap and grass shavings: a clean, hopeful smell. I try to find my way down into some good feeling, but the crowd is too loud.

AFTER THE GAME I lose ten minutes with Brent making an excuse for why I can't go out for a drink. He kisses me again, but this time he lands it right on the corner of my mouth, as if he wants me to think it might have been an accident. By then, the players have disappeared and there's a chokehold of cars funneling out of the lot.

I backtrack to the gym, hanging back near a picnic table scored with decades' worth of carved-in graffiti. The kids are in no hurry to get home: dozens of them circulate in packs, like wild animals, visible only by the flash and wink of their phone screens in the dark. A group of girls hunker down in the grass not far from where I'm sitting, and a group of guys doesn't leave them alone too long before arriving to spark up a joint and start passing around a water bottle that must be full of something else. Eventually, the stream of traffic onto County Route 12 slows to a dribble and the parking lot clears out. But the kids remain, disrupting the quiet with a Morse code of teenage shouting and laughter.

The football players, now showered and changed and carrying duffel bags, emerge from the locker room in pairs. But Monty comes out alone. I have to shout his name three or four times before he looks up, already scowling, as if he's still on the field and expecting to take a blow.

But then his face clears and splits into the exact same smile I remember from when he was a kid.

"Hey, Abby," he says, shyly, which is just how he used to greet me as a kid. As if all these years, he's just been waiting for me to show up.

I feel awkward hugging him, this half-grown giant, and remember anyway he didn't like it, so instead I just nudge him with my elbow.

"You've been doing some growing," I say.

He shrugs, but he looks pleased. "Football. What are you doing here?" he says.

"I came to watch you play," I say, and when a smile steals over his face I really wish it were true. "Good game."

"You shoulda been here for the real season," he says. Then his face darkens. "I haven't been playing as much. Not since . . ." He sucks back whatever he was going to say.

"You got in trouble, right? With Walter Gallagher?"

"You heard about that?" He looks at me sideways, and then, reading my face, says, "You talked to my mom?"

"I called her, yeah," I say. Monty shuffles his feet. "What happened?"

For a long minute, he just stares down at the space between his ragged sneakers, suddenly morphing back into a kid. "Last Halloween me and some friends snuck onto Gallagher's." He looks up at me through his eyelashes—dark, long for a boy's. "My friend Hayes wanted to steal one of Gallagher's four-wheelers. We weren't really gonna take one," Monty hurries to explain. "It was just talk. We were just pretending we were going to. You know what I mean?" When I nod, he seems to relax. "Anyway, it was kind of a tradition to mess with Gallagher on Halloween, we weren't even the first ones to do it."

"And you got caught," I say.

Monty nods miserably. "He let the dogs on us. Hayes almost got his leg taken off. But we were just messing around."

"And you were pissed," I say. He nods. "You said some stuff about Gallagher, threatened to get even."

He nods again, so droopy with obvious misery he looks like a cartoon bloodhound. "I wasn't serious, though," he says.

"Did you start that fire at Gallagher's?" I ask him, as gently as I can.

"No," he says immediately. "*Hell* no." And I believe him. "Sheriff Kahn's just got it in for me," Monty says, on a roll now, huffing with anger. "He's never liked me, ever since sixth grade he caught me spray painting this old wall behind the plant. No one even goes *back* there."

I take a deep breath. "Look, Monty, I have to ask you something. I need you to be honest, okay?" He nods. Despite the fact that he's six foot three, minimum, and broad as a plank, his face is sweet as a baby's. "What happened between you and Tatum Klauss?"

"Nothing happened," he says. He barely gets the words out. "How'd you hear about Tatum?"

I don't answer, and I don't let the thread drop, either. One of my law professors once told me you could defend any liar on the planet, so long as he didn't lie to you. "Did you threaten to hurt her?"

"I would never hurt Tatum," he says quickly, and he winces, as though the idea is painful.

"Sheriff Kahn says Tatum complained about you," I say. Poor Monty. "According to Tatum, you wouldn't leave her alone."

"Yeah, well, I was just trying to get her to listen." A hoot of laughter from the group of high schoolers seems to startle him.

I know that kind of laughter: like the hooting of an owl sighting a mouse. Sharp. Predatory.

"Listen to what?"

He looks away. A muscle tightening in and out across his jaw. "It was nothing. Some stupid game with her friends. But they aren't her friends. They don't give a shit about her."

The Game. A bad feeling scratches my neck. Probably coincidence. But still. "What kind of game?"

But Monty feels the currents changing. Despite his size, despite his football jersey, in Barrens, Monty isn't a hawk, but a mouse: and like all prey everywhere, he knows when there's danger in the air. The black mass of high schoolers is restless, shifting, swelling with sudden sound. "Look," he says, and I can tell he's impatient now. "It was just some stupid-ass game with some older dudes, piece-of-shit nobody suckfaces. But Sheriff Kahn didn't ask *them*, did he? Just because they got flashy cars and tighty-whities." He shakes his head. "I was just trying to help her. I was just trying to—"

He breaks off suddenly, as the mass of kids lobs a single word in our direction, again and again. *Freak. Freak. Freak.*

"Tatum's friends," he says, in a strangled voice. Then: "I gotta go."

He takes off to the parking lot at a half jog, sticking as close to the gym as possible, head down, as if he might slide by, invisible. Not that easy. Never that easy: a water bottle misses his head by inches, then an empty beer can, clattering off the side of the gym just as he disappears around the corner.

Chapter Twenty-Nine

"You should be careful, miss."

I'm not sure who says it. Turning, for a second I'm not even sure the comment was meant for me, but then a shadow comes toward me. A girl. With the calm air of all beautiful girls, as if the world is pouring toward them and they only have to stand there and wait. She repeats: "You should be careful."

"What are you talking about?" I say.

There's a pause. She picks her way across the grass, wobbling a little; she's drunk, or maybe just having trouble finding her footing in the dark.

She stops a good twenty feet from me, edging into the light.

I recognize the waterfall of blond hair. Wide-spaced blue eyes. A face uncannily like Kaycee's.

"I said you should be careful," she repeats. "He might kill you. He might burn you to death." When I say nothing, she adds: "He carries bombs in his backpack. He acts normal but his head is all screwed up."

"Who?" I ask automatically.

"Don't say I didn't warn you," is all she says, and turns away.

"Sophie." She freezes when I call her name. "Sophie Nantes, right?"

She doesn't turn back to me, but I can see her stiffen.

I swallow hard. "Congratulations on the Optimal Stars Scholarship."

She does turn around then, just for a moment. Just enough that I can see the way the words have taken her whole face and funneled it down into a hard look of hatred.

BACK IN MY day, the Game was an open secret, a tradition everybody knew about, even the teachers. But sometime around my senior year the Game took on a new dimension: instead of just the prettiest girls, the hottest girls, the senior boys started targeting the weirdos, the loners, and the unpopular girls, too.

But by then it wasn't just about the pictures anymore. The big scheme was in the shakedown that came after: money, blowjobs, and behind-the-stadium handjobs demanded as payment to keep the photos from getting back to parents, sisters, teachers.

That's what happened to Becky Sarinelli. And if Condor took the photos, he must have been the one to release them, too.

Which means: Becky was one of the few girls who didn't pay up.

It doesn't totally surprise me to find out the Game is still going on. Things like that have a way of carrying down, generation to generation, twisting the way viruses do, becoming more powerful and bleeding across borders to high schools around the world.

But Monty mentioned money and flashy cars, and I can't see that he would have talked that way about any of the local boys. Even the richest kids in Barrens are still lucky to inherit their father's old Ford when they turn sixteen.

So what kind of men is the Game attracting now?

It shouldn't matter. Joe's right. I should focus on what Optimal is doing now. Monty and his girl problems don't come within a hundred yards of my business.

Except I can't shake the feeling that they do.

Every time I close my eyes, I walk back through Kaycee's paintings and stop behind the largest one of all: a girl barely etched in pale color, a screaming mouth and eyes rolling wide like a panicked horse, and around her, a group of men, tall and narrow as tombstones. White teeth, clean angles. Flash.

Chapter Thirty

Monday morning, Flora comes to hail me at our brand-new office behind Sunny Jay's, where Condor works. Now not only is Condor across from me at home but he is next to me at work as well. Flora waves her arms overhead like an aircraft marshal trying to get me to wheel-in right.

"Environmental Testing Labs sent results of their tests," she says, before I've even cleared the door. "We've been calling."

"Already?" I ask. Normally getting results from ETL is like waiting for aliens to come to Earth with gifts.

"Lead," she bursts out, before I can ask. "Lead five times the legal limits."

"Is it true?" I turn to Joe.

He responds by wordlessly passing over the report: preliminary investigation of the chemical and hard metal composition of the Barrens, Indiana, public water supply. The document is short and straightforward: the reservoir is filthy, contaminated not just by lead but by trace amounts of mercury and industrial pollutants with unpronounceable names. Of course, the report makes no claims about the source of the pollution—it will be our job to link it to Optimal—but this gives us more than enough to take a formal complaint to the judge.

So why don't I feel like celebrating?

This evidence is enough to justify closing up shop and heading back to Chicago. We could easily do the rest of our work there, from our own homes and our own beds. I could get the hell out of here. And yet . . .

All I can think about is Kaycee. Coughing up blood. The dizzy spells, the passing out.

"Who'd you have to rub-and-tug to get these back so quickly?" I ask. There is the abstract truth: documents and numbers and theories. And then there is the *real* truth: Gallagher's ruined crops, the wreckage of his life savings; little Grayson, with a soft head and a malformed brain; Carolina Dawes and her son's itchy rashes.

"Actually, I can't take the credit on this one," Joe says. "Your prosecutor friend Agerwal leaned on them himself. It turns out he was serious about taking corruption out of Monroe County."

"An honest politician. Who knew?" Everyone's watching me, waiting for me to look happy. I keep rifling through the stack of pages, turning the words and charts back and forth. "What are the symptoms of lead poisoning again?"

"Skin irritations, for one. Rashes, like people have complained about." Joe ticks the symptoms off on his fingers. "Long-term exposure can lead to birth defects, major cognitive disorders."

"And Gallagher's complaints about his yield are in line with the agricultural effects," Flora puts in. "It all fits."

"It fits with what people are reporting *now*," Portland speaks up. Thank God I'm not the one who has to say it. "But it doesn't fit with what happened to Kaycee Mitchell."

Joe frowns. "Not you, too," he says to Portland. Then: "You guys, this is a slam dunk. CEAW's going to funnel some more funds into another round of testing. In the meantime, we can get out of here. If I never see a cornfield, or a shotgun, again, it'll be too soon."

"Snob." I try to make it sound like a joke, but I can't even force a smile. My mouth is dry. Tongue like a sock. I should be thrilled, but there's too much miring me here in Barrens: the freaking barn fire, and Monty, I believe, wrongfully accused. My dad falling apart before my eyes. Brent kissing me all the time like I'm his girlfriend or something. Misha. Condor and his daughter and her hula-hoop.

Shariah and her baby's tiny head. Lilian McMann's daughter, in nothing but her socks.

The bribes.

The Game.

"What about a corruption case?" I blurt out.

Joe shoots me a puzzled look. "Why do you think Agerwal took an interest? He's all over it already. I spoke to him this morning, and gave him your notes—on Pulaski and the connection between Optimal and Clean Solutions. Clean Solutions looks like a money dump, just like you said. Any luck, we'll be home in Chicago right in time for dollar oysters at Smith and Wollensky."

I can hear how truly excited Joe is about getting home—back to his life in Chicago, where a gay black man blends right in. Where he's easily juggling a rotation of seven boyfriends and can be seen with any one of them in public. Back to the perfection of his city apartment, filled with fabulous eccentricities, a state-of-the-art sound system, matching wineglasses, and an odd "water feature" that's essentially just a fountain.

It's another reminder of how different he and I really are. The prospect of returning to my condo—brand-new, impeccably clean, modern, and practically empty—fills me with dread.

I know now that there's a hole inside me. A hole that can't be patched or filled with files or paperwork or legal cases or new clothes or miles or happy hours or bartenders.

This was never about the water. It's not even about Kaycee, not really.

It's about me.

"This is exactly what we came to do, Abby," Joe adds, softer now.

But that's where he's wrong.

. . .

WHEN I WAS a kid, the reservoir was the biggest body of water I'd seen, and it was the center of the whole world. The south side was always the good side, the area with people whose parents had jobs as electricians and telemarketers and, later, at Optimal. On the west side is a wild nest of woods. The east side is where the skeleton of Optimal gradually rose up, like a shipwreck in reverse.

And to the north, there's an old dump of ramshackle homes, a lot of them empty, the trees growing thick between them. It's only a mile walk through the woods from my dad's house. A mile of woods that I played in as a kid—I would sit with my back against a rock, surrounded by trees, imagining I could live there forever like a fairy when I knew my mother was dying. Where I played hide and seek with Kaycee, and where we buried Chestnut.

I take the dirt roads instead of the woods, roads baked in heat. Flies buzz over something dead and, through the trees, the reservoir shimmers.

When I climb out of the car, I feel a little like I'm on the wrong side of a microscope. Here, too, the residents run their sewage straight into the trees down the hill. It can cost four grand for a new water hookup, and no one around here has that kind of money. They must be filling their taps and showers with water from the reservoir, like all the poorest families do. No wonder Shariah's kid was born disfigured.

Shariah Dobbs lives at #12 Tillsdale Road, which is hard to find because these roads are more like pathways and none of them have signs. She isn't home, so I scrawl a note on a scrap of paper I unearth from my bag and tuck it into her mailbox along with my business card.

Returning to my car, my eyes land on the one-story house across a yard littered with car parts. A mailbox leaning off the front door is labeled *Allen*. It's a common enough name, I know, but I hesitate, rolling my keys in my palm.

Cora Allen was one of Kaycee's and Misha's best friends. Misha told me that she wasn't doing so well, that they weren't in contact anymore. It's amazing how poorly the golden girls of Barrens High have fared.

Is it a coincidence? Or did something happen to explain how fast and how far they fell?

I have to know.

Dropping my keys in my bag, I cross the weedy lawn.

The house shows all its age and neglect: peeling paint, even a cracked window kept from shattering by two-by-fours. I might think it was abandoned if it weren't for the truck pulled up beneath a plastic carport.

Before I can even make it to the door, it opens, and there she is. Cora Allen. Or rather, some rotted version of her, scabby and grayscale. Only her eyes are the same: big and brown and thoughtful.

"Abby Williams," she says, before I can even lift a hand. "I heard you were back." She scratches at her stomach beneath her T-shirt. "Been expecting you to find me."

"Hi, Cora."

She turns around and disappears inside again, and for a second I stand there, confused about whether she means for me to follow. But then she leans out the door to gesture me after her. "Well, come on in. Let's get this over with."

I follow her inside, which is hazy with old cigarette smoke. The kitchen counter is cluttered with empty beer bottles and before she sits, she grabs a new one from the fridge. This isn't fun day drinking. This is something much darker. I have a quick look at the inside of her refrigerator: water, beer, orange juice, and a shriveled round of cheddar.

We take a seat in the main room, and she switches off the TV. She pops the beer against the coffee table edge, which is scored from hundreds of previous beers. She won't stop scratching, either. Misha wasn't lying. She's a drug addict. It's painfully obvious.

"So? What is it you want to know?"

I'm more and more puzzled by the minute. "It seems like you're the one with something to tell me?"

"You've been asking around about Kaycee Mitchell, huh?" She takes a swig of her beer. "What did all the others tell you?"

"Nothing. And all the same exact thing. That they haven't heard from her in years. That she was a liar. That they were glad to see her go." Cora flinches, just for a second. "How about you?"

For a second, Cora says nothing. We stare at each other until I have to look away.

"No. She scared me sometimes. But no." She takes a long sip of her beer. "We let her down, all of us. She was sick, you know," she goes on. Then, in response to my look of surprise, "Sick in the head. Her dad used to be too fond of her, if you know what I mean."

Suddenly my stomach drops. I remember Kaycee in fourth grade, proudly showing off tubes of mascara and lipstick, tucked at the bottom of her backpack. *My daddy gave them to me*, she told me. *He says I'm a big girl now so why not?*

I think of Kaycee, heating up a silver Zippo lighter, shocking my skin with the burn of steel. *You know it's love because it starts to hurt.* I was too young to understand.

The air is stifling—the smell of stale beer coats everything. I feel as if I can hardly draw a breath.

"She tried to tell us, too. What do you do about something like that? Misha accused her of wanting attention. Misha was always accusing everybody of wanting attention."

I clear my throat. "That's called projection," I say, and she laughs, throaty and surprisingly rich.

"I'd say." Suddenly she leans forward, putting her elbows on her knees, her eyes fighting their way to sharp focus. "I think that when she got sick, it was because of that. You ever heard about that? How the mind can make you feel bad even when you're not?"

"Sure," I say carefully. "But I thought she was only pretending?"

She leans back. All at once, she seems totally exhausted. "No," she says quietly. "It wasn't pretend. She was sick all right. We all were. It was no one's fault but our own." She directs the words toward her beer, as if it's proof of this.

Misha always said that what happened senior year was a prank that quickly spiraled out of control: as more and more girls began to get sick, no one knew what was real and what was pretend anymore. Cora's idea is that the sickness was a kind of punishment.

But for what?

She avoids my eyes and watches her beer drain toward empty with every sip, as if trying to figure out what's happening to it. No point in holding back now. "Was it because of the Game?"

Bingo. She jerks her head up to stare at me. "That was some sick shit. I remember when they found Becky Sarinelli hanging. I thought I was going to puke."

"Me too."

"It was Kaycee's idea, you know." She stabs a smoke ring with her pointer finger to dissipate it. "Not the Game itself. The senior boys had been competing for nudies for years. But the money part."

The cigarette smoke is making me nauseous.

"That was typical Kaycee," she says. "Always running some scheme." And I know she's right. Kaycee was always scheming for money, even when we were little. Her family was worse off than mine, or even Cora's. "She used to steal stuff whenever she could. We all did—beer and rolling papers and gum and shit like that. But with her it was like she couldn't help it." She shook her head. "So then Kaycee had this idea, right, that we could ransom back the pictures they took. Make the girls pay, or else. I didn't want to. But you know how Kaycee was . . ." She trails off, shrugging.

She doesn't need to finish, anyway. I know what she would have said: It was impossible to say no to Kaycee. She could talk you into anything.

Dogs like that should be put down.

"What did she do with the photos after people paid up?" I ask. "Did she actually return them?"

Cora frowns. "What do you think?" She leans forward to stub out a cigarette. "She kept them."

Chapter Thirty-One

On the way to Monty's house that afternoon, I get two calls from the same Indiana area code—Shariah, I assume, has found my note. Joe's face pops up cartoonish in my head, saying *focus*, saying this is about what's happening *now*, but I send the calls to voicemail instead.

The water results have bought us all the time in the world. We have nothing but time now: years of litigation, of grunt work, of remediation and blame-casting and bureaucratic red tape.

But I let Kaycee disappear once before. I can't let her disappear again—not when I'm closer than ever to finding the truth.

Cora's words play again and again in my head.

Her daddy used to be too fond of her, if you know what I mean.

Always running some scheme.

She's right about some of it. Even as a kid, Kaycee stole things— little things, trinkets from other people's houses, stuff from the cubbies at school. She was never sorry about it afterward. I remember when Morgan Crawley cried until her nose bubbled with snot over a pair of mittens her grandmother had knitted her—mittens Kaycee had showed me, gloating, at the bottom of her bag the day before.

"Then she shouldn't have been so careless with them," she said, when I confronted her about it. "If you love something, you have to take care of it and keep it safe." She was so angry at me that she took the mittens and threw them in a storm drain, and I'll never forget how she looked then, standing in the street while a rush of rainwater roared the mittens down into the sewer. "Look. Now they're not stolen anymore. Now no one has them." As if it had been my fault all along.

Nothing was ever her fault. She was immune to guilt, and her memory worked like one of those old gold sifting pans, shaking away all the dirt, all the bad stuff, leaving intact only the things she really wanted to remember, the things that made her look good.

That's why the thing with Chestnut's collar has always puzzled me, too. What made her keep the collar and then, so many years later, give it back? Why was that so important to her? It was as if Chestnut's death wasn't proof of something terrible she'd done, but proof of something terrible done to *her*.

But what? It didn't make any sense.

Your problem, Abby, isn't that you can't draw. It's that you can't see.

I FOLLOW THE school bus right to Monty's doorstep, expecting to see him pour out through the open door, all six feet of him. But only a girl disembarks, bent nearly double beneath the weight of an enormous backpack, and trudges across a browning yard to a neighboring house.

Maybe Monty caught a ride home with his mom: she works in the cafeteria at the high school and part-time in one of the toll-booths on Interstate 70, which runs between Columbus and St. Louis. She told me once she liked to wear her hairnet there, too, tried to dress herself down and look as plain as possible, so the late-night drivers coming through would be less tempted to stroke her palm when she was giving change or whisper dirty things to her.

Monty lives in a funny patchwork house that looks like two ranch homes got into a collision and never got unstuck. An American flag hangs over the door.

The house is dark inside. But his mom, May, comes to the door as soon as I knock, still wearing her hairnet.

"Abigail," she says, and gives me a huge hug. She smells like cinnamon airspray. I've always thought May was like a favorite quilt, colorful and comforting, soft to touch. The kind of mother who makes you feel, right away, like you're at home. My mother was exactly like that.

"It's good to see your face." She holds my cheeks briefly between her hands. "I came around the other day to visit your daddy but he said you had your own place . . . ?"

I nod. "Yeah, I rented a place behind the hair salon," I say. Feeling suddenly judged, I add, "I just didn't want to put my dad out. And I've gotten used to my privacy now, living in Chicago."

"Seems lonely to me," she replies, and I'm not sure whether she means it as a criticism. But a second later, she smiles.

"Come in, come in." She steers me into a cramped seating area wobbly with teetering sports trophies and framed family photographs: she must have tripled her collection since I was last here years and years ago. "Sit down. Make yourself at home. Can I get you anything? Water? Soda? I got some of my special tea!"

"Sure, tea is great," I say, as she bumps off into the kitchen. I sit down next to a shrine to Monty's incremental growth from grinning, gap-toothed child to enormous muscle man.

She returns a moment later with a tall glass of tea clinking with ice. "Monty told me he saw you last night at the game." She puts a coaster on the table and takes a seat across from me, sighing as she eases off her feet. "You know half the kids showed up today still smelling like beer. Alcohol-free zone, my you-know-what. Last week of school, too. Some of them don't even bother bringing books to class anymore."

"You didn't go?"

She shakes her head. "Football and more football. Seems like that's the only thing anyone can agree on."

"Is he at home?" I ask. But before she can respond, I get my answer: from deeper in the house, the crash of something heavy to the ground.

"Gimme a second," she says, stiffly, and pushes up from the sofa. She disappears and I hear a muffled dialogue, the rapid back-and-forth of teenage stubbornness. She returns looking not angry, just exhausted.

"Hun, he's not up for talking," she says in a low tone. "I had to take him out of school early today. He turned over his desk, got into a shouting match with the principal." For a second, she looks like she might lose it. "I'm just at my wit's end with him. But what do they expect, dropping that kind of news at assembly?"

"What news?" I ask, and she stares at me.

"Lord, I thought that's why you came by." She scooches forward on the couch and lowers her voice, casting a nervous glance in the direction of Monty's room, as if he might overhear. "Terrible, terrible thing. She'll pull through okay, though. Still, a girl so young . . . a good student, too . . ."

"What girl? What happened?"

"Tatum Klauss," she says, and my heart stops. The girl who accused Monty of stalking her, according to Sheriff Kahn. "Monty's had a thing for her for ages—since they were freshmen and they used to ride the same bus, before her parents divorced. Sweet as anything, and always so polite when she sees me in the line. Not like most kids. Look at you like you're trash. A bright student, too."

Talking to May has always been like trying to separate strands of spaghetti left to cool in a colander. Every idea leads to ten others. "What happened to Tatum?"

"Got ahold of a bunch of her brother's attention medicine and took them all at once—last night, when everyone was at the game." May makes the sign of the cross. "Thank God her momma wasn't feeling well and came home early. Found her puking her guts out and barely conscious. She rushed her right to the emergency clinic in Dougsville." The same clinic where I rushed my father, after his fall. "They say she'll be just fine. Can you imagine? And she's a straight-A student, too. Got one of them Optimal Scholarships. Supposed to be heading out to college in the fall . . ." May says "college" the way someone might say "heaven." In some ways, it isn't surprising. Around these parts, both are just as hard to get into.

I take a long swallow of tea, hoping it will wash down the sudden bitter taste in my mouth. "Do they know why?"

May shakes her head. "Sheriff Kahn was there for assembly, and that's all he said."

An image blinks in my mind, hundreds of hands passing photographs through the risers. And Becky Sarinelli, hurtling herself down from the bleachers, trying to escape—but not quickly enough.

Not nearly quickly enough.

Some things are inexplicable, Sheriff Kahn said that day. It seems there are a lot of things he hasn't been able to explain.

May adds, with sudden ferocity: "Well, he ain't gonna pin the pills on Monty, is he? Doesn't mean he won't try. I swear, if the sun turned green tomorrow he'd say it was Monty's fault."

"Has Sheriff Kahn told you whether Gallagher is going to press charges?"

"It isn't Gallagher," she says. "Even that old kook has more sense than that. Sheriff Kahn keeps saying they need to make him an example!"

"I'll talk to Sheriff Kahn again." I say the words automatically, though I know the promise in them is empty. If Gallagher isn't pressing charges, there's no reason to go after Monty. Unless Kahn's trying to cover for someone else.

"He won't eat," May is saying. "The school's saying they might keep him from walking at graduation. *If* he graduates." May's eyes well up and she swipes at them with the back of her hand. "Look at me, crying over spilled milk. I keep thinking of Tatum's mother . . ."

"Will you tell Monty I came by?" Suddenly I just need to get out of here. A hundred Montys grin at me from a hundred different pasts: a hundred idiot smiles, blissfully unaware of what comes next. "Have him call me, if he feels like it. Here."

She lifts my card by its edges, as if she's afraid to smudge it. When she glances up, I see a look of uncertainty travel all the way from forehead to chin. "Why did you come by, then, if not about what happened to Tatum?"

"No reason." I stand up, alarmed by a cloud of black that temporarily darkens my vision. I steady myself against the wall. "To say hi, that's all."

She nods. But I can tell she isn't convinced.

I'm already in the car when she pokes her head out again to shout, "You say hi to your daddy for me, okay?"

It looks like she says something else, too, but the engine swallows whatever it is.

Girls, games, poisons—the past is repeating itself, rippling outward like the surface of the reservoir.

I'VE MISSED ANOTHER call—not a local number, this time. I pull over onto one of the nameless dirt roads, so narrow that the fields slap my side mirrors. I cut the engine and listen to a faint wind sift the leaves. From here the road does nothing but disappear into cornstalks, and I imagine if I keep driving, I'll disappear too, just blink out of the world. Like Kaycee did.

The first voicemail is from Shariah, sounding uncertain. In the background, a baby cries.

Hello, Ms. Williams. I got your note. I . . . well, I'm calling you back, like you told me to. You can give me a call anytime at this number. Or if I don't pick up, I'm probably putting Grayson down. Okay. Bye.

The next message is a man I don't recognize: he explains he's calling for Abby Williams in a creepy-calm voice.

This is Dr. Chun, calling from Lincoln Memorial in Indianapolis.

Unconsciously, I straighten up a bit, check my rearview mirror, as if something might be coming from behind.

Dr. Aster sent me the results of a recent MRI for your father, and indicated you were the point of contact. Please call me back at your earliest convenience.

It's funny how quickly the whole world shrivels up to the inside of a car, to the space between ringtones. I watch birds streak across a washed-blue sky. Six of them. Then a seventh one, late.

I squeeze my phone until it turns warm beneath my fingers.

One for sorrow, two for joy, three for a girl, four for a boy, five for silver, six for gold, *seven for a secret, never to be told.*

I reach a receptionist. Possibly, it's the same receptionist at every doctor's office, rental car agency, and health insurance claim office I've ever called. Possibly, there is only one in the whole world, and she rotates her bored inflection from desk to desk, like a Santa Claus who brings nothing but *not giving a shit.* She informs me Dr. Chun will call me back when he can, in a way that suggests I will be very lucky if this occurs before Christmas.

But he does call me back, almost immediately.

"Abby? It's Dr. Chun, from the neurology wing of Lincoln Memorial. Thank you for returning my call. Dr. Aster sent over some scans for me to look at," he says.

Finally I find my voice. "I'm sorry. What kind of specialist are you?"

"Neurology," he says, and I almost, almost relax. Neurologists look at brain scans. Normal. But then he goes on: "Actually, my specialty is neurological pathologies. And oncology," he adds, almost apologetically.

I close my eyes and remember all the times I wished for my father to die. I open my eyes. The world is still there. A pickup truck rolls by, the truck bed packed with sunburned teenagers.

It carries a memory I must have buried long ago: me and Kaycee, maybe third grade, when my mom was still alive, the first and only time I was allowed to go to the Halloween Fright Fest.

I'd been scared out of my mind in the haunted house. Not because of all the monsters popping out in masks with chainsaws, but because Kaycee had run ahead, thinking it would be funny to pretend to disappear. I ran room to room, terrified and searching for her. There were coffins everywhere, and fake blood, and even a mannequin with blond hair hanging floppy-necked from a noose. She didn't even have a face, just drawn-on eyes and a lipstick mouth—but in my panic, in the dark, I thought it was her.

We took a hayride afterward. We were on the back of a wagon, just the two of us, because Kaycee's dad had gone to get another beer out of the car. Kaycee was sulking because I hadn't seen the point of the joke.

I scared you, didn't I? she kept saying. *It's a haunted house. Get it? I scared you.*

Then, suddenly, we were in the woods. In the quiet drip of the overhanging branches, paper ghosts nailed to the trees, she turned to me. "I'm not scared of dying," she said. "Not one bit. How about you?"

I had never actually thought about it before. My mom was dying, and that was enough to think about.

"No," I lied.

She reached for my hands. "When I die, I'm going to become an angel, so I can look after you all the time." Then she squeezed so tightly it began to hurt. "But first, I'm going to take revenge on everyone who deserves it. I'll frighten all of them to death, one by one."

ONE SECOND, TWO seconds, three: I open my eyes, and the world is still there. I'm still holding the phone to my sweating cheek. Kaycee is still gone.

"Do you think you can bring your father down here to see me?" Dr. Chun says.

"When?" I croak out. I'm praying he says, Whenever you can make it. I'm praying he says there's no rush. I'm praying he says, In a few weeks.

"I'm here until seven tonight."

Chapter Thirty-Two

Dr. Chun has obviously had a lot of practice making bad news sound like just the news you were hoping for. He is quiet and patient, warm and matter-of-fact. He doesn't stutter. He looks us in the eyes without blinking. And I believe that he cares.

He asks whether my father has experienced mood changes, whether he's had trouble sleeping, whether he's shown signs of forgetfulness. Whether he's fallen recently, or had trouble with his balance.

He explains that often in older people, the symptoms of glioblastoma multiforme are confused for other signs of mental deterioration like Alzheimer's.

He explains that the tumor has likely been growing for some time.

He tells us that the median survival rate is roughly fifteen months. But he also says, gently, that he expects, given the size and location of the tumor, that my father will have less time than that.

He tells us that our focus now should be on my father's quality of life, during the little quantity of it he has left, and I know, deep down, he is already dead.

Chapter Thirty-Three

We drive home mostly in silence. I'm full of a terrible burning, a frantic urge to blow something up.

One month. Six months. It's hard to know. But it will be fast from here.

My father can't be dying. My father is indestructible. He is the rule. He is the law.

He is all I have.

He dozes with his head against the window. His breath smells old. Something white is crusted to the corner of his lip.

The weather is changing. A bleak covering of clouds is rolling across the sky but the heat is still crackling, electric, and the air churning through the car vents smells like singed rubber.

When my phone rings—Joe again—my father startles awake. I thumb it silent. Then, after a pause, turn it off entirely.

"Who was that?" my father asks me. Catching sight of the name on the screen, he asks, "Joe? Is that your boyfriend?"

"I don't have a boyfriend, Dad," I tell him, for the ninetieth time. Since I've been home, my father has found creative ways to work my love life into nearly every conversation. *Does your boyfriend mind you work so much? Why don't you ask your boyfriend to help you with that steering issue?* I can't tell whether he's doing it deliberately, whether he's making a dig, or whether he really has forgotten, over and over again, that I have no one. Joe is the closest to a functional relationship I have—and he's gay, and mad at me more than half the time.

"A girl needs a boyfriend," he mutters, turning back to the window.

I think of what Dr. Chun said, and imagine my father's tumor like a chunk of hard metal, a residue of chemical waste.

"Did I ever tell you how I met your mother?" My dad speaks the words to the window.

"You did, Dad. A hundred times at least."

"—Back in 1980. The Reagan years."

"I know," I say. Call-and-response. "And she was working the line of drunks at the soup kitchen, and you saw her from across the street." *Amen.*

"No. This was the middle of winter. She was in the kitchen, stirring the soup. Her hair was loose and I asked her what if she got some in my food and she laughed and she said we've got bigger problems, you and me."

This is nothing I've heard before. I wait for him to correct himself. The way the story goes, my dad saw some chewed-up alcoholic, whose hands were shaking so bad he could barely keep hold of his cup, hitting on my mom at the shelter, complimenting her hair. My dad saw what a saint she was and swooped to her rescue.

But he goes on with this new version. "She must have seen something in me, because she put her hand on mine and told me I was gonna be all right."

This is backward. It was my father who, moved by a message God sent straight into his heart, crossed the street to *her.*

Except that all at once I know that *this* story is the truth. The one I heard my whole life was the inversion. He was the alcoholic. He was the one who needed saving.

"You know I never touched a drink again after she put her hand on me like that? That was God touching me, too. I felt it. It's like her hand weighed fifty tons but didn't weigh a feather."

I cycle through a hundred different questions, trying to land on one that makes sense. I'm sweating and freezing all at the same time, like even my body can't tell what's real.

My father is the no-name, gutted drunk of his own stories.

I don't know what it changes, exactly, and at the same time everything feels different. I feel like I did the first time I found out that every time we played ring-around-the-rosie we were calling up a plague of cholera and miming people drowning in their own blood, chanting for the smell of their ashes. I have feared my father and hated him and, only recently, begun to pity him.

But I have never, before this, felt sympathy for him.

I think he might be sleeping again. His eyes are closed, and his head nods with the rhythm of the car. But then he says, "I'm not afraid to die, you know."

It reminds me of Kaycee.

"And don't say I'm not dying," he adds, before I can. "I heard what the doctor said."

"There is no death," I say. "Just God." It's a line he often fed me.

He sits there, rocking, eyes closed. Like he's listening to music I can't hear.

"Two Septembers ago I found a cat in the old shed. Pregnant to the point of bursting. She was in bad shape. I put a blanket on her, gave her water and some milk. The kittens came—six of them, smallest things I'd ever seen. Some of them could've passed for bugs, except for the fur." He shakes his head. Still squeezing his eyes shut. "I made a little nest for them, just some cardboard and old blankets."

I expect him to finish but he goes silent. We're passing into Barrens now. And even from here, from the other side of town, the smoke from Optimal's chimneys is visible, like fingers splayed into a gesture, but I can't say what it means.

"What happened to them?" I say finally.

He opens his eyes. "Big storm came through. Overnight the temperature dropped forty degrees. There was no warning, nothing on the reports. Just a change in the wind and a freeze knocked all the leaves from the trees and made it winter overnight." He brings a hand to the window and presses it to the glass, then pulls away to watch his prints disappear. "They were all dead by morning, every one of them, six tiny kittens and the mother, too."

"I'm sorry," I say, and I am, but puzzled, too: out here you get used to things dying. There are farms buzzing with flies, cows and pigs and chickens slaughtered to fill deep freezers. Deer hunted in the winter, cats killed in the road, and birds dropped from the sky.

"I don't know if there's a God," he says. We're still moving, punching through a great big hanging picture toward nothing. "I used to think it was a plan. And even the bad things that happened, your mom getting sick, a kid getting mowed over, it was all part of the plan. But what kind of plan is there for kittens to freeze like that? They meant nothing to nobody. What kind of God would do that. Why not leave them unborn in the first place?" For a second, anger tightens his face, and he looks like the man I remember. "There's evil in this world, Abby. You remember that. You look for it. You look so it can't look for you."

The world exhales. This sounds like the father I know. Smoke unwinds against the clouds. "I'll remember."

He leans back in his seat, satisfied. As we pass the clutter of tire shops and fast food outlets and new restaurants, Optimal lurches out from the distance again, an ugly sprawl between the trees.

"Look at that," he says. "All that smoke. Chemical spew. Disgusting." He shakes his head. "They killed her, you know," he goes on. "Oh, I know everyone says they didn't. But they did. They killed her with all their filth. Poison and greed, that's all it is."

Mom died right before Optimal finished construction. The day we buried her, the first bit of smoke came up from the chimneys, and I remember thinking at first it was a kind of celebration.

"They didn't kill her, Dad," I say, though I'm not sure why it matters. "Mom got cancer before."

"I'm not talking about your mother." He leans back in his seat and closes his eyes again. "I'm talking about that girl, the one everyone always fussed about. Kaycee Mitchell."

Chapter Thirty-Four

Only when morning comes do I realize that it must have been night. I remember drinking. My dreams were full of bright-colored bodies. Shades of blue and orange and red. There was fire. It smelled like paint.

In my living room, a girl deformed by terror is leaning on the armchair, screaming: and then I startle up and I realize that I'm the one who screamed. The girl is Kaycee, embalmed in oil on one of her canvases. A self-portrait.

I look around. On the table, another two stacked canvases, a half-empty bottle of Jim Beam, and cigarette butts floating in a filth of dirty liquid.

I haven't smoked since college. But I can taste the smoke in my mouth.

I try to shuffle back through my memories, but all the images feel like balloons, slipping out of my grasp. I don't remember going back to Frank Mitchell's unit at the U-Pack but I must have: I don't remember why and whether I was seen, whether I was careful, what on earth could have compelled me to steal the paintings and bring them home with me. I'm moved by a desperate, enormous desire to hide them, to burn them, to get them out. But they are staring back at me, refusing to be moved.

I fall onto the couch.

Ten years, and my dad never said a word to me about Kaycee's disappearance. I tried to press him for information but he had little to offer: only that he turned up Kaycee's bag down by the reservoir, half concealed by overhanging brush, and thought she must have forgotten it there after a bonfire. He expected her to come looking for it, only to learn everyone was saying she'd run off.

Who runs off and leaves a wallet, cell phone, and driver's license behind?

I asked him why he didn't go to the police, and he only shrugged. *It wasn't any of our business*, he said. *That girl was nothing but trouble, anyway.*

I hardly remember the drive back to my rental, then to our makeshift office. Time is moving in jump cuts again. The rest of the team is already assembled when I burst through the door, and the words are out of my mouth before I can stop them.

"Kaycee died."

Joe sits very still, like the way small prey freezes at the approach of a predator. "What are you talking about?"

"Kaycee Mitchell. She didn't disappear. She didn't leave town. She died," I repeat, and as soon as I do, I'm sure it's right. The words feel right. They feel as if I'm taking out a piece of shrapnel from my chest. "I think she died here, in Barrens. Because she *was* sick." Joe's face hasn't changed, so I plunge on. "I think that her family was paid off to lie about it. Maybe Misha, too. Maybe even her boyfriend, Brent."

"Did you get any sleep last night?" Joe asks, in a way I don't like.

"I'm fine," I say, because I am, I think I am, and all my memories feel like dreaming so they must be dreams. And I tell him what my father told me about finding her bag near the reservoir.

"Abby, your dad is sick," Joe says, very slowly, as if he's holding a fishing line and just begging me to follow the hook. "We can't exactly assume he's dealing in facts. Doesn't he have Alzheimer's?"

This isn't the time to correct Joe, so I don't. The symptoms are the same. But my father hasn't lost his grip on the past; it's the present that seems slippery.

"Kaycee and her friends played an awful game in high school," I say, ignoring his lead. "They weren't the first ones to play. But Kaycee was the one who thought of a way to make money off of it." Briefly, I tell him, tell the whole room, what Cora Allen told me. "Blackmail," I finish, out of breath.

For the first time I realize how strange I feel. But I won't sit down; if I do, it would be like admitting that Joe is right, that the interns with their shifty glances are right, that I'm standing here babbling nonsense instead of trying to explain that I've finally seen the truth.

"Sorry." Joe rubs his forehead. "What does this have to do with the Optimal case?"

"Blackmail," I repeat. "Don't you see? It was her *pattern*. She'd gotten a taste for it when she realized she could use the Game to get payouts from people terrified their photos would go public. But how much could she possibly have gotten? Forty, sixty bucks a pop?" I'm filling in holes as I go. "Kaycee must have heard about the case Optimal settled back in Tennessee before they moved to Barrens, and she set her sights higher. So she comes up with her little scam to pretend to be sick, maybe persuades her friends to go along with her, thinking they could go to Optimal for a payout. But she didn't understand how serious things would get. Optimal was working its own scams, flouting environmental regulations, cutting costs, hiding money, bribing officials to look the other way. They couldn't afford publicity. They couldn't afford the *scrutiny*."

"So they killed her." Joe's face is blank.

And here, under the painful bright lights next to crates of file folders and office supplies, I have the sudden sensation of drowning: It sounds crazy. Of course it does. But I'm right. I have to be. "Or they hired someone to do it. For all I know, they paid off her fucking *father*. But it fits."

For a moment, there's silence. I can feel my heart jumping rhythms in my chest.

It's Portland who speaks up, slowly. "But the school nurse said Kaycee was really sick," he says. "The pictures prove it."

"The pictures prove she was a good actress," I snap, although once again I see Kaycee on the bathroom floor, a swirl of blood in the toilet. And then another image of Kaycee shuffles up from the past, this time from when we were kids. Kaycee's face, shuttered like a closed door, when I confronted her about Chestnut. *I didn't do it*, she said calmly, biting off all the edges of her words so instead they sounded like a brag. *You must be really screwed up, Abby, to even think I would do it.* "She was a liar. She was always a liar. Maybe she made *herself* sick."

Still, no one looks at me. Anger rises like a quick tide: I want to bury them in it.

"I'm telling you, you didn't know her. We were friends when we were little. She was fucked up. She killed my dog with rat poison."

This, finally, startles Joe into speaking. "She what?"

"She lied about it for years, and tortured me for refusing to forgive her, and then before she died, or before she was killed, she left me *proof*, just so that I would know for sure."

Joe stands, scraping the chair back from his desk, and I run out of air and stand there panting and sweating, and I realize I'm about to cry.

"Can we talk in private?" Joe sounds as polite as a stranger. I have no choice but to follow him, like a child.

Outside, a blaze of heat and sun warms my face. The door swings shut behind us with a *bang-snap*. Across the parking lot, Sunny Jay's is already open. I wonder if Condor's inside. And if he is, I hope he doesn't come out and see me like this.

"Look." I take a deep breath. "I know what you're going to say. Okay?"

"I don't think you do." He sounds worried. He screws up his mouth like he's trying to digest. "You've been working too hard."

My heart drops. He doesn't believe me. Not even a little. "Joe, this is important." My throat is so tight I can barely choke out the words. "Kaycee Mitchell died. And everyone has been lying about it. For years."

But he isn't listening. He squints into the distance. "I've known you a long time, Abby. You're a friend. You know that, right? Since our very first day at CEAW, when I told you I hated your shoes. Remember?"

I can't keep the tears back anymore, and I don't try. I stand there, humiliated and exhausted and furious, feeling as if in just a few words he's stripped me of my skin and left me raw and open in the hot wind. My father is dying, and Joe won't listen; I came back to bury the past, but instead the past is burying me.

"I'm worried about you," he says. "You need a break. When was the last time you took a vacation?"

"I don't need a vacation! I need you to listen!"

"You're not well, Abby." His voice gets a little harder. "I don't want a repeat of what happened our first year."

Despite the sun, a sudden chill runs through me. "That's not fair."

"Isn't it?" When he turns to me his eyes are dark. "You stopped sleeping. You started drinking too much. You were pulled in a thousand directions—you thought Bromley had encoded messages in the *invoices*, for God's sake—"

"I'd been awake for seventy-two hours." My voice cracks on the still air. "Look, I know I lost it. I was eating Adderall. I was a mess, okay? I admit it. I admitted it then." *And you, fucker, promised never to hold it against me.* "But this is different."

"It's not a negotiation." Joe's face morphs, flowing into a stranger's eyes and lips, a stranger's sharp tongue and cruel expression. "I've already talked to Estelle about it. You're going home. To *Chicago*." He emphasizes this, as if I may have forgotten. "We're all going home. I'll continue to run the investigation from there. They'll bring on Casey Scheiner as support."

He might as well have punched me. The air goes straight out of my lungs.

"Fuck you." I can only whisper it.

Joe sighs. He doesn't even get angry. That makes it worse, in a way. "You're not in trouble," he says, as if that's what I'm worried about. "You still have a job. But you're going home, and you're going to get well, and forget about fucking Kaycee Mitchell." He starts to turn back to the door, then pivots around to face me again. "Oh. That reminds me. Kaycee called you. Apparently she lives in Florida now." Joe's smile is cold and narrow, bleak as thin-shaved ice. "She left a number for you, if you want to call her back."

Chapter Thirty-Five

I'm sitting in my car staring at the sun reflecting off the glass of Sunny Jay's and my fingers are shaking so badly I twice misdial the number Joe has given me, reaching first a Florida tanning salon and then a man who fires off some quick Spanish at me before hanging up. My throat is dry as dust. I wish I had something to drink, a beer, a shot, something, but if I drank now it would mean I was really falling apart, and I'm not.

I won't.

I *can't* be.

The third time's the charm. I close my eyes and feel my heart heavy in my throat. Count the ringtones. One, two, three, four. She picks up after four, and a bad feeling stutters in my chest.

"Hello?" Kaycee's voice is lower and raspier than I remember. A voice you expect to hear whispering dirty things on a phone sex line. Still, my heart beats faster just hearing it. I can't say it isn't her. I thought I would know instantly.

"Is this Kaycee Mitchell?" I ask, and I hold my breath, waiting for her reply.

"You got her. Who is this?"

I go silent, suddenly dizzy.

"Umm . . . This is Abby Williams," I say, and she laughs, and I hold my breath again, trying to pin the sound to my memory.

"Abby. Wow. You sound different." This is either the truth or some perverse form of cleverness. Or both.

"Where are you?" I ask her, and although the area code was one for South Florida, I pray for a wild second she'll surprise me and tell me she's come home, like me. Just like that, the urge to see her—not so I can prove anything, but just because—stretches up from a dark space and puts a hand around my thoughts.

"Not far from Sarasota. Been here for a couple of years now. I moved around a lot after I left Barrens."

Sarasota. A sudden sense of déjà vu momentarily doubles my vision. Sheriff Kahn just returned from Sarasota. Coincidence?

"Why did you leave?" I blurt out.

"Why not?" Kaycee says, with another laugh. "I always wanted to. Don't you remember? Mrs. Danforth used to catch me trying to sneak out the windows when I used the bathroom pass. Even in third grade, I always wanted out of there."

I had forgotten Mrs. Danforth, and how Kaycee used to try to shimmy out the windows next to the gym during the school day since the doors were manned by a rotating list of hall monitors. Sometimes she even made it.

I fumble to punch the window down, but still I can't get enough air. It's her. It has to be her. Kaycee ran, like everyone said, and I'm wrong, and probably going crazy. Kaycee is alive, sun-kissed, still beautiful; Kaycee is lounging on a patio or sitting by a pool somewhere south of Sarasota. There was no deeper meaning to any of it. She just left. She shook off Barrens like a sweep of dust. She never looked back.

And in this, too, she proved she was better than me.

"Who told you I was looking for you?" I ask, through the leaden feeling in my chest.

"Misha," she answers, after a pause.

"She told me she never spoke to you," I say.

"I asked her to lie." Kaycee says this casually, easily, as if it should be obvious. "I didn't want my dad knowing where I was, or bugging *her* to give me messages, or asking me for money, or any of that."

A stupidly easy answer that never even occurred to me. Of course Kaycee wouldn't have wanted her dad to have any way of tracking her—he was half the reason she was running in the first place.

Easy arithmetic. So why do I feel that *she's* the one lying?

"So you had questions for me?" Kaycee asks.

"I just wanted to understand why," I say. "Why you lied about being sick. Why you ran off without a word."

Kaycee sighs. Behind her, a man's voice is barely audible. I imagine her tilting her head away from the phone, to listen for a husband or boyfriend calling her inside.

Or, maybe, to listen for instructions.

The idea comes to me suddenly, impossible to dislodge.

"Look." Kaycee presses her mouth up close to the receiver. "I don't remember why I did any of it, okay? That's the truth. It was a long time ago. I was screwed up. I wanted attention. Maybe I thought there was money in it."

She might as well be reading from a book: *All the Reasons Kaycee Mitchell Might Have Run Away.*

"I'm sorry," she says, a little quieter, and the whole world goes white for a moment. "I'm sorry for everyone I hurt and all the people who wasted their time looking for me. I'm sorry for *you*, Abby."

"Don't be." Alarms are blaring in my head.

Kaycee Mitchell is sorry.

But Kaycee Mitchell is *never* sorry. I never once heard her say the word.

She missed recess for a whole week rather than apologize to Matt Granger for stealing his crayons. She couldn't apologize. She didn't have it in her.

Kaycee Mitchell is immune to guilt.

Whoever's on the other end of the line, it isn't Kaycee Mitchell.

"Well, look, you know where to find me," she says.

"Just one more thing." My heart is beating so heavy and huge I can barely breathe around it. "It's stupid, I know. But I've always been curious." One, two, three heartbeats. Sun streaks through the windshield and across my lap. I remember the warmth of Chestnut curled beside me on the front porch. "What really happened to Chestnut?"

There's a long moment of silence.

Then Kaycee again—or whoever is pretending to be Kaycee—this time sounding uneasy. "It was a long time ago . . ."

"Does that mean you don't remember?" Beyond the windshield, the world goes on.

She gives a staccato laugh. "Remind me."

"My dog," I say shortly. "The one you killed."

There's another short silence. "I have to go," Kaycee says abruptly. "Sorry I couldn't be more helpful," she says. There's that word again, *sorry*.

"Don't worry," I tell her. "You did enough."

SOMEONE IS GOING to an awful lot of trouble to prove that Kaycee's alive.

Which means, almost certainly, that she isn't.

The Kaycee impersonator, whoever she is, said that Misha had told her I was looking. And I'm willing to bet that this, at least, is true. Someone had to feed her the information. And the best liars ride as close to the truth as they can.

Besides, the example Misha chose when we met at the new community center to prove her point about the complexity of right and wrong couldn't have been random. Misha plays dumb, but she's anything but. *Let's say Frank Mitchell had a customer, a normal man. And let's say that what he's really after are the younger girls.* She'd said pictures were better than them going out and finding the real thing.

But was she really just talking about Frank Mitchell? Or was she actually defending *herself*, too? It might have been a kind of confession. It was definitely a hint.

Back in the day, when the Game was heating up, Kaycee kept the photographs for herself, even when her victims ponied up cash.

Maybe Frank Mitchell found a way to turn a bigger profit on them. It would certainly explain her father's nice, new house. And why he's so eager to tell everybody who asks that Kaycee ran off on her own.

And what does Misha have to do with it?

I remember the secretary who poked into her office that day I went to visit the high school. Misha collects student phones . . . to prevent cyberbullying, she'd said.

But could she really be looking for new targets?

It all comes back to the Game.

I can think of one person who might be able to help: Tatum. Monty mentioned that she and her friends were involved in the Game. I need to know whether the rules have changed, who the other players are, and who's keeping score.

I point my car toward Dougsville, and the clinic where May mentioned that Tatum was taken. I'm feeling a little better, a little more in control. I don't need Joe. I don't need anyone. All I need is the truth. Still, the periphery of my vision keeps warping in the heat, shimmering into a mirage. Lack of sleep, nothing more.

Dougsville is twelve miles from Barrens, accessible only by the kind of flat roads that make speed limits seem like an inside joke. Corn whips by, tossing its green arms toward the sky. I think of my dream. Was it a dream? Of heat and fire. I think of Kaycee's portraits scattered around my rental.

My phone rings almost continuously: first a call from Joe, then a local number, then Joe's again. He's probably wondering where I went. I silence the ringer.

Growing up, the Dougsville kids struck us all as stuck up: Theirs was the first Walmart in the whole county, and on its heels came the clinic, then a brewery. Their football team was always number one. It's really little more than a single long strip, all car dealerships, aboveground pool installations, and churches. The clinic shares a parking lot with a big hunting and fishing retail; a sign in the window directs customers to the back for licenses and ammunition.

I head to the Walmart for a plastic-wrapped bouquet of flowers and a Get Well card. The flowers look pretty but exhale a moldy vapor, and for a second that's just how I feel, like some rotten thing plastered over with a bow and good intentions. I should turn around. I should leave Tatum alone. I should let her get better.

But I don't.

The clinic is small, bright, and clean. A receptionist at the desk politely asks me whether I'm a family member when I request to see Tatum.

"I'm a lawyer," I say. The word *lawyer* is like the word *police*: the verbal equivalent of a bomb. No one wants to be the one caught holding the package. "Is Mrs. Klauss here?"

She shakes her head. Her eyes have widened into a caricature of alarm. "Go on back," she says. "I'm sure it's all right." So I skirt around the desk and pass through the double doors.

The clinic has only a few examination rooms and Tatum's room is the last one on the left. It has been transformed into a hothouse of cards and carnations. Tethered to an IV in a hospital bed, Tatum looks young, and very small. Beautiful, too. I think she must be sleeping, but as I ease the door shut behind me, she opens her eyes. They are a shocking, startling green.

"Who are you?" she asks. But it isn't an accusation. She sounds genuinely curious.

"My name is Abby," I say. I lift the flowers so she can see them. "I brought these for you. Looks like you don't need them."

She closes her eyes and shrugs. I clear a space on the counter for her latest offering.

"I don't know you," she says again, as if she's observing the facts from a distance. I wonder if they've sedated her.

"No, you don't." I stay where I am, not too close, giving her lots of space, letting her size me up. "Listen, Tatum, I don't pretend to know what you've just been through."

That, at least, gets something of a normal teenage eye roll.

"I wish everyone would stop making such a big deal out of it."

"You swallowed a handful of pills."

"Just a dumb idea. I wasn't trying to die. I just . . . had a headache." When she looks at me then, her expression sharpens into one of distrust. It's as if, for the first time, she is seeing me. "Who are you? What are you doing here?"

"I'm from Barrens, too. I left for a while. But I'm back now." I hate how final the words sound. But aren't they, after all, the truth? My condo in Chicago feels as far away to me as a dream. "I'm a lawyer. I came home to find out what happened to a girl a decade ago. She went missing."

"Kaycee Mitchell?" she says, and of course I realize she would have heard of her. I can only imagine the lore, and how the stories of Kaycee were transformed. "She faked being sick and everyone else started faking too. So, what? You think I'm faking?"

"Not at all," I say. I take a deep breath. "I think Kaycee was in trouble. And I think you are, too." This gets her attention. She gets even stiller, more alert, as if she's listening for music playing far away. Then: "I know about the Game, Tatum."

For a second, her mouth opens wide, and I'm worried she'll scream, or shout for a nurse. But then, all at once, she relaxes.

"Who told you?" she asks.

"Monty Devue." This gets another eye roll.

"He's been obsessed with me since, like, seventh grade." But she doesn't sound afraid of him, only annoyed. For a long time, she sits there, obviously debating whether to say more. Then, suddenly she sits up in bed. "You didn't tell my mom, did you? She can't know. You can't tell her!"

"I haven't said a word."

She sinks back against her pillow. She stares down at her hands, clutching and unclutching them. "I feel so stupid."

"Is that why you did what you did?"

"I got scared." Her voice drops to a whisper.

"Why? Is someone threatening you?"

She waves this idea away. "No. Nothing like *that*." As if she, Tatum Klauss, is beyond threatening. "But I got worried everyone would find out . . ."

I take a gamble. "Because of the pictures?"

Now she looks up. "How . . . ?"

"The Game has been going on for a long time," I tell her, and she sucks her lower lip into her mouth, chews it like a kid. "Tell me what happened."

She shrugs. "I heard about the parties back when I was a freshman . . ."

"What parties?" I ask. She twists the sheets between her hands, and I can see her trying to swallow back the words. "You can trust me," I say, a little more gently. "Okay? I don't want to get you in trouble. I want to help."

I count long seconds. In the quiet, I can hear a distant mechanical beeping.

Finally, Tatum lets out a big breath of air, and I can tell she's made a decision. "They were supposed to be invite-only," she says. "Special parties, you know, for the scholarship girls."

"What about the boys?" I ask. "Were they invited?"

"Just girls," she says, in a voice so quiet I nearly miss it.

"Who threw the parties? What were they for? Who else was invited?"

I can tell right away I've leaned on her too quickly. She clams up. "I don't want to get anyone in trouble," she says. Then: "We *wanted* to go. Nobody made us."

"Okay. I get it." I take a deep breath and slowly pull up a chair next to her bed. When she doesn't react, I take a seat slowly. Now she's forced to look at me. "Look, Tatum, the truth is that you *are* in trouble. Right? Isn't that why you're here?"

Suddenly, her eyes fill up: she looks so small, drowning in all those white sheets. She whispers something I can't make out.

I lean forward, holding my breath. "What?" She's crying now, though, and only hiccups when she tries to speak. "Take a breath, okay?"

"I just wanted a new phone." Another sob rocks her. "My phone was such crap, but my mom . . . my mom said I would have to buy it myself . . . I thought . . ."

"Tatum." I place a hand on the bed, wishing I could hug her instead. This poor kid. "Tell me about the parties."

But suddenly, with a gasp, she goes still. Listening. Then I can hear a chorus of high-pitched voices move toward us from the hall.

"Tatum." Now I want to reach out and shake her. "Tatum, please."

It's too late. The door swings open and I recognize two of the girls who pour into the room, all sunshine and smiles, as Optimum Stars. One of them is Sophie Nantes.

"We brought donuts," Sophie says, but stops short when she sees me. It's amazing how someone so pretty can look that ugly in an instant. "What are *you* doing here?" She whips around to glare at Tatum. "What's she doing here?"

Tatum swipes her face with her forearm. "She brought flowers," she says, as if that explains it.

Sophie tosses the bag of donuts on the counter and leans up against it. Even I feel her presence, how it works like an eclipse to stifle all the light. The other girls jostle to be the one to stand next to her.

"She was at the PowerHouse game, too, talking to Monty," Sophie says, addressing Tatum directly. "I guess your stalker club is growing."

Tatum looks away. I stand up, happy with this small advantage: I'm a head taller than all of them, and in better clothes. Still, Sophie's eyes sweep me as if I'm an insect hovering too close to her picnic.

"Tatum and I were just talking about the Game," I say. My voice sounds overloud. In my head, I could flatten them with it.

Several of the girls look at one another. Not Sophie, though. She's too good for that.

"I don't know what you're talking about," she says coolly. Then she peels away from the counter and sits on Tatum's bed, placing a hand gently on the IV coil flowing liquid down into Tatum's blood.

My mouth goes dry.

"Poor Tatum," she says, cooing. "You're crying."

"I'm fine," Tatum says mechanically.

Sophie shakes her head. "Aw, honey. You can't lie to me. I'm your best friend, remember? Tatum's a terrible liar," she adds, to me. "It doesn't stop her from trying, though. She's, like, pathological."

She turns back to Tatum. "But we love you, anyway, no matter what." She leans forward to stage whisper to her. "Even if you're a slut."

"Get away from her." I have to ball my fists to keep them from flying at Sophie's throat.

Sophie turns to stare at me. "You're the one who shouldn't be here."

"Tatum, please." I turn back to her, beg her to listen, to look at me. "I can help you. If you'll tell me the truth . . ."

"I asked her to leave. I told her I had nothing to say." Tatum's hands fumble across the sheets toward Sophie, who leans over to touch her face, releasing her grip on the IV. A shiver travels through Tatum's whole body, as if Sophie's touch carries a current.

Even before she begins to scream, I know I've lost her.

"Help!" Tatum throws her voice as high as it can go. "Help! Help!"

"Tatum . . ." I try, one last time, to reach her. But even as I start for the bed, Sophie steps in front of me. For a long moment, her eyes hold me there. And it's in that moment that I know who this girl is—*what* she is. She's *their* Kaycee.

She smiles. She draws a breath. For a second, she looks as if she might apologize. "Help! Help!" She's only inches from my face. I can smell coffee on her breath.

Like dolls animated by the sound of her voice, the other girls begin to echo her. "Help! Help! Help!"

I burst through the door. I trip, running down the hall. I push through a swarm of descending nurses, careen off the reception desk and hurtle toward escape.

HELP.

The word keeps echoing in my head, even when the clinic is far behind me.

The sun is huge, red, terrible: like a mouth opening to swallow the horizon.

A long-haul trucker blowing toward me leans on his horn before I realize I've drifted into his lane. I jerk the wheel and slam on the brakes as his horn blast rolls into silence.

I pull over for a bit, just to let my heartbeat catch up.

Help, help, help.

From the bottom of my bag, my phone lets out a few insistent beeps. I've missed another call. I thumb over to voicemail with shaking fingers.

Ms. Williams, this is Sheriff Kahn. I was hoping you could stop down at the station today, or give me a ring back. I got a complaint from the night manager over at the U-Pack, says there was some kind of scuffle and you disobeyed his order to stop your vehicle. The pictures of the fence look pretty bad, and he's got security video, too. I'd like to hear your side of the story.

Chapter Thirty-Six

Condor comes to the door even before I've knocked.

"Jesus Christ! Come in, before you beat my door down."

Maybe I did knock. My knuckles are raw-red and sore. My throat swollen as if I've been screaming. My mouth tastes medicinal. Vodka. Or whiskey.

I remember a bar, dimly, but I can't haul the image into focus.

Hours are dropping away, siphoned into darkness.

I remember seeing two calls from TJ, my dad's friend. I remember letting my phone ring and ring, letting the sound of it drown beneath the noise of the bar.

"What happened to you?" Condor says.

What's happening to me?

"You lied to me," I tell him. I count the drinks I must have had by the slur of my speech. Four maybe five maybe six.

"Sit down. You need some water. *Sit.*" He pilots me into an armchair, and the room slows its turning, like a merry-go-round reaching the end of its cycle. The living room, warm and comfortable, its cheapness buffed and brushed up by details everywhere—pictures of Hannah, framed photographs cluttering the walls, old books stacked high on the shelves—fills me with a sudden shyness.

Condor's living room is like a weather-beaten dock, and I am washed-up wreckage.

A glass cabinet filled with ornate feathers catches my eye and holds it there; silver, gold, purple, blue. As he returns with a glass of water and watches me finish it, he catches me staring.

"Fishing lures. Always have better luck if you make your own."

The water has cleared my head, just a little. "Thank you. Where's Hannah?"

"With her grandparents for the week." He gestures for the glass. "I'll get you some more."

I can remember, now, leaving Dougsville, and finding a bar on my way home. I can remember the first drink but not the others. My stomach drops. I think of Misha's pink shoes and how they ended up on the floor next to my bed after the bonfire in the woods. A sick feeling moves through me, like the world is tilting. "Something stronger," I say. "Anything you got."

"I don't think you need it."

"I'm telling you I do." I make an effort to sharpen my words. "Come on, Condor. I'm fine. I can spit and hit my front porch."

He makes me drink another water first, then opens a bottle of wine and pours me some into an old jam jar. He takes a seat across from me. He moves as if his body hurts.

"Well, what are we toasting?"

I can't think of a single thing. "To Optimal," I say, meaning it as a joke. But my voice breaks. "Those fuckers."

"Those fuckers," Condor repeats, solemnly, and touches my glass before drinking.

For a while we sit in silence, as the night passes through the room, and the occasional sweep of headlights on the main road cuts through his windows.

"My father's dying," I blurt out after a while. I didn't even mean to say it. I didn't come here to confess. Then again, I'm not sure why I came at all.

Condor's hand tightens momentarily on his cup. "Fuck, Abby. I'm . . ." He trails off, and when he looks away I can see a muscle working in his jaw. "You've had some couple of days."

I look down because looking at him only makes me want to cry, and wanting to cry makes me want to disappear. "I should be with my dad," I say. "But I can't. I couldn't."

Maybe I did come here to confess, because suddenly the urge to be understood is overwhelming. "I hated my father. I wished him dead all the time. I used to pray for it. He would send me to my room for hours to pray. Sometimes he'd lock me in a closet, because he knew I hated the dark, and he told me that sinners lived in darkness forever. And instead I would pray that he would drop dead of a heart attack or fall off a roof."

"It's not your fault, Abby," Condor says.

"How do you know?" I take a sip to keep from choking. "Maybe there is a God. Maybe my prayers worked."

"God doesn't answer prayers like that. That isn't what he hears," Condor says quietly.

"What does he hear, then?"

He hesitates with his glass at his lips, watching me over the rim. "The little girl, alone, and frightened of the dark."

He's nice enough to look away, pretending he doesn't notice that I'm on the verge of tears. He just sits there studying his glass, the walls and the ceiling, while I breathe through the urge to cry like the little girl I was then.

When I get it together I don't risk looking at him. I focus instead on the square of rug between my feet. "Optimal's been fattening the bottom line by dumping waste in the water supply," I say. "Probably for years now. The tests came back and proved it."

Condor stares at me. "They all said the water was safe."

"They all lied." I remember Kaycee and I once found a bees' nest, abandoned, lying in the woods. She poked it with a stick until it caved in. Kaycee said the queen leaves her hive after laying her eggs and the children kill one another. This time nobody won. "It's a nest. It's all corrupt. Optimal, the local agencies, and some of the federal agents, too. They're all in on it."

"Money?" Condor asks.

"What else?" I say. But I can't shake the thought of Lilian Mc-Mann, and her daughter posing naked in those ugly socks.

Those girls shouting in unison, *Help, help, help.* The word oozing from the corners of their pretty mouths.

"We're going back to Chicago," I say. "We'll do the rest of the work from there. Now that we have proof, we'll have help from other firms, other agencies, deeper pockets."

"That sounds like good news," Condor says.

"It's *bad* news." I practically shout it. Condor sits back in his chair, watching me without expression. Another memory surfaces, of passing the principal's office and hearing Kaycee's voice float through the open doorway. *I'm not lying. I'm not making it up. Why won't you believe me?* "There's more. I know there's more. If we could only keep digging."

"And then what?" Condor shakes his head. "It's not your job to fix every evil. You did your job."

"The world is full of people just doing their jobs," I fire back, "and look what we're left with."

"Sure," Condor says evenly. "And if all of us dig, guess what happens? We all get buried."

He's right. But what he doesn't know is I'm already buried. I'm not trying to dig down. I'm trying to dig *out.*

"Why did you lie?" I ask him, and he glances up at me, surprised in the act of refilling my glass. "Why did you tell me you were the one to take the photos of Becky?"

He finishes pouring, carefully, wiping the bottle lip with a thumb.

"I didn't tell you," he says. "You told me."

"You let me believe it. You let everyone believe it."

For a long time, we sit in silence, and the house breathes as houses do, in ticks and clanks and creaks.

"She asked me to lie," he says at last. I don't know what I was expecting, but this, the simplicity of it, pulls the air from my chest. "We were friends. Our moms worked together at the prison before it closed. They stayed close." He checks his cup, as if he might find something different inside of it, then takes a hard swallow. "I kind of lost track of her in high school. I had my own problems. But I gave her a ride sometimes, hung out when her mom came over to gossip." He shrugs.

"Why did she want you to lie?"

He sighs, long and hard, as if the truth is something heavy he's been carrying. "When she heard about the pictures, she freaked. She was worried her mom would find out, so she wanted to just pay up and be done with it." His eyes click to mine. "I was the one who talked her out of it," he goes on. "I told her just to talk to her mom. To explain. We agreed her parents would take it easier if they thought I was responsible. Like we were hooking up, hanging out, getting drunk, and I did it for a joke to show her later. It sounds stupid now." He looks away. "When it turned out the photos were from a party with all those people standing around, she just . . . couldn't take it."

I imagine a circle of kids, laughing, faces red from alcohol: in my head, it's Kaycee's paintings I see, the predatory grins, a girl in the fetal position on the ground.

"I didn't think they'd actually send the photos around," Condor says, and I feel sure it's the first time he's made the confession out loud. "I thought they were bluffing. There you have it. My dirty secret."

"Not so dirty after all."

"Dirty enough. She's dead."

"It's not your fault," I say, unconsciously parroting his own words back to him.

He gives me a narrow smile. "Thanks. Feels like it, though." He finishes his drink. The bottle is empty. He stands up to get another.

"Fuck it, right?"

"Kaycee Mitchell is dead." I can't keep it in any longer. "I'm sure of it."

For a long time, Condor says nothing. "Kaycee Mitchell ran away," he says shortly.

"No. That's why I can't find her anywhere. She never left in the first place."

"So everyone in town is lying?" Condor's voice is curiously flat, as if he isn't really asking the question. He pours another glass and slides it across the table to me.

"Only the people who matter. Everyone else just believes what they were told." My head is already spinning. "She was murdered."

There. I've said it.

But Condor doesn't look shocked. Just tired. "Oh, yeah? Then who killed her?"

I can tell he doesn't believe me, and I say so.

Condor sighs. He rubs his eyes hard with his fists. "Why would someone murder Kaycee?"

"I—I'm not sure yet," I admit. "But I know it had something to do with Optimal. And with the Game, too."

"You think Kaycee was killed for some high school hustle?"

"No. It was bigger than that. I think her father was selling the pictures Kaycee and her friends collected. I think he found a new market. And I think he killed her when she threatened to tell."

"That's insane," Condor says.

"He used to hurt her." Almost immediately, I'm ashamed. It feels like a betrayal of a secret Kaycee would have sworn me not to tell.

"I don't doubt it," Condor says, and his tone softens. "I'm telling you it's impossible. There's no way Frank Mitchell killed his daughter."

"So you're a mind reader, now." I don't even care how I sound. I'm sick of being doubted, disbelieved, and made to feel like I'm imagining things. "Did you have to get a special degree for that?"

The words hang sharply between us. Condor didn't get a degree at all, and he knows that I know it.

"Look, I saw Frank every day for months after Kaycee disappeared. Every morning, he bought a six-pack and a pint of vodka. For a while, it was a twelve-pack and a pint. It was like watching someone commit suicide in slow motion. One day I couldn't help myself, and I told him drinking wouldn't help him forget Kaycee."

He interlaces his fingers, squeezing so tight his knuckles stand out. "He looked at me like I'd lost my mind. You know what he said to me? 'I'm not drinking to forget,' he said. 'I'm drinking to believe.' I didn't know what he meant at first. 'Believe what?' I asked him. 'Until I believe she ran off, until I believe she's somewhere doing just fine.'" Condor is quiet for a second. "Don't you get it? He said she ran because he wanted to believe it. He needed to. But he didn't know. He was terrified of not knowing."

I stand up quickly. My body feels like it belongs to someone else.

"Forget it." I shouldn't have come. I don't know why I did. Everything is collapsing everywhere I turn. "Forget I said anything."

Condor gets to his feet, too. "I'm trying to help you—"

I cut him off before he can finish. "I may be wrong about Frank Mitchell. But I'm not wrong about Kaycee. They wanted her out of the way, they knew she could expose them—"

"Who's 'they,' Abby?" He looks at me like he's afraid of me. "Optimal?" In his voice, I can hear how it sounds. In his eyes, I'm a shrunken reflection, desperate and small. "And Sheriff Kahn? And Misha? And all of Kaycee's friends? And *Brent*?" He spits the name out like a curse.

"You don't get it. You don't know—Optimal owns everything in this town—it's everywhere—"

"*You* don't get it." His voice cracks against a note of pain, and it touches a place deep inside me and suddenly I realize that the anger is just grief, just fear, just worry. "Fuck Kaycee Mitchell. Dead, alive, burning in hell, wherever she is. Fuck her. She ruined enough. Don't let her ruin you, too. Don't—"

I kiss him. Taking the words off his tongue with brute force. We knock a pile of books off the table, crash down to the chair and then onto the floor. We topple the lamp and it shatters on the ground, making the room go dark.

"You can't fix yourself on me," he says, undoing his belt. "You know that, right?"

"I'm not here to fix myself," I say, pulling him closer.

Because maybe I can't be fixed at all.

Chapter Thirty-Seven

Knocking. Someone is at the door, knocking again and again.

I'm in my own bed, but the smell of Condor is everywhere and all over me.

More knocking.

My phone's dead, and I have to find the microwave to read the time: 8:12. Only bad news comes this early.

I twitch open the blinds with two fingers and my heart stops. Sheriff Kahn is scowling at my door as if it's been talking back. I can tell just from how he's standing that he's been there awhile.

The paintings are still sitting in my living room: each of them looks like something ripped from a body, like some horrible inner secret.

Kahn starts knocking again before I've shuffled one of them beneath the sofa.

"One minute." Sweat sticks my hair to my forehead. I'm wearing the shirt I had on yesterday, but inside out. "One minute." I shove the other two paintings under my bed.

I look for a lie, for an excuse, for something to say, but there's nothing. One time I lost control of my car on Lake Shore Drive, and after a few seconds of panic, while my car was spinning over black ice toward the ditch, I landed on a moment of peace just like this one. The collision was inevitable. All I had to do was wait for it. It was almost a relief.

"Abby." Sheriff Kahn looks like a mourner at a funeral he's secretly excited about: like he's trying a little too hard. *Some tragedies are inexplicable. People run. Girls run away all the time.* "I'm sorry to bother you so early."

The morning light feels like a terrible uninvited houseguest. I stand there blinking and sweating, while Sheriff Kahn refracts light from his shoulders.

"Not as sorry as I am," I say, and then immediately regret it. I try again. "Can I help you?"

"I have some bad news," he says. I watch him force himself to look directly at me.

"I saw you called." I pause, taking in his expression, but I can't read it. "And honestly, I have no idea what you're talking about."

Kahn flinches. He waves a hand as if to shake off a fly. "I'm not here about that." The pause is long enough to contract the whole world into a heartbeat. *Not here about that* means *here about something else*, and I make a sudden pivot to possibilities I didn't even know I should fear. For a wild second I think he must be here about Kaycee Mitchell, or whoever was pretending to be her.

"I have some bad news about your father."

What's funny is that right away, it feels like I was waiting for him to say it.

"Can I come inside for a minute?" he asks, in a softer voice.

IT'S AMAZING HOW many different ways there are to suffocate. You can suffocate in water as shallow as a puddle, by smothering and by choking. You can even suffocate by breathing if you're breathing the wrong air.

It was TJ who found him. He went to see him just a few hours after our meeting with Dr. Chun. It was part of their routine. On Mondays he usually went over to inspect the trees of course and for a ginger ale. It seems important for me to tell Sheriff Kahn this, about the routine of it. It seems important for me to prove I *knew* his routine—at least, some small part of it.

I don't know why I feel the need to give off the impression that I know more about my father's daily life than I actually do—like when I justified renting my own place to Monty's mother. Strangers make you feel like family should be the most important thing. Blood is thicker than water, that kind of thing. How are you supposed to act when it's not?

TJ's story is short. He says my dad seemed moody and confused. He talked a lot about my mother. He ranted about cancer and the government, how the disease was invented by a U.S. lab back in the fifties to try to get people off their Social Security.

He gave TJ his hacksaw as a gift, one of his favorite tools.

And then TJ called me twice, with no answer. Sheriff Kahn doesn't say that part. I doubt he knows.

My head is full of ringing echoes, voices I can't make out, someone screaming for air.

Sheriff Kahn tells me that TJ cried in his office. *He feels guilty*, he tells me, *for taking the saw.*

When TJ found him this morning, the car was still running in the garage, coughing out its last vapor of gas.

Sheriff Kahn tells me that he would have felt no pain. It's a peaceful way to die. He tells me it's just like sleeping.

I wonder whether when he opened up to me in the car, he'd already decided.

For a moment, I can't remember if I hugged him when I said good-bye.

But I know I didn't.

Chapter Thirty-Eight

I don't sleep. I don't eat much, either. But somehow a day slips by, and then two.

My father committed suicide two days ago now. Choked to death on his own car fumes. Maybe it was the confusion, maybe he was just too proud to be taken to the ground, or maybe his loss of faith was too dark to bear.

Sheriff Kahn is nice enough to give me those two days before returning to arrest me. Breaking and entering. Vandalism. Maybe he feels bad for me because he skips the handcuffs and just reads me a sworn statement made by the night manager at the U-Pack. Zombie-like, I watch Kahn's lips move as he explains what I did. That I failed to stop my car and present identification to the night manager. When he tried closing the gates, I steamrolled right on through them any-way. They don't seem to know about Kaycee's paintings, and how I hauled them off with me. Shitty security cameras, apparently.

The paintings are still stashed under my sofa and bed—I can almost smell them. I can't bring myself to confess or return them. I'm even afraid to see them again—afraid that, like dead bodies, they'll have started to rot.

"To be honest, what they're after is a check. Frank Mitchell's another story, though. He's a wildcard. I know I don't have to tell you that. He could press charges."

Wildcard. The word makes me think of playing cards with Kaycee, sitting cross-legged on my porch. Whoever had won the last round got to pick a wild card, and Kaycee always picked the king of hearts. "Suicide King," she called it, because of the knife drawn straight through his head.

"What were you doing out there, anyway?" Sheriff Kahn asks.

I'm too exhausted to lie. "Frank Mitchell got that unit right after Kaycee supposedly ran away."

"Supposedly, huh?" Sheriff Kahn stands up, working his hat around and around in his hands. "I thought you wound up tracking her down."

"Who told you that?" I say, feeling a spark of interest—the first spark in days, like a cigarette flaring in a dark lot.

"Your partner. Guy with the, ah, *shirts.* Said Kaycee gave you a call when she heard you were looking." He pops his hat into place with one hand, like a cowboy in an old western movie.

"Joe's not my partner anymore," I say. "I'm suspended."

"I'm sorry to hear that," Sheriff Kahn says carefully. "What'd I tell you about rooting around in old messes? Let sleeping dogs lie. That's what my grandma always said. Don't get up," he adds, though I haven't offered to. "I'll find my own way out."

Before he can slip outside, I blurt out, "Don't you want to know where she is?"

He stops, pivots, frowns at me. "Where . . . ?"

"Kaycee Mitchell." I force myself to look at him. "You're not even curious where she ended up?"

"Not really," he says, with a thin smile. "None of my business."

"Florida," I tell him, and for just a second, he freezes. Another ember sparks in the darkness. "Sarasota. You've got a timeshare down there, don't you? Or was it a friend who loans you a place?"

"Take care of yourself, Abigail." Sheriff Kahn opens the door. "Try and get some sleep. You're not looking too good."

. . .

I'VE BEEN AVOIDING Condor's calls, along with everybody else's, and hiding out whenever I see him coming, no matter how long he stands on the porch. Now—three days after my dad died—he finally gives up knocking. But I hear a rustling sound and, after I'm certain he's gone, I swing open the door to the night air. Tucked behind the screen door is an envelope marked with my name. Inside, enfolded in a soft bit of cotton, I find a beautiful fishing hook and a handmade lure, feathered and beaded in rich stripes of gold and blue, work my dad would have found impressive.

A short note is attached. *I hope you catch your big fish.—Dave*

Seeing his first name, a name he almost never uses, jolts something in me. I suddenly think I'm going to cry, am overwhelmed with the memory of his mouth on mine, the urgency of him, his anger, his concern.

Carefully, I rewrap the fishing hook and stuff it into the pocket of my dad's old work vest. It still smells a little like he did: like car oil and Old Spice and wood shavings.

The note, too. I can't bring myself to throw it out.

Dave.

THE TEAM RETURNS to Chicago, and I bury my father with only TJ in attendance, under a bleak sky hinting at a storm that never comes. Although a few other people expressed interest in showing up for the funeral—Monty's mother, Condor, and Brent among them—I know I won't be able to stand the weight of their sympathy and how little I deserve it. Besides, it seems fitting that my father's burial is as lonely and brutal as his death.

Afterward, I stop at the gas station for two six-packs and what my dad would have considered party food: frozen mozzarella sticks, Hostess crumb cakes, nacho cheese dip from a jar, salsa and chips. The house is hot, and it smells. I haven't yet been able to bring myself to start cleaning, and there are week-old dirty dishes in the sink attracting a swarm of flies.

Instead, we set up on the back porch, overlooking the woods.

TJ brings Jim Beam, and he and I take turns sipping straight from the bottle, feet up on the railing, creaking back in the rocking chairs my dad built for my mother when I was a baby. My father's mess has even spread to the porch: stacks of plywood, old air-conditioning screens, salvaged pipes, and electronics that haven't worked in decades. The view has hardly changed since I was a kid, only gotten a little wilder, a little overgrown. I can see the hard glint of the sun off the reservoir—not the water itself, exactly, but little solar flares, as if something behind the trees is catching fire.

If I breathe deeply, I imagine I can smell the lingering smoke of a bonfire.

Only the present is solid. The past is smoke.

"You need any help sorting through your dad's stuff, you let me know," TJ says. He twists to grab the whiskey bottle with his "good" hand and we drink for a while in silence.

"What happened to your arm, TJ?" I ask him, when I'm drunk enough to think it's a good idea. I've heard of phantom limb, of course, of people feeling a twinge in their missing fingers or getting an itch on an amputated kneecap. But I never heard of anyone with the opposite problem.

"IED," he said. "Iraq, 2004. Blew up half our unit. I got lucky." Then: "My friend Walt lost his head. He always made me swear I'd take his wedding ring back home to his wife, but I couldn't get it. Too many bodies, and people blasting us from all sides. Eventually we had to pull out."

I nod, even though his story doesn't answer my question. Maybe the past doesn't have to explain everything. Maybe it can't.

IT DOESN'T TAKE me long to pack up the rental. The hardest part is trying to move Kaycee's paintings. I can't just carry them openly. So I wrapped them and tied them all together, but now they have a gruesome kind of weight to them. I imagine I'll have to cart them with me wherever I go, forever.

Hannah, Condor's daughter, has returned from her grandparents' house with a new toy: a plastic tablet she keeps about an inch from her nose. But she glances up from her perch on the front stoop when I wheel my suitcase out to my car.

"Are you leaving?" she asks me, very solemn, and when I nod she scrunches up her face. "Are you going back to Chicago?" She says Chicago like someone might say the moon.

"Nah." I still have to dispose of my father's things, get his house in order, sort through the accumulation of his junk. But my rental contract in Barrens is up and there's already a new tenant scheduled to move in.

Maybe all along this is what my future held—what I tried so hard to escape, and what, ultimately, is inescapable. Time isn't a line, but a corkscrew, and the harder I've pushed, the more I've drilled back into the past. "I'm going home."

Chapter Thirty-Nine

TJ borrows an industrial-size Dumpster off a friend with a roofing business, and the next morning, I sort and dump. Mostly dump.

My father's belongings hold no nostalgia, no feeling at all besides shudders of bad memories. Mismatched plastic place settings, holiday mugs, frayed chamois shirts, stained towels, a La-Z-Boy, a three-legged bookshelf: these are my inheritance. I chuck the contents of my dad's refrigerator and spray the whole kitchen down with disinfectant, chasing insects out of the open windows with misty clouds of Windex.

I would throw out the whole refrigerator if I could lift it.

I'm lonelier than I've ever been in my life. My inbox fills up with e-mails in the days after my dad's death—even Portland sends me a note, morbidly titled "Digging," which I don't bother to open—and then the communication, predictably, slows. Brent calls stubbornly, every day, always leaving a version of the same message. *Hello, it's Brent, I'm worried, please call me.* An arrangement of flowers arrives, a wreath of lilies appropriate to an enormous church service. They go right in the trash.

I don't want to see anyone. I can't.

Ironically, Barrens has never been fuller; first the local news channels arrive to speculate about a growing corruption scandal.

Protesters begin to gather outside of the Optimal gates, preaching the importance of clean water, and every day their camp swells. Then come ambulance chaser personal injury lawyers and lobbyists with their talking points and political agendas.

All of it seems distant, as if it's happening in some other town. The few times I turn on the local news I'm surprised by Joe's face, conferencing in from Chicago to give updates, and even by footage of the whole team hard at work looking busy and official in the Chicago office. No one on the team even mentions me.

The one exception is the county prosecutor, Dev Agerwal, suddenly the darling of Indiana news: he never fails to mention that a local woman, Abby Williams, tipped him off to long-standing corruption in the office of his predecessor and inspired his current mission to end Optimal's influence in local and state politics. One enterprising reporter from WABC even tracks me to my father's house. When I answer the door, carrying a trash bag rattling with junk from the bathroom cabinets, he takes a step backward and nearly tumbles off the porch. I tell him he has the wrong Abby Williams.

My days are achy and hot. Wearing my dad's work vest, sleeping on the couch in the indent left by his body weight, sorting his belongings, making coffee that tastes like scorched grounds in the crappy drip machine: I feel as if I'm slowly slipping into my father, becoming him, bringing him back to life.

The only other company I have, besides TJ, is the mailman, who knocks on the door to tell me he can't get anything in the mailbox because it hasn't been emptied in two weeks. There isn't any more to say, but still I find myself trying to delay his departure.

"What's the strangest thing you've ever had to deliver?"

He hardly blinks. "I don't open the mail, ma'am. That's a federal crime."

"You must have some idea, though," I persist. "Bloody hearts gift-wrapped for exes, exploding glitter bombs, anything like that?"

He glances at the beer in my hand.

"Forget it," I say. "Dumb question."

"Nah. I'm just thinking. Trying to remember," he says. "Every

Christmas some of the kids send letters to the North Pole. I get letters to the tooth fairy, too."

I wish I hadn't asked. Loneliness turns from an ache to a hard punch. I think of all those rose-cheeked children, all those families at their dining room tables making wish lists: snowglobes of normalcy.

The mailman lifts his cap to palm some sweat off his hairline. "I once knew a widower kept sending his wife letters," he adds. "A few months after the funeral the letters started coming. He'd leave one for me every day. No address, just a name and Rome, Italy. He'd convinced himself that she'd run off with somebody else. He told me she always wanted to go to Rome." He shakes his head, plays with the buttons on his uniform with stained fingers. "He wrote her every day until he died, begging her to come back. Funny, isn't it? He'd rather she had an affair. He wanted her alive, even if it meant she'd done him wrong." He shakes his head.

"Funny," I echo.

He nods and turns back to his truck.

I stand there for a while, looking out over nothing, leaving sweat prints on my father's mail, thinking about that old man sending letters to his dead wife, thinking about Misha and Frank Mitchell, everyone insisting Kaycee had run away. Maybe Condor was right—maybe it wasn't so much a lie as it was wishful thinking. Maybe they just wanted to believe she'd escaped.

Wanted to believe they'd let her.

My father's mail is all coupons and junk mail, plus a flyer—obviously recent—calling for residents to show up to a town meeting about the water crisis. I'm about to chuck all of it when a manila envelope slides out from between a wedge of leaflets and skitters across the floor.

There's no address, only a name marked in neat Sharpie: *Ms. Abigail Williams.*

As I reach for it, my whole body seems to pour down into my arm, into my fingers fumbling off the tape keeping it closed. Instinct. Premonition.

Inside, there is no note, only a dozen Polaroid photographs, all of high school girls. High school girls topless, posing, making kissy faces despite the obvious drunken blur of their eyes. Girls unconscious on couches, legs splayed so their underwear is visible. One naked, entirely, her face obscured by the glare of a flash.

Sophie Nantes is in one of the pictures, her skirt hitched to her waist, hair catching in smeary lipgloss, eyes half-lidded from alcohol. I sort through the photographs carefully, more than once, even though it turns my stomach.

Apart from Sophie Nantes and a girl I identify as one of the friends who tailed her in Tatum's hospital room, I recognize three other faces.

All of them have pictures hanging in the new community center.

Five girls, all of them the new bright stars of Optimal's youth scholarships, hand-selected by the vice principal of Barrens High School.

Chapter Forty

Lilian McMann looks surprised to see me, though I called to let her know I was coming. Or maybe she's just surprised by how bad I look. Catching sight of myself in the mirror mounted behind the reception desk, I get a sudden thrill of the unfamiliar: a girl with hollow eyes, blue-tinged skin. A stranger who bears only a passing resemblance to the reflection I remember.

It probably doesn't help that I'm still wearing a pair of paint-splattered jeans and my dad's work vest.

"Come in," she says. "Can I get you anything? A water? Tea?"

I accept a water. I'm still a little buzzy from the beer, and I need to clear my head, need to focus. As soon as she sits down again, I get right to the point. "I'd like to talk to your daughter about what happened to her before you left IDEM," I say, and she freezes with her water bottle halfway to her mouth. "I need to ask her about the messages she received, and about whether she knows of anyone else—any other girls—who were targeted."

She lowers her water without drinking. For a moment she sits there in silence, and I'm worried she'll say no. But she simply says, "You believe me, then? You think she was targeted deliberately?"

"I think Optimal has been using girls. I think they've been using them for entertainment. For bribes. They've been trading pictures, for sure. But I've heard rumors of parties, too, that some of the girls attended as part of the scholarship program." I can't think about what might have happened to them when the camera lens was turned away. "That's how Optimal got so many people to protect them. It wasn't just money. It was girls. Everyone is implicated. Not bribery." I swallow. "Blackmail."

For a long time, Lilian sits in silence, gripping her water tightly. And now, in the silence, I can hear my heart beating. I'm worried she won't believe me.

"How?" she asks finally.

"I think Misha Jennings, the vice principal, got the idea from her friend Kaycee Mitchell, ten years ago," I say. "It was a game she and her friends played when they were in high school—a very sick game they invented. They preyed on younger girls, underclassmen, people who wanted to belong. Invited them to parties, got them drunk, convinced them to pose. Then they ransomed the photos back, or threatened to release them."

I can hardly stand to look at Lilian. Her face is cold and tight and furious, and I can't help but feel she's blaming me—for bringing the news, for failing to stop it. "But the photos were never returned. I understand that it might sound crazy, but I think that through Kaycee's father, they found a revenue stream and exploited it. Some Optimal execs were hunting around for young girls."

If Misha proposed selling the photos through Mitchell's store, Kaycee might have tried to stop it. Not out of moral duty, but because that was like her: to change her mind, to want something one day and then stop wanting it as soon as other people agreed. Plus, she hated her father; maybe she saw this as a chance to stand up to him. Or she was simply afraid of getting caught. But I can't remember that Kaycee was ever afraid.

And if Condor is right about Frank Mitchell, that leaves only Misha with a strong enough motive to kill her: Misha, who always had a thing for Kaycee's boyfriend; Misha, the crueler, coarser, uglier version of her best friend; Misha, who lied to Brent about speaking to Kaycee on the phone; Misha, who tried to focus my attention on Kaycee's dad by hinting to me in the community center; Misha, who only plays dumb.

Misha, who might be the smartest of all of us.

I wonder if Annie Baum and Cora Allen suspected what happened, or whether they even helped. It might explain why they've spent the past decade trying to drink or drug themselves into forgetting.

That leaves the question of whether Brent knows, too. But I just can't believe it. No matter what he says now, he must have loved Kaycee once. He's been trying to help me, even though it must pain him. He's been trying to help Misha, too. And I can't believe he would help her if he knew she was a monster.

"I think Misha kept the Game going all this time," I continue, "changing the rules, using the scholarship money as incentive—and insurance." I remember the day I visited, how her secretary was collecting phones, turning them over to Misha as punishment for texting in class. Likely targets for a much bigger operation.

Lilian stands abruptly and moves to the window. There's no view to speak of: just a half-empty parking lot.

"We transferred Amy to a private school after it happened," Lilian says. "She doesn't know anything."

"She might know more than you think."

"She put all that behind her." Lilian's voice breaks. "It nearly killed her. She's finally happy . . ."

"This is bigger than just her," I say, as gently as I can.

To her credit, Lilian doesn't cry. I see the urge move through her, bucking her spine and shoulders. But when she speaks again, she sounds calm.

"Should we call her together?" she asks. "Or would you prefer to speak to her alone?"

IN THE END I opt not to speak to her by phone at all. Culver Boarding School, where Amy has stayed on for a summer arts immersion course, is two hours north of Indianapolis; it's early evening when I arrive and though I haven't been sleeping I feel more alert than I have in weeks.

It takes me fifteen minutes to locate the student center where she has agreed to meet me for coffee. I worry she'll have lost her nerve in the time it took me to drive up here.

But she's there. She stands and shakes my hand firmly, making me feel a little like she's the adult and I'm the kid who just arrived for an interview. Even as I'm working out how to explain why I've come, she beats me to it.

"My mom said you wanted to talk about what happened sophomore year?"

"Not exactly. I'm here about the photos," I say. "Not just yours. Other photos of girls your age. Circulated. Sold, too."

She looks away. "None of my friends did that kind of stuff."

"But did you ever hear about it?" I ask her. "Did you know other girls who did?"

"People tell stories," Amy says slowly. "I don't listen. Half of what people say is a lie, and everyone would rather believe the lies sometimes. Like, how come if a guy has sex he's a hero, but if a girl does everyone says she's a slut? It's not fair."

"It isn't," I say, hoping that will prompt her. But she just picks at the corner of the table with a chipped nail, avoiding my eyes. "So you never heard about something called the Game?"

Amy looks up. "Sure, I heard about it," she says. She sounds genuinely confused. "But that had nothing to do with the pictures."

I stare at her.

"The Game was about the *scholarships*," she says, as if it's the most obvious thing in the world.

"What do you mean?"

"Mrs. Jennings is the one who recommends students for the scholarships." Misha. "But everyone knew it didn't always work that way." She looks embarrassed. "There were . . . parties. Events for the girls who wanted to be considered."

Tatum Klauss's words in the hospital come back to me. *The parties were only for the girls.*

"There were always people from Optimal there. You know. Older people." Her eyes briefly lift to mine.

"Older men," I say, and she nods.

"So that was the Game," she finishes. She chips at the edge of the table with her fingernail. "To try and get selected."

"How?" My throat is so dry I can barely get the words out. "What do the girls do to get chosen?"

"I never went," she says. "I wasn't pretty enough." A sad smile skates briefly across her face. "I guess that's why when the whole online thing happened, I was flattered."

"So the Optimal Scholarships aren't about grades," I say, trying to keep my voice neutral.

This makes her bark a laugh. "Are you kidding? Half the girls who get scholarships are barely passing until they get special tutoring through the program."

I can picture it now: Misha and the parade of girls in trouble, girls who see this as their only chance. I close my eyes, gripping my chair, finally understanding: how she might then have controlled them, used proof of these past mistakes to manipulate and intimidate.

"Besides, have you seen them? They're always the prettiest girls in school." Amy shakes her head. "You know how they call the scholarship kids the Optimal Stars? Some of the guys in school had a different name for them."

"What?" I ask, even though half of me wants to cover my ears, to beg her not to say anything more.

She smiles grimly. "The Optimal Skanks," she says.

Chapter Forty-One

As I drive home, the road starts to blur. I'm so dizzy with disgust that I have to pull over.

I'm now convinced that Misha knows exactly where Kaycee is. Sheriff Kahn might even be in on it, or at least have been persuaded by Optimal to look the other way.

It all makes terrible sense: Kaycee's game, and the chance to make some real money. It likely started with a single buyer; one of the head guys at Optimal might have told Mitchell what he was looking for. One buyer became two, and then three, and then more than that. At some point, the demand for photos morphed into a desire for the real thing, and grew into its own kind of culture, into its own economy. Optimal executives could use this special kind of sexual entertainment—deeply forbidden, deeply illegal, and, to a certain kind of person, doubly appealing—to keep the regulatory agencies and government higher-ups happy while they did whatever they wanted.

But however things began, Misha—and her contacts at Optimal—are clearly the ones now running the show. The Optimal Scholarship is bait. It's how they fish for targets.

What would someone like Misha, the vice principal, the person in charge of doling out scholarship money to at-risk students,

247

be able to convince the *girls* to do? How easily might they confuse what was happening for friendship, for attention, the way Amy had online?

I can't imagine. I won't.

It's small comfort to think that Kaycee died—must have died—because she refused to keep participating.

I can't call Joe; he'll just say that I'm grieving or that I've finally lost it. I can't go to the cops because Sheriff Kahn is in Optimal's pocket—he must be. Who knows how long he's been covering for them, or how many others in the sheriff's department are in the know? I trust Condor, but I don't know whether he'll trust me. He freaked out when I suggested Kaycee hadn't left town, and practically accused me of being a conspiracy theorist—what will he think if I tell him I've exposed an actual conspiracy?

Still, I pull up Condor's number before I can second-guess myself. The phone rings six times and then rolls over to voicemail. I hang up, then wish I hadn't. I redial, hang up after one ring when I realize he'll think I want to see him.

I send him a text instead. I decide on the truth, or something close to it.

There are enough lies in this town.

You said I was chasing a conspiracy. I found one. I don't know who else to talk to. Call me back. I add *please*, then delete it. Too desperate.

I press Send.

Is it possible that Kaycee pretended to be sick because she was trying to communicate a message about Optimal? Was she not so much pretending as *signaling*? A way of making Optimal the focus of attention without implicating herself directly?

As soon as I think it, I know it must be true. It fits. Kaycee loved that—secret messages, cryptic ways of communicating. The summer after fifth grade she tried to make up a whole new language that only we would be able to understand, and was so frustrated when I couldn't learn it fast enough that she threatened to stop being my friend, only relenting when I burst into tears. She was always all tricks and codes and clues. The kind of girl you could only get close to the way you have to creep sideways toward a wild animal, not making eye contact, so it won't run away.

However screwed up she was, however much to blame for starting the Game in the first place, she regretted it. Maybe for the first time in her life, she was trying to do the right thing.

And she died for it.

My phone rings.

I catch it on the first ring and don't even have time to glance at the name before I answer.

"Condor?" My voice is still croaky.

There's a slight pause. "It's Brent," Brent says. He doesn't bother keeping the hurt from his voice. "Sorry to disappoint."

"Brent. Hi. Sorry." My chest tightens. Does he know? Could he possibly know? I think of what he told me at the football game: *I'm beginning to think you're right about Optimal . . . there's something funny going on in accounting.*

"I've called every day. I've been worried about you."

"I know. I've been . . . busy." An obvious lie. By now, Brent must know I'm off the Optimal case. "I'm okay, though."

"You don't sound okay," Brent says matter-of-factly. "You sound like you've been crying."

I hesitate. Brent works for Optimal. He's friends with Misha. He dated Kaycee for years—and yet, he kissed me.

On the other hand, he's never blamed or punished me for investigating Optimal, or tried to warn me away. He admitted Misha always had a thing for him. Misha is an expert liar. Why wouldn't she be lying to Brent?

"Abby?" Brent sounds as if he's pressing his mouth into the phone, trying to reach his way through it. "Are you still there?"

"I'm here," I say. Can I trust him? Yes or no. Heads or tails.

I count seven crows on a telephone wire. *Seven for a secret, never to be told.*

"Talk to me," he says. Warm. Concerned.

"You're right. I'm not okay." Then, before I can regret it: "How much do you know about the Optimal Scholarships?"

"The . . . ?" Now Brent sounds bewildered. This definitely wasn't what he expected me to say.

"The scholarships," I repeat. "What do you know about them?"

Brent clears his throat. "Not much, honestly. I know Misha manages the program and our CFO oversees the financing. But why on earth . . . ?"

And I'm sure, now, he isn't faking his confusion. He can't be.

"I need to know I can trust you." My phone is hot in my hand. "I need you to promise."

"Promise what? What is this about, Abby?"

And finally I can't bear to hold it in anymore, can't bear the weight of it alone. "They're using the girls, Brent." My voice cracks. "They're using them as—as collateral. Currency. Bribes. It's been going on for years. I think—I think Kaycee knew about it. I think she was killed. I think that's *why* she was killed."

There's a long silence. "What you're saying," he says finally, "it doesn't make any sense. It's . . ." He sucks in a breath. "I can't believe it."

It's the first time I've ever felt sorry for him. I think again of the time I caught him with Misha in the woods behind the school. What lies was she feeding him then?

"I'm sorry," I say. "It's true."

More silence. When he speaks again, he can hardly manage a whisper.

"I always wanted to believe . . ." His voice breaks. "I always wanted to think she was okay." He clears his throat. "Jesus. Can we meet up? Can we talk in person?"

He doesn't think I'm crazy.

"Okay," I say, "I'm at my dad's house." I guess it's my house now.

"I'll come as soon as I can. Don't—don't tell anyone else, okay? If you're right . . ." His voice cracks again. "We can't trust anyone."

That word, *we*, lights up my insides. I'm not alone anymore. Brent is on my side.

"I won't," I tell him, and hang up.

. . .

MY FATHER'S HOUSE is cool and quiet. It smells like Pine-Sol and Windex. I've almost cleaned away the past.

I've tucked my mother's jewelry box on the top shelf of my father's closet, behind the few items of his that I intended, only a few days ago, to keep. Now I see there's no point. There is no meaning attached to his belt, or his tie, or the two-dollar bill he kept folded in his wallet, just as my mother's ghost has not imprinted on her jewelry, just as Kaycee cannot be resurrected through her fingerprints on Chestnut's collar.

I loosen the collar from the tangle of cheap necklaces—junk, all of it. The past is a trick of the mind. It's a story we misunderstand over and over.

I find a shovel in my dad's shed and set out for the reservoir with Chestnut's collar coiled around my wrist. Years ago I set out to bury it; instead, I let Brent kiss me, and from that moment on, without knowing it, I've been stuck in place.

I remember burying Chestnut close to the shore—I insisted on it, because he loved the water—and my dad marked the grave with a pile of rocks he pulled from the underbrush. But I can't find the grave anywhere. The rocks must have been moved—used to line a fire pit, maybe, or as part of another kid's imagined fairy world.

In the end I just pick a spot that seems nice, a place where the dirt hasn't quite given out to mud, and I start to dig. A small hole will do it, but I shovel until my arms ache, until my hands blister and I'm suddenly aware of the sun kissing the tree line.

The hole is absurdly large. Grave-sized. I'm not just burying the collar. I'm burying Kaycee.

I drop the collar into the dirt. And then I cover it, tamping down the earth until you would never know it had been disturbed.

I've only just returned to the house when I hear the distant sound of tires crunching up the studded dirt road. Brent. I have just enough time to tuck the shovel back in the shed before he comes around the side of the house, looking out of place in his work clothes, his shiny shoes covered with mud and grass.

"Abby. Thank God." He practically runs to hug me. "I was

banging on the front door. You weren't home. No one answered. I thought—" He doesn't have to tell me what he thought.

"I'm okay." I mean it this time. "Just doing something I should have done a long time ago."

"Your phone call . . . I can hardly think straight." He shakes his head.

"Inside," I tell him. He nods and follows me.

The living room is mostly empty, now stripped of everything but the furniture that was too heavy to move to the Dumpster. Brent waits while I splash water on my face. I'm surprised by my reflection. I look pale and wild, my eyes sunken from too much booze and not enough sleep.

When I return to the living room, Brent has poured two tall glasses of scotch.

"Macallan," he says, gesturing at the bottle. "I had it in my desk. I was saving it for a special occasion . . ." He laughs, but there's no humor in it. "Well. This is an occasion."

I don't feel like drinking, but I take a few sips anyway.

"Tell me," he says. "Tell me everything."

So I do. I tell him about Tatum Klauss, and Sophie Nantes, and what I found out from Amy McMann. About the Optimal Stars, and the parties where they were carefully screened, and Misha taking some of the most troubled girls under her wing. I repeat the story she told me about Frank Mitchell, and the so-called hypothetical instance of a man wanting younger girls. By the time I've finished half my story, and half my glass, Brent is refilling his for a third time. His eyes are red, and he's sweating through his shirt.

By the time I get to Kaycee, to how it fits, he can't take it anymore and stands up.

"I need a minute," he says, gasping. "Give me a minute." He hurtles through the screen door. I hear him pacing, spitting out his nausea in the grass. I know exactly how he feels.

The night has come without my noticing; we've been sitting in the half dark, and when I stand I can hardly see to fumble on a light. Brent is still outside. No longer on the porch, he is standing motionless by his car, staring out into nothing.

Sudden dizziness forces me to sit again. My mouth is chalk-dry. The scotch doesn't help. I reach for my bag, and the water bottle inside of it. When was the last time I ate anything? I can't remember.

I shouldn't have drank; I need to stay focused. We need to make a plan.

My hand lands on my phone, flashing with new alerts. Three missed calls from Condor. I must have silenced the ringer. He's sent a text, too, heavy on the punctuation—for some reason it takes me a minute to tack the words down into place, to make them stop blurring together: he wants to know if I'm all right.

Just as I'm about to put the phone down, an e-mail lands. Portland again, forwarding his last message, the one whose subject is *Digging*. I open it half by accident, squinting at the grid of paragraphs, fighting against a growing blurriness in my brain.

I wanted to be sure you saw this. Could be important.

Below that is his original message. Words leap out at me—*Kaycee. Poisoning. Symptoms.*

The words circle and I have to pin them down, one by one, staring them hard into place.

I did some more thinking about what you said about Kaycee's symptoms. You're right. Her symptoms never corresponded to lead exposure. But they're identical to the symptoms of mercury poisoning. Check it out.

Tremors.
Confusion.
Aphasia (short-term memory loss).
Balance problems, uncontrolled body movements.
Nausea, vomiting.

Then:

I'm not sure how she could have been exposed, or why she would have been the only one affected. I did some digging and found out that mercury was used decades ago in paint. Didn't you say she was an artist?

I have to read that line, again and again, before it makes any sense.

Or rather—I have to read it, again and again, hoping it will *stop* making sense.

All at once Kaycee roars back to life, like I always half expected she would. She is everywhere, urgent and afraid, breathing in my hair, whispering to me, holding tight with sweat-damp hands to my shoulders, willing me to understand, to listen, to see.

Your problem, Abby, isn't that you can't draw. It's that you can't see.

Look, look, look.

See.

See Kaycee, working alone, thumbing paint across a canvas, dizzied by the smell.

See Kaycee, painted head-to-toe in school colors for graduation.

See Misha and Brent, the way his hand tightened on her knee, the way he spoke to her. Reassuring.

In control.

See Brent coming through the woods, his hair wet, his shirt damp, as if he'd been swimming.

See the way he reached out to kiss you.

See flashes behind your eyelids. Firefly bursts, but brighter.

Flashes. Flashlights. People on the water.

No.

Someone in the water.

We have to make sure . . .

The scene at the bonfire must have stirred up an old memory, the faint words, a scream, quickly stifled, all of it drifting to me dreamlike on snatches of wind . . .

We have to make sure she's not breathing.

See the way you stood in front of the mirror later, tracing the places where he'd touched, trying to figure out if it was real, wondering whether he'd left a mark on you.

Wondering whether you still smelled like his fingers.

Like the beach.

Like paint.

Chapter Forty-Two

The screen door creaks when it opens. A warning, but one that arrives too late.

Brent's footsteps are heavy. Slow. Deliberate.

"Abby?" He says my name casually, all his fake shock and anger discarded. Somehow I've made it into my old bedroom. I'm holding on to the door, trying to stay on my feet. But the floor isn't a floor: it's water, and it's breaking up beneath me.

Run. I think the word. I think the word and I break into a sprint. I skim through the house, barrel out the door, sprout wings in open air, and fly. I'm running, I'm sure I'm running, and yet when he edges down the hall and sees me swaying there, I realize I'm still holding tight to the walls, still pinned inside the house.

"You're still awake," he says.

Fuck you, I try to say. But the words turn into stone; as they drop, my body collapses.

I don't even feel it when my head cracks the floorboards. I only notice the dust stirred by my breath, and his shoes coming toward me.

"That'll be one hell of a hangover," he says.

He drugged my drink.

I am in a dark sea.

I am on the floor.

I wonder where he got the climbing rope, and why I can't feel my arms.

And then I lose the rope, and I lose my arms, and I lose my whole body. I fall down into a hole so deep it swallows me up completely.

I WAKE TO a slosh of water, and to the steady vibration of an engine. I'm on a boat.

The sky is scattered with stars. A high moon burns through the cloud cover.

Brent is captaining slowly, probably so we don't make too much noise, and trailing the stink of exhaust behind us on the water.

He's humming.

Fear rattles through me but I can't move. There's a screaming pain in my head, and the burn of vomit in my throat. My clothes are soaked, and my wrists chafed from the nylon cord lashed around them. He's bound my ankles, too, and wedged me down between the bench seats.

In the distance: the thud of pounding music. The smell of wood smoke carries to me. Someone is having a bonfire.

I need to get out of the boat. But I'll never be able to swim with my hands tied. I'm not even sure I could tread water, even if I get free—my body feels like a sandbag.

Still, I have to try.

Brent turns away from the wheel, cutting the engine. I can't begin to reach the side of the boat to roll over. I aim a weak kick with both legs and miss him entirely. The effort blackens my vision. The thud of the music, even from a distance, makes my head throb.

"This would have been a lot easier if you'd just finished your drink," he says.

"Please." My voice sounds foreign. I'm not even sure what I'm asking. "Please don't hurt me."

I've been so stupid. All along I had the answer: Kaycee gave it to me. She left it for me in my locker.

Chestnut's collar, poor Chestnut, the dog she'd poisoned. She wasn't gloating. It wasn't about hurting me. It was about asking for my help. It was a *code*.

Someone was poisoning her, and she didn't know who or why, and she couldn't trust anyone she was close to.

So she trusted me—because I was friendless, because I was innocent, because she thought I would be able to help if something happened to her.

Brent shakes his head. Dismissive. Annoyed. "You didn't have to come back here," he says. "You could have left it alone. You could have forgotten all about Barrens. So why didn't you?"

"She was my friend once," I croak out.

Brent stands there, staring down at me. "You're an idiot. She wouldn't have pissed to save you. You know that, right?" He has to raise his voice above the noise of the engine, and I have a brief, stupid hope that the people at the bonfire will hear us.

Why isn't he worried that they'll hear us?

But immediately I know: he must have built up the bonfire and blasted the music himself. He's not worried because there is no one there to hear.

He turns away again. Panic seizes me, bringing a fierce tide of nausea: Whatever he drugged me with, it was strong. I need time—to talk to him, to convince him to let me go, to find a way to escape, to get the drug out of my system.

"Why did you do it?"

"You know why," he says. "You explained it to me tonight. You just got the details wrong. Mitchell never had anything to do with it."

So Condor was right after all. I should have listened to him. "You were the one who proposed selling the pictures to Optimal, weren't you?"

"Wrong again. They were the ones who proposed it to me." He smiles. But he's not as cool as he looks; when he angles his face to the moon, I can practically see tension oozing off him. "Everyone knew I hung around with all the hottest high school girls. So once I landed the internship, some of the older guys came after me looking for a piece of the action. Everyone loves hanging with pretty girls, and they're even more fun the drunker you get them. I've always believed in sharing."

I can't believe I kissed him. I can't believe I ever found him attractive. I wonder how much Optimal has given him, promised him for his continued loyalty—what final tally of promotions, kickbacks, and perquisites has outweighed all that he's done.

And even as I think it, another piece of the puzzle falls into place. That must have been why Kaycee threatened to go to the police. Not because she felt bad. Not because she began to regret it. Just another thing I've misunderstood. "Kaycee wanted a bigger cut, didn't she? She and Misha were sharing in the risk, but you were the only one getting all the perks."

Brent's smile is like a predator's: shiny in the dark, all sharp teeth and hunger. "She was always a greedy little bitch," he says. "That's why I liked her so much."

I swallow the taste of vomit. "Did you kill her, or did Misha?" I ask, even though I think I already know the answer. I bet Misha has barely blinked in the past ten years without worrying what Brent will say about it.

And now I remember thinking that Misha's baby, Kayla, was surprisingly blond. Almost as blond, it occurs to me, as Brent.

Does Misha really believe that she might make Brent love her, by doing everything he says, by feeding girls into some sick program where they can be abused and passed around, by covering up for Brent? Does she think he's even capable of love?

"It was Misha's idea to put mercury in Kaycee's paint," he says calmly. "She thought it would be funny to convince Kaycee she was going crazy. And like I said, she always had a thing for me."

No wonder I've been so sick. Kaycee's old paintings have been shedding mercury all this time and I've been inhaling it.

"We weren't thinking of killing her then, though." He sounds bored. "Just making her look like a nutjob, to keep her from going to the cops, and to make sure they wouldn't listen even if she did."

Whenever he glances away, I work my wrists back and forth, to loosen the restraints. If I can just get my hands free I can jump, and worry about my ankles once I'm in the water.

I can almost slip a hand free. All I need is another minute.

"So why kill her, if you were convinced no one would listen to her?"

"You," he says, and I almost forget where we are and what he's come to do. "The last day of school, you remember what happened? Kaycee put that stupid dog collar in your locker."

I stop moving. I never knew *he* knew.

He looks at me as if I'm on the other side of a telescope. "You told Misha that Kaycee had left it there for you as a clue."

"I didn't," I whisper.

But of course I did. I remember now: flying at Misha, trying to hit her, trying to claw my fury at Kaycee out on her best friend's face. *What the fuck is your* problem? A cluster of students gathered in the hall to stare. Misha drove me backward against the wall, I wasn't strong enough to fight her. *Are you deranged?*

I was screaming at her. Inches from her face. Trying to bury the words inside her skin, trying to cut her with them. *It wasn't enough she poisoned my goddamn dog. She had to leave me a clue, just in case I forgot?*

I remember Misha's look of blunt shock, and thinking, for a second, that I'd finally gotten through to her.

Brent's right. I *am* an idiot.

I close my eyes. The boat rocks with a wave, then falls still again. Rise and drop. Kaycee *had* left the collar as a clue, or as a cry for help—but not to prove to me that she killed Chestnut. It was, I see now, a kind of insurance. If something bad happened, she could be sure I would wonder about the collar and why she'd left it for me. She hoped that I would spot the connection. The common factor—between Chestnut and her.

Both poisoned.

But that day in the hall, I unwittingly revealed to Misha that Kaycee had begun to suspect someone was trying to kill her the same way Chestnut had been killed—with poison. Misha must have been in a panic. If Kaycee had left a clue for me, some loser she hadn't spoken to in years, who else had she told—and what, exactly, did she know?

"That night in the woods," I choke out. "When you kissed me . . ."

"Couldn't have you getting too close to the water," he says matter-of-factly. "She made a lot of noise as she was going down. I could have sworn she was dead before we loaded her into the boat, but I guess I was kind of in a rush."

She won't stay down.

We have to make sure she's not breathing.

I remember now. Why couldn't I remember before? I'd convinced myself my own memories were suspect. I'd convinced myself to ignore the terrible suspicion that something was very wrong in the woods that night.

He moves toward me. When he leans down, I can smell the sourness of his breath. For a terrible second, I think he is going to kiss me again. And now it's too late—too late to get free, too late to escape, to survive. "But I did always think you were cute. In a pathetic kind of way."

He seizes my wrists and I shout—an instinct, a useless one.

Too late, I see he has a knife.

"I've always liked the broken ones, I guess." He brings the knife to my wrists. With one clean sweep, he frees me.

Chapter Forty-Three

Iaim a punch, but Brent swats my hand away easily, almost amused. He examines my wrists, keeping a grip on me so tight it brings tears to my eyes.

"Good," he says. "No marks."

He releases me again and stands, folding up the knife and returning it to his pocket. I haul myself up to sit but have no time to launch into the water. Almost immediately, he straddles me, leaning his full weight on my chest, catching my wrists again with one hand when I try and push him off.

"It's important there are no marks." He seems almost as if he's reciting the words. His weight on my chest is crushing. I can hardly breathe. "It's important that you drown."

I spit directly in his face. He jerks back, just an inch, and then the wind shifts slightly in my favor and sends another ripple across the reservoir. The boat rocks and he rocks with it. To keep from toppling over, he releases me and steadies himself against the deck. Just for a second, he has to shift his weight forward, rising onto his knees, giving me space to move.

A second is all I need. I drive both my knees hard at his groin, catching him with just enough force to knock him off balance. Instinct curls him up and I twist out from underneath him, clawing for the side of the boat. He launches at me, grabbing my ankles as I hook an arm over the side of the boat, dragging me backward so I crack my jaw against the deck and taste blood in my mouth.

"Bitch." He flips me over onto my back and slams me down again, sending a shockwave of pain through my body. For a second, everything goes white and I have the strangest memory of my mother. It was the winter before she died; she was still well enough to move around, and my father had made a fire pit in the back, clearing a drift of snow, so that she could have s'mores for her birthday.

The fire was so high at first that we couldn't get close. We'd stood back, waiting for it to calm, as my dad used a piece of steel tubing to spread the logs apart.

Isn't it amazing? my mom had said, pointing to the very center of the fire, where it was blue. *All of that burning, just because it wants to breathe.*

In my memory, her hand is very cool, and it's clear what she's really saying: if I don't fight, I'm going to die.

The pain ebbs. Brent has a rag in one hand. I catch a whiff of chemical scent. Chloroform, or gasoline.

I wrench my head to the side, gasping for clean air, fumbling for something, anything, I can use as a weapon, striking out with my fists, my legs, writhing and twisting, on the slickness of the deck.

He tries to shove the rag into my mouth but I cough it out. I slither away from him. But he's too strong, and I'm too tired. I'm a fish, lashing out in its last moments still tethered to a hook.

The fish hook.

I'd forgotten the fish hook and lure Condor made for me, still nestled in cloth in my front pocket.

I tug the zipper open just as Brent clamps the rag, wet with chemicals, tight to my face. Instantly, I'm blind; the acrid scent takes over, gagging, the rag suffocating.

And just before I slip entirely, I swing with the fish hook latched between my fingers.

Brent screams and draws back. Oxygen floods my lungs, drives off the darkness, brings the world back into focus. Something warm hits my face. Blood. I've slashed him just below the eye, a gaping, ragged cut.

I scrabble backward and the hook spins out of my grip. Before I can find it he gets his hands around my throat—no longer worried about marks. He crushes my windpipe in his fist.

I feel along the filth of vomit and blood until the fish hook bites back in response.

This time I aim more carefully.

His eye makes a slight popping sound, like a grape bursting, when I drive the metal through it.

Chapter Forty-Four

I tumble over the side of the boat and plunge beneath the surface of the water. Even then I can hear him screaming. My ankles are still bound, and my clothes are so heavy I nearly don't make it up for a breath. I struggle out of my father's vest and let it drop. But I can't get my ankles free, not with my fingers half-numb and my body still heavy with drugs.

When I surface, I see the bonfire blazing in the distance, and not a single person standing there to watch. Like I thought. No point in screaming. The stereo is blasting "Sweet Caroline." I've always hated that song.

Brent has stopped screaming. I can't see him at all. The boat rocks on the wind-ruffled water, its silhouette dark against the sleek reflection of the moon in the water.

I slip under the water again and come up coughing. I try to fumble off my shoes but this takes me under again. Each time it's harder to break through to the oxygen above, so I give up.

I start to swim toward the shore. For a second I imagine I see a flashlight blinking through the trees. But the light blinks out again as soon as I try and focus on it.

My heart feels like it, too, is swollen with water. Head down, head up. My jeans weigh a thousand pounds. The shore seems to be getting farther, not closer. I'm gasping for breath, choking on my fear, wishing for things I haven't wished for in forever: for my mother to hold me, for my father, for God to save me—for anyone.

I sink. Fight for the surface. Sink again. Up and down. Barely making any forward progress. If I can just make it, I can hide in the woods. I can lose him; I know these woods better than he does, better than anyone does.

But even as I think it, an enormous amount of light dazzles the surface of the reservoir, illuminating even the logs floating in the shallows a hundred feet away.

I turn around and am blinded by floodlights: Brent has powered them on, lighting up a clear path between us. The hum of his engine grows to a roar as he wheels around.

And points the boat straight at me.

"Help!" There's no point in screaming but I do anyway, taking in another mouthful of water. "Help!" The boat comes so fast it cleaves a wake behind it. Thirty feet away. Fifteen.

I'll never make it. I have no strength to swim anymore.

It's the craziest thing: just before I drop, before I let the water take me, I swear I see Kaycee Mitchell step out of the trees, almost directly on the place my father and I buried Chestnut. Not Kaycee as she was the last time I saw her, but Kaycee the child, Kaycee my best friend, skinny and long-legged, just a flash of blond hair and a strong, urgent message she sends out across the water.

Swim.

Brent's boat sends a surf of water up to meet me, and I fall down under its weight, tumbling. The underside clips my shoulder, missing my head by inches.

Underneath the water, sound becomes vibration: a shudder, a distant boom that makes the whole reservoir shiver. I open my eyes. The floodlights have cut their way down into the depths. A peaceful place to die. Green with old growth. Weedy and silent. There are letters embedded in the silt, large white letters, a hieroglyph I understand intuitively, a message that fills me with a strange joy.

I have learned how to see.

. . .

"ABBY. ABBY. CAN you hear me? *Abby.*"

A whirl of lights and color. Fireworks. Explosions of sound.

"Just hang on, okay? You're going to be okay. I'm right here with you."

A web of branches above me.

I'm a child again, bundled in a white sheet, rocking.

"Keep the oxygen coming."

"Radio the bus to come down Pike Road, it'll be quicker."

My mouth is made of plastic. My breath mists inside of it.

"She's trying to say something. She's trying to speak."

A stranger touches my face. She looses my mouth from its plastic cage.

"Don't worry, sweetheart," the stranger says, "you're going to be just fine." She has a smile that reminds me of my mother's.

It takes a second to work out what my tongue is, how to move it in the right direction.

"I found her," I whisper.

"What'd she say?" I know that voice. Condor. "Abby, what's the matter?"

She frowns. "Found who, sweetheart?"

"Kaycee." I close my eyes again. I see the letters written at the bottom of the lake: the white of her bones, so clean, so fine, almost glowing. "She's been waiting for us to find her. She's been waiting for us in the reservoir."

Epilogue

It's September before I finally pack my car with my suitcase and my duffel bag, my mother's jewelry box, and a cardboard box of my dad's belongings I've decided, after all, to save.

Why not? The past is just a story we tell. And all stories depend on the ending.

And for the first time in my life, I truly believe that the ending is going to be just fine.

Hannah gives me a sheath of drawings bound up in a three-ring binder: a superhero named Astrid who wears a purple cape and a pair of leather boots and goes around rescuing kids drowning in ocean waves or stranded by mounting floods on the roofs of their houses.

"I tried to make her look like you," she tells me shyly, before briefly squeezing me into a hug and then darting off.

"You didn't say good-bye," Condor calls after her, but she's already vanished, disappearing inside the house.

"That's okay," I say. "I don't like good-byes, either."

It's a bright day, full of classic Indiana colors: gold and green and blue. The month of August seemed determined to make up for the drought, as if twelve months' worth of rain had just been piling up waiting to spoil everyone's last bit of summer. But when the storms passed, they left fields wild and lush. The reservoir is approaching normal levels again, though it's still testing too high for lead and other contaminants, and the people of Barrens are still drinking and washing in bottled water trucked to town by the state and various charitable organizations. Protesters even set up camp in the playground that, ironically, still welcomes visitors with an *Optimal Cares!* sign. (Though after a recent graffiti modification, it now reads *Optimal Scares.*)

I never found out who sent me the envelope full of photographs that finally set me on a path to understanding the truth. But I suspect Misha might have had something to do with it, just as I suspect it was Misha who tried to run me off the road, though I doubt I'll ever know whether she was finally sick of covering for Brent, whether she'd simply realized that he would never love her in the way she kept hoping he would, or whether she simply thought she could get me out of the way, even if it meant implicating herself. All I know is that she has been cooperating with the federal investigation into the nature of the Optimal Scholarships and the abuse perpetuated in their name. Maybe she's cooperating in an attempt to redeem herself. Maybe it's just an attempt to reduce her sentence, although, given the number of girls affected, it's unlikely she will ever leave prison again.

And then, of course, there is Kaycee's murder, and the charges related to it. Now that Brent's dead, Misha will stand trial, alone.

I almost—*almost*—feel sorry for her.

An awkward silence stretches between Condor and me—uncharacteristic, since we've spent weeks talking, eating dinner together almost every night, bonding over the strange and sudden bubble of publicity that made us into a makeshift family. It's funny: through all of this, we fell into an easy intimacy, the kind of friendship I've always craved and have had only intermittently with Joe.

I'm not ready to leave him, or Hannah, or even Barrens.

But I have to.

We both know I don't belong in Barrens. Condor has his whole life here; I have my little sterile condo waiting for me in Chicago. Who knows? Maybe I'll hang a photo or two. Maybe I'll make Joe buy me dollar oysters. Maybe I'll let him buy me dollar oysters for a year, with a big side of groveling—he's promised he owes me a lifetime supply.

Maybe I'll finally get through my inbox, and all the new complaints, environmental reports, and potential new cases awaiting my attention. You want a clean world, someone's got to filter out the crap.

Good thing I've gotten used to getting my hands dirty.

I clear my throat. "She seems so much better," I say.

When he smiles, the corners of his eyes crinkle. "Kids are amazing, aren't they? Resilient as hell."

I flip through the book of drawings again. She's actually very good—she has a talent that reminds me of Kaycee's at her age. "Not a spot of blood," I say.

"No loose body parts, either," Condor says dryly. After that night on the reservoir, Hannah couldn't stop drawing the terrible things she had seen: flames and blood, a body broken on the deck of a foundering boat.

It was Hannah I saw in the woods, Hannah who in my exhaustion and terror I'd mistaken for Kaycee as a child. The crack I heard just before going under was a gunshot: a single rifle shot, aimed from the shoreline one hundred feet away at a target moving fast in a motorboat.

Condor was born and bred in Barrens, and Barrens taught its boys how to play football, and how to aim a gun. One shot was all it took.

He'd told me the whole story in the hospital the day after it happened—how he'd grown worried after seeing my calls, especially when I didn't answer his. How, after several hours, he'd become so agitated he decided to drive to my father's house to make sure I was okay. He hadn't wanted to leave Hannah by herself—but she was a fussy sleeper, prone to nightmares, and he was worried she might wake up and discover him gone. So he'd woken her and packed her in the back seat of the car.

"I was sure I was just being paranoid," he told me. "I figured we'd find you tucked into bed, turn around, and go home."

"Then why did you bring your shotgun?" I'd asked him.

He'd simply shrugged. "You ever gone camping without a flash-light?"

I shook my head.

He smiled. "Me neither."

Later, I heard the story repeated by the news channels, on web-sites, blogs, and late-night segments. Everyone was captivated by my narrow escape on the reservoir—and more than a little enam-ored of Condor, the gruff good-looking single dad who played the role of the hero.

The story was embellished, edited, and exaggerated, but the basic facts remained the same: arriving at my father's house, he'd found Brent's car, and mine, but the door hanging open and tracks off the back porch, leading across the grass, suggesting some-thing—or someone—had been dragged into the woods.

He had commanded Hannah to stay in the car. He hardly ever gave direct orders, and she never disobeyed them.

That night, she did.

When I got out of the hospital, I tried returning to my dad's house, which had been cleared by then of the police tape that for days had encircled it. But already, curious tourists were arriving. I would wake in the middle of the night to a sudden flash, only to see a stranger at the window and be pulled into a well of panic, replay-ing the entire event over and over in my head.

When Condor suggested I stay with him, I agreed right away. I made coffee in the mornings. He made eggs. I slept in his bed. He took the foldout couch. Hannah and I drank warm milk at midnight when the nightmares had startled us awake. Condor and I sat on the couch, watching old episodes of sitcoms without paying any at-tention to them, after endless hours of giving evidence, interviews, help to a tidal wave of federal investigators and prosecutors, sexual assault survivors' advocates, corporate watchdogs. It was as if ex-posing Optimal and its economy of teens used for entertainment, and nearly getting killed in the process, had all been part of some master plan to snag my fifteen minutes of fame. Barrens, and its dirty not-so-little secrets, was suddenly everywhere. The fall of a multimillion-dollar company, the exploitation, the corruption, the girls, the ten-year-old murder—it was a ratings jackpot.

But the attention would fade—it already had begun to—and so would whatever this was between Condor and me. It was never meant to last, at least not in that way. Condor and I had already made lives in different places. That's the funny thing about home: you've always arrived just as soon as you stop checking the compass.

"I'm going to miss you," Condor says now, his mouth all twisted up, like it always is when he has to say something serious.

I give him a quick hug. Barely a squeeze—anything longer, anything more, and my thoughts spin down places too murky and lonesome to understand.

He raises a hand. Framed by a huge billow of Indiana sky, he looks truly beautiful. I will always remember this moment, I tell myself, but already know that I won't.

He pivots just before he gets to the front door as I slide into the car. "Try to stay far away from boats."

"Try not to shoot anyone," I call back. He blows me a kiss.

I key on the ignition.

Before heading out of town, I take a familiar turn toward my dad's house. As I get closer I can see the same ever-so-slightly crooked split-level and the gravel driveway, but the brown and overgrown yard has been cleared of weeds. The house, with TJ's help, shines with a fresh coat of pale blue paint.

I hardly recognize it.

This isn't home anymore.

A *For Sale* sign juts from the mown lawn at an angle, optimistic, and perhaps absurdly so.

Eventually a new family will move into this house; a new child will run through its halls, stare out at the line of trees in the forest from her bedroom, ride her bike down the path to the reservoir, collect little items that are important to her, and maybe, sit down to dinner and hold hands with her parents as they say grace.

Or maybe there won't be any kind of grace in that house again.

I roll down my window and breathe in the smell of the reservoir through the wood line for what I know will be the last and final time.

A formation of crows pinwheels on invisible currents through the sky. Together, they form an arrow, pointing north.

I turn my car to follow them.

Barrens grows smaller in my rearview mirror until, at last, it disappears.

Acknowledgments

I have a lot of people to thank for helping and supporting me through the process of writing this book. Thank you to Lauren Oliver for working tirelessly with me on *Bonfire* from inception to completion. Thank you for your amazing ideas and every late-night pep talk—I never could have done this without you. I also want to thank Lexa Hillyer and the entire Glasstown Entertainment team, also Stephen Barbara at Inkwell. Thank you to Molly Stern, Jen Schuster, and everyone at Crown for believing in me and for this amazing opportunity. Thank you to Dave Feldman and the rest of my team for supporting my dreams, especially Kyle Luker and Steve Caserta, each of whom must have read seventeen drafts of the book as it evolved. I also want to thank my dear friend Gren Wells for her notes and feedback and for encouraging me along the way. Thank you to my adorable sister, Bailey, for taking my author photo. Thank you to my best friend, Lauren Bratman, for cheering me across every finish line. Thank you to Rachael Taylor for the incredible book recommendations. Thank you, lastly, to Adam and Mikey for all the love at home.

About the Author

KRYSTEN RITTER is known for her starring roles in the award-winning Netflix series *Marvel's Jessica Jones* and cult favorite *Don't Trust the B---- in Apartment 23*, as well as her pivotal role on AMC's *Breaking Bad*. Ritter's work on film includes *Big Eyes*, *Listen Up Philip*, *Life Happens*, *Confessions of a Shopaholic*, and *She's Out of My League*. She is the founder of Silent Machine, a production company that aims to highlight complex female protagonists. Ritter and her dog, Mikey, split their time between New York and Los Angeles.